Semper

MINE

A SONS OF WAR NOVEL

Lizzy Ford

ISBN-13: 978-1-62378-142-2

Dedication

For my family, the reason I'm able to do what I do!

CHAPTER ONE: SAWYER

S *AVE PETR.*

I can still hear Mikael Khavalov's final words. There's a reason the military doesn't put brothers on the same special operations team, but that night seven days ago, it didn't matter. A routine mission with a second team put the twins both under my watch, and every commander's worst nightmare happened.

Sergeant First Class Mikael Khavalov – known as Khav-One – was one of four service members that died to give the rest of us, including his wounded brother, Petr – Khav-Two – a chance to make it to safety.

An early spring chill tickles my ear, a reminder that I'm in Massachusetts, thousands of miles from the war zone. The sky is unusually clear, blue and cloudless, with the scent of flowers in the air. My gaze sweeps over the men and women dressed in black, gathered for the final farewell to Mikael.

Nothing is quite as moving as a military funeral: the aching wail of a coronet, twenty one gun salute, and the piercing silence that follows. I've attended too many the past year, four this week alone. There's a sense of peace in the final solemn, disciplined display that thanks a man or woman for the ultimate sacrifice before lowering him or her into the ground.

This one is unlike the others for a few reasons, and I feel out of place where I normally don't. There's no *Taps* or salute, no one else in uniform, and the flag that flew back with Mikael's body is tucked under one of my

1

arms. The wealthy Khavalov family declined the Arlington burial in favor of having their son laid to rest in a private, walled cemetery, behind the mansion where the rest of the immediate family lives. It's a completely civilian affair, and I am out of my element.

A true blueblood, Khav-One had a degree from Yale, a sports car I wouldn't be able to afford with ten years of wages in hand, and was friends with the families of politicians and celebrities, some of whom are in attendance today.

God knows what made someone with his background *enlist*, of all things, let alone pursue the grueling, gritty, elite path of a Green Beret, aside from a love of his country, mixed with a side of crazy. Whatever it is, it runs in the family. Mikael didn't survive the worst night of my life, but Khav-Two did. He's in a hospital near here, stuck in a medically induced coma to keep him stable after his leg was blown off near the hip.

It's certainly the most peaceful graveyard I've visited yet. It feels more like a garden with hedges, stately statues and obelisks, a fountain at its center and a stone pathway that weaves among the dead.

I knew his family had money, but I had no idea they *had money*. It makes me think he was crazier than I first gave him credit for.

The ceremony ends with a Catholic priest blessing the sleek black casket covered by a blanket of flowers. I stand to the side, the only one in uniform. Khav's father is someone I know better than my own from the stories the spirited twins used to tell. He's a burly, former Russian KGB officer with white hair and bright blue eyes who defected to the States when he fell in love with an American heiress, a ballerina training with the Bolshoi Ballet group in Moscow.

Everyone in our unit knew their story. Fairy tales have a place, especially in war, and this was a nice, rosy one that was real enough for us to touch. A man leading a life of war and violence meets a beautiful ballerina and finds peace and happily ever after? Who doesn't want that someday? Avid storytellers, the twins kept the morale of their respective units up with the sheer power of their upbeat personalities. I can't imagine going back without them.

The Khavs' sister, whose name I can't remember, is standing beside her father, a veil covering her face. She's small, like I expect of the daughter of a ballerina, and dressed in black. She leans into her father in a stance I've seen too often lately, one that makes me hurt for those like her. The only thing I recall Khav-One saying about her was never to eat the cookies she sent the unit, but not to tell her the cookies got tossed, because she has a temper.

The twins were known to exaggerate, though, and I didn't believe it until I tried one. I've never met a cookie I didn't like, especially in a war zone. The taste was nothing compared to the bellyache hers gave me after I choked a few down.

I wish I knew something else about her. I try to say something personal to everyone I meet at funerals. It seems like an oversight right now not to have something more thoughtful to express than *please don't send more cookies.*

"Thank you for your service, Captain," one man says, approaching me. I recognize him from television. He's a senator. I haven't been stateside in four years, so I'm not sure from which state.

"It's an honor, sir," I reply.

"Force Recon Marine at a Green Beret funeral? Things have changed since my day." He smiles.

"We recruited the best of the best from all services for our special team, sir. It was an honor to serve with him."

"Well said, Marine." We shake hands, and he leaves. Two more men and a woman approach and shake my hand.

The people begin to drift away, talking quietly, while the two immediate family members remain. I stay with them, wanting to do what little I can to help, even knowing there's nothing that can really be said. They hug, and I turn away to give them some privacy. I notice the rose bushes lining one wall, the source of the subtle scent has been tickling my nose since I entered the graveyard.

Whenever I leave the battlefield, I notice things I never did before. Right now, I'm mentally measuring how symmetrical the different hued flowers are and am fascinated by how something as delicate as a petal can survive in a world like ours. Things are so green here, it almost doesn't seem real. Like a dream. One I would give anything to wake up from and feel whole again.

Behind the façade that earned me the nickname *Ice Commander, Iceman, Captain Icee* and others from my men, I'm raw, like a severe rope burn has cut straight through my soul. My first mission as a newly minted commander, and I lose four men.

The opposite of the twins, I'm not one to talk much. Even if I knew how to express my thoughts, the emotions run too deep for me to name. So I breathe in the scent of roses and let myself stay in that one, peaceful moment in the garden, knowing it'll be gone soon enough.

"Captain Mathis." It's the voice of Ms. Khavalov, the sister of the Khav brothers. There's an edge to it, one I recognize too well from other funerals.

I'd rather deal with insurgents than grieving families. It's a cold thought stemming from trying to keep myself numb this week. I'm here for the family members as well as my fallen men, but I never thought it'd be so hard.

I turn to face her.

The stinging slap she lands across one cheek is a definite first. It's enough to jar me but not enough to knock me out of my stance at attention. I can take a blow pretty well after a lifetime filled with them.

"You were supposed to bring them both back alive!" she says in a choked voice.

"I am sorry for your loss, ma'am," I say calmly.

She pushes up her veil, and I stare.

The twins look like their father, and I can only assume their sister resembles their mother. She's stunning, from the light hazel eyes to her chiseled features and the delicate, quivering chin. In her twenties, she's got the determined set of her jaw that I know from the twins and a gleam in her eyes that tells me she's just as smart.

"That's it?" she whispers. "You're *sorry?*"

"He died bravely, ma'am," I add.

Her eyes widen. "One of my brothers is gone and the other may never wake up!"

Trust me. I know. I don't say anything. Part of the grieving process is anger, and I've been the target of it for a great many family members. If it helps them sleep at night, then I don't mind.

God knows I don't sleep anymore. Someone should.

"Forgive Katya. She does not know what we do about war, Captain Mathis," her father says, approaching. His Russian accent is heavy, his words slow. His bushy eyebrows twitch. "It is not those who were lost but those who were saved that should be counted."

"Don't patronize me, baba!" Katya snaps. With a furious look at me, she marches away, breaking into a run after a few steps. I can hear her sobs.

I hate seeing women cry. It makes me edgy. Turning my attention to her father, I hold the flag out to him.

His eyes mist over. "Thank you. You are a good man, Captain Mathis." He takes it and kisses it. "Come." He takes my elbow and guides me towards the gate she fled through. "Tell me how he died defending his country and his men." He gazes at me with sorrow and compassion mixed with hope.

"He did, sir," I reply. "He saved many lives, including mine and Petr's. We wouldn't have made it out without his sacrifice."

"I knew it." His eyes sparkle with tears, but he's proud. "A soldier wants a good death, eh?"

I don't answer, not expecting him to be quite so understanding. I know the Russians we worked with occasionally in Iraq view life a bit differently, in a more grounded if not cynical way, and I'm kind of grateful for it right now. The past week has been brutal. First the firefight that cost me half the super specialized, well-trained men fighting under me, and then four funerals and families I personally visited to convey my condolences.

The damn counselor I was assigned after the suicide mission says part of what I feel is survivor's guilt. I'd characterize it more as commander's guilt, if such a thing officially exists.

Mr. Khavalov opens the gate of the private cemetery, and I glance towards the massive stone mansion that resembles a castle a short distance from us.

"My Katya, she is a good girl. You are fortunate all she did was slap you. Her mother could throw a shoe halfway down a football field and hit you anywhere she aimed." He grins, affection crossing his features. His eyes are on his daughter, who is racing across the field separating the graveyard from the stately mansion. "She will understand one day."

I've never quite met someone like this, who doesn't seem to blame me, who seems to comprehend what war and death are like. Who almost seems to be trying to comfort *me*, when he's the one who lost a son.

"You will come to the wake?" he asks.

"Thank you, sir, but no," I reply, thinking of Katya. "This is your time to be together. I needed to say farewell but won't interfere."

"He told me a lot about you. They both did," the older man says.

I hear the sadness in his voice. I know his thoughts are as much on Petr as they are on Mikael.

"It was my pleasure to serve with them," I reply. "It was my first command, and they taught me how to be a better leader." I stop walking and face him, intending to go to the driveway rather than the house. "Sir, I want you to know ..." My voice breaks, and I clear my throat. Today has been hard. "... excuse me. I just want you to know that I will be checking in on Petr. When he pulls through, I'll be here to help him. If there's anything you need, sir, anything at all, please don't hesitate to contact me." I give him my card with my email address.

Mr. Khavalov accepts it, his features warm. "You are always welcome in my family, Captain Mathis." He pats me on the arm. "Petr told me you have none of your own. You brought him home. You can consider this your home, too." He waves towards the mansion.

I nod briskly, not certain what to say. I brought one son home in a box and the other in a coma. How that earns me any sort of consideration from a man like this, I don't know.

But his words touch me. He's right. A ward of the state from the age of two until I was eighteen, my family is the Marine Corps and the elite, multi-forces group I command. They are the only family I need, and yet, I appreciate how generous he is being, given the circumstances.

I can't respond, so I bow my head, turn crisply and walk away. I find myself reaching for my good luck charm and stop, knowing it's lost somewhere in the deserts of Iraq after the gunfight a week ago.

It is not those who were lost but those who were saved that should be counted.

As much as I like the sentiment, I don't think this, either, will help me sleep at night. With a glance at my watch, I realize I've got about six hours to grab my gear and be back on base, before I'm headed back to Iraq.

This has been the most draining week I've ever been through. It's not in my nature to second-guess myself, but recalling the amount of pain in Katya's eyes ...

Save Petr.

I need one of the Khav twins to pull through, for my own sake. A family can't lose two sons at once. It's just not right.

I can't wait to get back. War I understand. There are no down moments for me to think about the suffering of men like the twin's father and women like their sister, whose lives are forever destroyed by one decision I made.

That's all it takes to change someone's forever. One choice.

I've never been this fucking tired.

CHAPTER TWO: KATYA

JULY

EVERYONE DIES AROUND MY BIRTHDAY. I lost my mother a week before I turned nine and one of my brothers three days after my twenty-fifth birthday this year. I don't think I'll ever get over either of the two times in my life where I've seen my strong father cry.

I get lost in my head a lot, unable to close the door on these memories the way I ache to. I've been tempted to take down the pictures in my bedroom with my two brothers, hoping that helps me move on, but can't bring myself to do it. If I take down Mikael's picture, I'm afraid he'll disappear forever. It's silly, the same thought I experienced after my mother's death, because I know they're already gone.

But if I keep the pictures up, it's like they're still around somewhere, maybe just outside my room, and I can pretend all I have to do is open the door and they'll be there waiting.

A hard smack of flesh on metal snaps me out of the melancholy thinking.

My surviving brother, Petr, is playing with his prosthetic leg like he's a five-year-old who got the best birthday present of his life. It doesn't look like a real limb and kind of weirds me out, which is why I'm grateful he's in jeans this time and not boxers. It's made of some sort of resilient, lightweight metal and reminds me of the robot troopers in the latest round of Star Wars movies. The design is purely out of some science fiction

7

magazine or comic book. If I hadn't seen him run on it, I never would've believed it'd hold his body weight.

"You're going to knock your leg off," I snap at him. "The doctor said not to mess with it!"

Petr rolls his eyes. "This thing is cemented to my bone. It's not coming off." He slaps his new leg harder, and I flinch.

It just doesn't look sturdy.

"Your meds," I say and hold them out. He's been avoiding them, I think because they make him a little less … hyper. He's been insisting for days he's ready to return to duty, while the medical staff wants him to wait another month before letting the military decide what he can and cannot do, if they let him back in at all.

At a little over six feet tall, he's got my father's heavy features, a nose that's been broken more than once, and a lopsided grin that makes him charmingly roguish in appearance. His hair has grown out some since he came home four months ago, but there's no way he resembles anything other than the soldier he is.

He's regained the muscle mass he lost while in the coma for three weeks and managed to put on more weight. He works out every day like he's going to return to the war that killed our brother and nearly cost Petr his life, too.

Over my dead body. I'm the youngest in the family, but you'd think I was the mother. Probably because I took over the role of taking care of my thickheaded, stupid older brothers after our mother died. I was nine, and they were fourteen, old enough to be in trouble every weekend.

"Kitty-Khav, I'm a trained killer. I can take care of myself," he reminds me and takes the meds, only to put them back on the tray. His blue eyes sparkle with mischief, the way they always have, though there's a shadow in them that wasn't there before Mikael's death.

The death of our brother haunts us both.

He stands, moving away from the hospital bed as if he's not wearing a fake leg that looks like it could collapse at any minute.

"You shouldn't be going to the retreat at all, Petr," I tell him, not for the first time. "What if you trip in the forest or something?"

He ignores me and puts on a knit cap. I'm not sure what his obsession with knit caps is lately, but he wears one every time he leaves the hospital.

"Petr, you have to be careful." I'm worried about him, have been since I

8

sat by him every day he was in a coma. I never left his side, and I've been a wrench in his spokes since then, knowing the doctors can't influence my stubborn brother the way I can.

"I love you, sis," he says with a wink. "You can throw as many shoes as you want at me, but I'm going."

Pursing my lips, I'm about to put my foot down and remind him *exactly* what the doctor said, when there's a knock at the door to his room.

"This isn't over," I warn him.

I'm hoping it's the nurse he's been eyeballing, the only other person who might be able to convince him to wait until the end of the week, after his final round of tests, before he tries to break in the new leg doing something stupid.

Opening the door, I spot the dress uniform of a Marine and frown, then look up at him. Dark hair and eyes, olive complexion, heavy jaw, tapered nose, full lips and a low brow. He smells clean and of some light, sweet cologne that reminds me of coconuts. He's got the lean physique and wide upper body of a swimmer that I'd drool over, if he were any other man.

"You," I hiss.

Captain Sawyer Mathis has an intensity and calmness around him that infuriates me, especially when I think of how detached and cold he was at Mikael's funeral, like saying farewell to my brother was a chore. His brown eyes are on me.

He's as handsome as he is good at taking out the men of my family. Why Petr and Baba like him, I have no idea.

"Ma'am," he replies.

"You here to make sure my other brother ends up six feet under?"

"No, ma'am. I'm here to check in on him."

"These are family only visiting hours." I slam the door closed, or try to.

His foot is jammed in the door. "With all due respect, ma'am, your brothers saved my life, which makes them more than family in my book."

"With all due respect, *Captain,* I think you've done enough for my family."

I swing the door open, realizing his foot isn't about to budge. Planting my hands on my hips, I'm not about to move from the doorway.

Seeing him reminds me too much of Mikael and how I'll never see my brother again. I'll be damned if I'm going to let the man who got Mikael killed come near my Petr.

Captain Mathis' jaw is clenched. I'm not sure what he can be thinking, but he sure as hell isn't expressing anything that makes me think he's more human than he was at Mikael's funeral. I don't know why he bothered showing up that day.

"If you want in, you'll have to move me out of the way," I tell him.

"You can't weigh more than one thirty. I've carried packs heavier than you." His gaze sweeps over me. "I'll be out of your way in five minutes, ma'am," he adds calmly. "But I won't leave until I get that five minutes with your brother."

"Violence and threats are the weapons of choice, I see. Guess it comes naturally to someone who thinks invading some sovereign country over oil and getting innocent people killed is the right thing to do."

A flare of something crosses his gaze and vanishes quickly. "And I imagine you think saving the whales is more important than funding the equipment people like your brothers needed to stay alive in a hostile environment."

"There wouldn't be a hostile environment if we had a policy of peace rather than war," I point out.

"I didn't start the war, ma'am, but I will win it so people like *you* can maintain your way of life."

"You aren't going to win if you keep killing off your own men!" *God, what an asshole!*

We glare at one another, the air between us charged and thick. I hit a nerve with him and sense it. I'm happy for it. I hate this man, because he came back when my Mikael didn't. Not even Captain Mathis' thick biceps and broad chest can make up for him being what he is: the representation of everything I despise about the military and war that took my brother away.

"Step aside, ma'am." The order is gravelly, low and quiet in the resolute tone of a natural leader. It cuts through my anger. His gaze is piercing.

He's not like my brothers and father. He's not backing down.

"Oh, Kitty-Khav, I think I need some … Tylenol." Petr says from behind me, pain in his voice. "Can you get the nurse?"

At once, my attention shifts to my brother. He's seated on the bed, forehead in one hand. I panic at the sight of him in pain. There were so many times I thought we were going to lose him … I'd do anything to keep him from going through the misery he's spent the past four months in.

"Yes, of course!"

Captain Mathis forgotten, I push by him out of the room, intent on finding the nearest nurse I can, even if I have to drag one out of someone else's room.

CHAPTER THREE: SAWYER

I T TAKES ME A MOMENT TO RECOVER. I've never wanted to put hands on a woman before and talk some sense in her or worse, take her out onto the battlefield and show her what *real* war is like. I can't recall the last time someone got under my skin like that. It doesn't help that it's impossible to take my eyes off her. Katya Khavalov is stunning, more so when she's angry, and I hesitated long enough for her to set up the battlefield to her advantage. I gave her enough time to mount a pre-emptive attack and do what no insurgents can: piss me off.

I gotta get better at dealing with civilians. Or maybe just this civilian, if I'm going to spend the week with Petr. No more giving her a chance to lure me into a minefield.

Refocusing mentally, I step into Petr's room.

Petr bounces to his feet. "Hey, sir." He's grinning and moving around like the new leg is a part of him already. It's nearly impossible to keep a spec-ops guy down for long. I know this and am proud of him.

And relieved.

"We've got about sixty seconds before she comes back," he says and grabs his wallet off the stand. He picks up a pack half the size of his sister and slings it over one shoulder with ease.

"So you're not hurting," I guess, a smile spreading across my face.

"I'll throw myself on a grenade for you, but I will not get in her line of fire," Petr replies. With a quick, efficient walk, he leads me out of the room and down another hallway quickly, using techniques we employ in a war zone to evade detection in order to avoid his sister.

Not that I blame him. They weren't exaggerating about her temper.

"Freedom!" Petr breathes when we step outside the hospital. It's a private clinic I read about online with specialists that only families like Petr's can afford. When I asked him why, he said it was because he could afford treatment that most other injured soldiers couldn't, so to save the government resources for them.

They did him up right, I have to admit. He's happy, healthy, strong and fully recovered.

"You drove, Iceman?" Petr asks with a glance over his shoulder.

"Black F-350." I point to the largest truck in the parking lot.

"She'll find us, but it helps to have a head start."

I laugh. "Three tours in Iraq, and you're running from your sister."

"You heard that tongue. Before, it was divided between Mik and me. Now there's just me. I've had no peace since waking up from the coma."

"I take it she's got no boyfriend?" *Why did I just ask that?* I want nothing to do with his sister, let alone care about her life.

"She did, but he left her. She spent weeks with me at the hospital and not enough time with him. We know how that goes."

"Unfortunately." Life in the military is as hard on those in it as it is on those who support loved ones who are deployed. I don't know any member of the team who hasn't gotten a *Dear John* email at some point over the past few years.

Unlocking the truck, I open the door and slide into the seat. He tosses his pack in the back then climbs into the passenger's side.

"You move like you've got no problems at all," I say, curious about his new appendage. "How does it feel?'

"Amazing. I want two legs like this."

"According to your sister, hanging around me will probably get you another one."

"The louder she yells, the more it means she loves you," he says. "Baba says so, at least. She means well."

"I suppose." She comes across more like a spoiled bitch with a two-dimensional view of the world to me, but I'm not going to tell him that. I'm not sure how the Khav twins can be related to her. They're laid back, adventure seekers who never complained a day they were in my command. They definitely didn't have the liberal indignation of their sister.

I'm pretty sure Katya and I would be at each other's throats before the end of the first day, and I'd kick her off my team faster than I'd dive on a grenade for her brothers.

"Did I mention she runs fast, too?" Petr says with a grunt.

I glance up from adjusting the climate control dials. I can't get over how much I miss AC.

Katya is close enough that her run slows to a walk as she nears the parking lot. Her glare is on *me,* like I'm kidnapping her brother. Her features are flushed in a way that brings out her hazel eyes even more, and I find myself looking at her too long again instead of taking the opportunity to escape.

Without the bulky black dress from the funeral, I can see the hourglass shape of her body beneath the tapered leggings and Bohemian style blouse she's wearing. She's got an incredible body, looks to kill, and a mouth bound to drive away any man with sense who wants a piece of that otherwise perfect package. Though I have a feeling she'd be worth the effort.

Irked by the thought, I clear my head. *It's been over a year since I've gotten laid. That's all this is.*

"Shit," Petr says. "It was worth a try."

"You've seen me combat drive. Not an issue," I reply and start the truck.

"Well ... except I'm her ride," he says. "She can't drive my motorcycle. If you don't want her in the truck, I'll take her on the bike she doesn't know I own and will yell at me about."

The *last* thing I want is her in my truck, but I'd do anything for my guys, even manage Petr's sister for him.

"I'll handle it."

Petr glances at me, surprised. "I'll give the eulogy."

I'm not about to shy away from a little girl half my size who happens to have scared her spec-ops brothers and a former KGB officer shitless. If I can handle the super-alphas on my team, insurgents and the politics of being an officer in today's military, I can handle *her.*

I close the door to the truck, calm as ever before a mission, and circle the vehicle.

She stops, glaring up at me, hands on hips again. "My brother is *not* going with you."

"You've got a choice, ma'am," I tell her. "You're welcome to accompany us in *silence*, or you can walk to the retreat."

"He's not well enough to leave!"

"That's not up for debate."

"But Petr –"

"Not. Up. For. Debate," I repeat more slowly.

Her eyes narrow. "I know he didn't invite *you* to the retreat." She's referring to the reason I'm in town. After Mikael's death, her family opened up a foundation in his name to help underprivileged children of military families where a parent had been lost. The first annual camp for the kids is kicking off this evening.

"As a matter of fact, he did," I reply. "I'm the keynote speaker giving the initial address and sticking around for the week to help out as a camp counselor."

Her fiery look goes to her brother.

"So, ride with us quietly or walk. Your call." I'm using my calmest command voice, the one I've used to defuse situations between friendlies and restless allies.

"I'm not riding with you."

Normally, I wouldn't care how she got there. But I've got a competitive streak, one she managed to poke awake in the hospital. Our disagreement has elevated to a matter of principal, and I'm going to win this round.

"It's twenty four clicks from here. You aren't walking." *Jesus. How did they grow up with her and stay sane?* "I'm going to count to five. Have your ass in the truck by the time I'm done, or I'll put you there."

She rolls her eyes. "You got any other tactics except for resorting to violence, hero?"

I don't take her barb this time. Instead, I take off my cap and set it on the hood of the truck.

"One." It's followed by my dress jacket, which I fold neatly and place beside it. "Two." I've got her attention now. She's eyeing my biceps, which I will freely admit are huge, thanks in part to training I did with her brothers. I taught them to swim like a SEAL, and they helped me bulk up. "Three."

"Petr said you jarheads are crazy." She's watching me as if trying to figure out how serious I am.

I suspect no one in her family has ever told her no or failed to give in when she yelled. But I'm not like anyone else she's met before, and she's about to learn that.

"Four." Off go the shoes.

Katya moves slowly towards the truck, muttering something I'm pretty sure I don't want to hear. She opens the door to the back, gets in and slams it.

I'd like to think she's got the sense to know when she's outmatched, but I think she's more interested in making sure I don't kill her brother between here and the retreat.

Damn civilians. I take my time to replace my clothing and rein in my temper before getting in the truck.

It's quiet in the cab. I'm not sure why I'm so surprised.

Petr looks at me like I'm crazy but doesn't speak, as if afraid to provoke the can of worms seated unhappily in the back seat.

"One big happy family," I mutter and pull out of the parking lot.

It's days like these where I'm almost glad I'm an orphan.

CHAPTER FOUR: KATYA

C APTAIN MATHIS IS AN ASSHOLE with awesome biceps. I'm normally a thigh girl, but I have to admit – I could be swayed, if he wasn't such a dick.

I want to think I'm old enough not to mope, but well, I'm pissed. This is my world, my brother, my retreat! When he's involved, members of my family die. It's taken every minute of every day to help get Petr healthy again, and I'm still scared that something might go wrong, that he, too, might be taken from me.

"Seatbelt," Captain Mathis directs.

I pull it on.

Damn Marine. Not satisfied with killing people. He's gotta kill the environment, too. I'm reduced to being a silent prisoner in the back of one of the eco-unfriendliest vehicles on the road.

No one speaks for a few minutes. It's tense again, the way it was when I confronted him in Petr's room.

My brother clears his throat. "It's a beautiful day," Petr says. "Will be fun getting back into the forest. Always loved it there." By the smile on his face, I know he's thinking about how he and Mikael built an insane obstacle course in the forest and would race each other through it every time they were home. "I'm definitely testing out the new leg this week," he adds.

I open my mouth to protest, knowing the brutal, three-mile course is the last thing he should do before his final tests next week.

Captain Mathis gives me a warning look in the rearview mirror.

"Fifteen clicks."

I don't exactly know what a *click* is, but I'm assuming it's some military way of measuring distance. I do know that the asshole driving us would dump me on the side of the road in a heartbeat. If there's one thing I sense about him, it's that he doesn't give idle threats.

I stare out the window, clamping my mouth closed.

Petr twists to glance at me. "First time for everything," he says, impressed.

Biting my tongue, I lean forward and slap him on the back of the head.

He laughs. "Captain Sawyer Mathis, meet my sister, Katya."

"We met at your brother's funeral," Captain Mathis says quietly. "She slapped me."

"Katya!" Petr exclaims.

I ignore them both.

"No worries. Like a mosquito bite. Barely felt it," Captain Mathis replies.

Get your jabs in now, jackass. The minute I'm out of the truck …

"Choking down the cookies she sent was worse."

I gasp, staring at him.

"Ex-nay on the ookies-cay," Petr says, laughing too hard. "They were a nice thought, Kitty-Khav. We all appreciated them."

Hurt, I glare at Captain Mathis. I'm tempted to slap the back of his head, too, but something tells me he's more likely to go ninja on me than my brother will. I'll settle for making his life hell this week, since we'll all be spending it together.

There's nothing wrong with my cookies. Baba loves them. He's the one always encouraging me to send them overseas to help cheer up deployed soldiers. I guess I shouldn't be surprised a man with a nickname like *Iceman* doesn't like cookies. He probably steals candy from kids and tells five year olds there's no such thing as the Easter Bunny.

"Baba always asked what it'd take to keep you quiet, Kitty-Khav," Petr says, smiling. "I guess the answer is a Force Recon Marine. God knows two Green Berets couldn't."

I'm glad he's smiling. I just wish it wasn't at my expense.

They chat about people they know, rattling off names of other service members. I've heard Petr mention a couple of them but can't recall much about them. Gazing out the window, I watch as we exit the highway for a winding road leading through a forest. My family owns a lot of land along here. Our house is situated on about four hundred acres, a quarter of which was annexed from an old summer camp then renovated earlier this summer.

Mikael would love this camp idea.

Thinking of him makes me hurt inside. My chest gets tight, and my heart aches so much, I rub my left shoulder. I haven't been to the forest since Mikael's death. It didn't seem right to return to his favorite place without him.

We turn down a dirt road, and Petr, too, falls silent. I have a feeling he's thinking the same thing. I've gotten good at sensing his mood after sitting with him for most of the past four months. I was there when he awoke from his coma and when the night terrors seized him. He'd wake up screaming, and I'd crawl into the hospital bed with him and hold him until he stopped shaking. I helped him eat and take his meds when he was too weak or fevered to do it himself, and we developed our own little language for those days where he was too tired from the many surgeries to speak.

My eyes are blurring as I stare outside the window at the forest. I blink back tears.

"Kitty-Khav," Petr says, stretching his arm back over his head towards me.

I reach forward and take his hand. He squeezes.

"We've never been out here without Mikael," he explains to Captain Mathis.

He doesn't deserve to know. I want to say something, walking be damned, but there's a lump in my throat that prevents me from speaking.

Captain Mathis catches my eye in the rearview mirror. His attention lingers for a moment before shifting back to the road. He doesn't say anything, and I glare at the back of his head.

Of all the people my brothers served with, why does *he* get to be here?

"We'll be okay, Katya," Petr tells me gently. "You keep making cookies, and I'll keep working out."

I don't want to smile, but I do. I love my Petr so much. I didn't simply put my life on hold for the past four months, I straight out ditched everything to be with him. I'd do it again in a heartbeat, too, even if I'm not sure how things will ever go back to normal. My life is a disaster right now.

Deal with that later, Kitty-Khav, I tell myself. Someday I'll have to pick up the pieces but not today.

"Oh, god, you didn't invite Harris."

I lean to see what Petr is looking at. The camp is less than a quarter a mile ahead, and a group of men and one woman are out front of the log cabin welcome center, at the flagpoles. There are three men clumped together, guys I recognize from pictures Mikael sent home. Even if I didn't know they're members of his and Petr's teams, it'd be obvious by the way they were built and how they moved.

"We're even," I reply.

"I can't stand him, Katya."

I'm not about to tell him I didn't invite Harris Westwood the Third, either. I had nothing to do with the list of camp counselors, or Captain Mathis never would've made the cut. I imagine one of our father's assistants put together the list of camp counselors and chose Harris because of how close his family is to ours.

"Who's Harris?" Captain Mathis asks.

"A friend," I reply curtly.

"He's been stalking you since you were sixteen," Petr retorts. "Like a wolf after a sheep. Not the good stalking."

"You've never spoken to him for more than five minutes, and I traveled to Europe and South America with him," I point out. "He's not a wolf or stalking me. He's a friend." *Sorta.* In truth, Harris makes me uneasy sometimes, because he can be a little too intense. Not sexy-boyfriend intense. More like ... obsessive serial killer intense. "You'll get along well with him, Captain Mathis."

"I trust your brother's judgment," Captain Mathis replies.

"Maybe I should show him my leg, let him know how painful it is to have a limb cut off," Petr says.

"Keep that thing in your pants, Petr," I respond.

Captain Mathis chuckles. "I don't think your team will let anyone near your sister, Khav."

"I can take care of myself," I reply. "I don't need violent meatheads running my life."

Petr says nothing, probably knowing there's nothing safe to say.

"Remember. No jumping. No running unless it's on the track or treadmill. Any pain or discomfort, and we –" I start, going down the list of things the doctor warned me about.

Petr pretends to listen. I have a feeling his attention is on his friends, who he hasn't seen since he came home.

Captain Mathis parks, and we all exit his monster truck. He goes to greet those he knows, while I wait with Petr. My attention shifts briefly to the flags flying above us. The US flag is at the top of the pole. Beneath it flies one with Mikael's picture, like he's looking out for us. It's a nice thought, one I hope is true.

My foolish brother, Petr, is already lugging around packs as big as I am. He hauls it out of the truck bed with no apparent strain.

"Do you want help?" I ask, itching to assist.

"No, sis." He grunts and slings it over his back. "You didn't bring a sleeping bag?"

"Why would I?" I reply.

"Um, if you're a counselor, don't you sleep here overnight?" He gazes down at me, amused, his blue eyes sparkling.

Shit. I glance at the forest. I love it during the day. At night, when there are bugs and spiders and it's cold, I'm not as much of a fan.

But if Petr's staying, so am I. "I guess." Sometimes I worry too much about him and end up messing up my own circumstances.

"Have Zach bring you some stuff," he recommends.

Zach is one of our father's assistants. Nodding, I pull out my cell and type him a note.

Petr goes to the others. Their loud greetings and bear hugs draw my gaze. I smile, thrilled to see the huge grin on his face. Captain Mathis is the only one in uniform, which doesn't surprise me. He strikes me as the kind of guy who is never really off the clock.

"Not your usual ride," Harris says, approaching. Handsome and lean, he's got a trust fund the size of mine and aspirations of following his father into the family business one day. He's smiling, but there is never warmth in his eyes. It's one of the reasons that I sometimes don't like being around him. He can be moodier than me, too, which I have no patience for.

"No," I say. "Good to see you, Harris." I give him a quick hug.

"Always happy to help your family, Kat," he responds. "None of us knew how to show our support, so we jumped at the chance when Zach called."

Then he says something sweet like this, and I tell the little voice inside me that thinks he's creepy to shut up. With a father who doesn't trust anyone and brothers convinced terrorists live in our basement, it's sometimes hard for me to forget that normal people don't suspect everyone around them of being up to no good.

"Thank you so much, Harris!" I squeeze him hard.

He laughs. "Anything for you, Kat."

"Katya!" Petr calls.

I release Harris to see Petr waving me over. The others are gazing at me, except for Captain Mathis, who is looking at Harris.

I go and wrap my arms around Petr.

"My sister, Katya," he introduces me and bear hugs me back. "Hasn't left my side in four fucking months."

"Language, Petr," I murmur.

He rolls his eyes. "This is my team. Captain Mathis you met, Riley Holland from the Navy SEALs, Ian Schneider from Air Force special ops, Carson Gray – a Green Beret Mikael and I trained with – and of course, Army Captain Harper Jacobson. She's our bridge between the no man's land where we operate and the rest of the world."

"Nice to meet you all." I shake hands with everyone except Captain Mathis. Knowing how rough things are where my brothers operate, I'm surprised to meet a woman among those he considers his teammates. Harper is toned and taller than me with a quick smile. I like her at once, especially knowing her job was to take care of my brothers.

"Oh, and Harris." Petr motions to the man standing a few feet behind me. The way he says it irritates me, but I keep quiet for once, wanting to know a bit more about those he considers friends.

There are eight of us total to act as camp counselors and kid wranglers for the one-week program. I'm starting to think I should've paid more attention when Zack and Baba were explaining what being a counselor entailed. I'm not too keen on camping.

Petr is so happy, though, that there's no part of me that's about to complain about being stuck in the forest for a week.

Since joining the military, Petr has a life I can't relate to. I felt left out many holidays when he and Mikael would return with stories about people they knew and places they'd been. This time, I get to meet his friends, and to spend a week with the man he's become …

… while also ensuring he doesn't do anything that the doctor has forbidden. I may not have brought my sleeping bag, but I've got a list in my pocket with activities he's not allowed to perform and emergency numbers if he does.

"Welcome!" My father's booming voice draws everyone's attention. He's standing on the porch of the reception and activity center. His eyes are glowing, his burly form dressed in jeans and a light sweater. "Come in, all of you!" Larger than life, my father is the reason my brothers turned out to be the characters they are. I take after my mother, who my father describes as more delicate.

I just remember her temper and how disappointed she was that I didn't have her talent to become a ballerina. And of course, the night she died in a fire. The scarring on my back from that horrible night is the reason I don't wear anything but long-sleeved shirts. No bathing suits or t-shirts or pretty little blouses.

Father shakes hands with everyone then hugs Petr and me before we go in. There are six chairs at one long table with a full bag in front of each. Sitting beside Petr, I look through its contents.

There are a couple of polos we're supposed to wear to identify us as counselors, emergency first aid kits, dangerous insect and animal identification sheets, lists of children's names with special information by each, emergency procedures and contact information for everyone here …

I pull out the black belt. It's got a couple spots for attaching water bottles, knives, and I'm not sure what else. I try it on to make sure it fits and leave it. With some irritation, I see that the polos in my bag are all short-sleeved. There's a reason I don't wear short sleeves, one that everyone who might've put together the bags should know.

It doesn't take a rocket scientist to figure out who made sure I got short sleeves. She's standing in front of me, smiling.

"You'll be partnered up and work in teams with your assigned kids," Brianna, the eighth counselor, already wearing a polo, says, handing out team assignments. Beautiful and perky with light brown hair and more makeup than I think belongs in a forest, she dated Mikael and Petr both over the years.

We never really got along for a few reasons. In addition to tormenting me in school about the scars on my back, she crushed Mikael's heart to date Petr then dumped him last year, after he thought they were getting married some day.

He still likes her. It doesn't hurt that she's gorgeous and successful.

Which are all reasons why I can't stand her. Aside from her screwing over my brothers, she also likes to remind me that I never really know what I want to do with my life.

"You'll be joined at the hip with your partner for the extent of this," Brianna continues. "Since part of what we're doing is a competition, we tried to match up the teams so it's not too easy for one team to win." Her gaze is on the guy Petr introduced as Riley, the SEAL.

He winks at her with a smile. The biggest of all of them, it's no wonder she's gunning for him first.

But it pisses me off, knowing my brother still cares for her. She didn't visit him once in the hospital.

"It's okay, Kitty-Khav." Petr leans over to say. With all the time we spent together, he's able to read me as easily as I can him. "I'm over that." He's smiling and appears to be sincere.

If I had any doubt, the bitch would be on the floor right now, unconscious.

Brianna reaches me and hands out my team information. Six kids are listed on the page.

And then I see who my *partner* is.

No way in hell.

CHAPTER FIVE: SAWYER

*F*UCK. NEXT TO MY NAME on the sheet the cute brunette handed out is Katya's name. Being around her is about as pleasant as being pinned down in a firefight – without any weapons. Of the three civilians I could've been paired with, I'd take Harris over Katya, even knowing how right Petr is about the guy. I don't need to talk to him to sense there's something really off about him.

War brings out courage in those who never thought themselves capable of it. It can also shine a light on the darkness in someone's soul, when they're pushed to the point where they don't just snap, they take everyone down with them.

Harris is one of those men. If he hasn't snapped yet, he will one day, and it won't be pleasant.

I could really use my good luck charm this week. I'm still upset with myself for losing it in the battle that took Mikael's life. It was given to me by the Marine who inspired me to join, an heirloom of sorts passed to him from his grandfather, who served in World War One. I had carried it with me for ten years, since I was sixteen.

"Can we swap partners?" Katya asks.

Equally dissatisfied with my luck, I'm surprised she has the balls to ask for a new one. I'm not the one who's wearing heels and forgot a sleeping bag, and I'd never throw mud on her or disrespect Petr by admitting out loud I don't want shit to do with her.

"Who you got?" Petr asks, leaning over to see her paper. His gaze flies up to mine. He smiles. "Everyone here wants Captain Mathis. He's always got his shit together and never loses."

"Then someone here will be happy to swap with me," she replies coolly.

The guys exchange looks around me, not sure what to make of her insistence.

"I'll trade you, Sawyer," Harris offers.

"Nope. No swaps," Petr says quickly. "Captain Mathis is the best man out here, and that's who you're teamed up with."

By the astonished look on Katya's face, her brother has never put his foot down before.

I'll admit, as childish as it sounds, the fact she wants nothing to do with me provokes the side of me that wants to show her why she's wrong. Again. I'm not sure how this girl gets under my skin, but she does.

"I need long-sleeved shirts," Katya says, peering with dissatisfaction into her bag.

What is with her? I'm ready to write her and her shirts off as crazy when Brianna responds.

"Something wrong with short sleeves? Fat arms or a few scars you don't want anyone to see?" she laughs.

Katya's face is red. I'm thinking there's some knowledge between the two about the shirts. I can't begin to guess what it is, or why I have a feeling Katya and Brianna are going to be at each other's throats this week.

The awkward silence that falls is interrupted by Mr. Khavalov.

"It is with my deepest gratitude that I thank you all," he says in his thick accent. "Mikael meant the world to Petr, Katya and me. That you all have come so far to honor him, honors us, too. We are here to honor Mikael and use his legacy to help children who have lost a parent. He was a noble man, and this is a noble cause."

It's truly an incredible thing they've done here. It makes me view Katya in a little better light, knowing that her general hatred towards me stems from love for her brothers. I respect her loyalty, even if her anger leaves me wishing for a new partner for the week.

"I think I speak for everyone here when I say it's an honor to be here today, Mr. Khavalov," I respond. "Mikael would be proud, and this is a touching way to remember him and help others."

Mr. Khavalov smiles. "I like you, Captain Mathis." He chuckles. "Come! Brianna will show you all the grounds."

We all gather our bags and trail the sexy brunette out of the welcome center. She leads us around the small but modern campsite, explaining everything. While the log structures and stone walkways are quaint, the camp has modern amenities like private showers, air conditioned dorms with high quality beds and wardrobes, and a mess hall that I immediately wish I'd had at any point in my career. There's an immense obstacle course, swimming pools, horse stables, and other activities, in addition to the camp sitting on a lake with pristine paddleboats loosely corralled by a rope near a new dock.

It's clear the Khavalovs put a great deal of money into the camp, another sign of how serious they are about honoring Mikael.

Each set of partners is assigned a dorm, where we'll stay with the kids on our team. We're given an hour to set up then instructions to go to the reception center for some team building exercises.

I go to my truck to grab my gear and return to the barracks I've been assigned with Katya. Each entrance to a barracks is decorated by a flag in a different color. We're the blue team.

Walking around the interior, she's got her arms crossed and is peering into corners.

I'm not even going to ask. I go to the back, where there's a break room stocked with healthy snacks and water, a laundry room and a second room for the counselors with two bunk beds and two sets of dressers. We have our own bathroom while the kids have a larger, community one they share with the others.

I'm not sure how the two of us are going to sleep in the same room. She seems like the kind who might try to kill me in my sleep. Might be a good thing I rarely sleep.

"Any preference as to which rack you want, ma'am?" I call.

"No."

I claim one side of the room. It takes me ten minutes to make my bed, position everything in drawers, and stow the rest out of sight, ensuring an aesthetically pleasing room.

"You don't have to do that," she says from the doorway.

I glance at her. "Do what?"

"That." She's pointing at the corners of my bed, which are crisp and tight. "You can relax."

"Discipline stems from routine," I reply automatically.

"Right. They don't let you jarheads think, do they?" She sighs and walks in, gazing around, unimpressed with our comfortable quarters. "You allergic to peppermint?"

"No."

"Okay, good." Katya goes to the corner and pulls a dark glass bottle from her large purse. Pinching the top of the dropper-lid, she deposits a few drops of something into the corner.

"What is that?" I ask.

"Peppermint oil. Keeps spiders away."

No sleeping bag or halfway decent shoes, but she remembers bug repellant? I don't think this woman has an ounce of sense.

This isn't going to work. I watch her deposit oil into each corner then under the window, unable to find a polite way to tell her that her priorities suck.

When she's done, she faces me. The tension between us isn't normal. She doesn't look at me; she glares. There's always fire burning in the depths of her gaze, and she's tense. There's a tiny part of me that wants to say something to help her.

The rest ... well, I'm not sure what to do. I can't remember anything ever feeling so awkward. Unaccustomed to dealing with civilians, I have a feeling my preferred way of handling her won't go over well.

"This is gonna be a long week," she voices what I'm thinking. "It's not too late to go back to Iraq. You won't be stuck with me."

"I'm not afraid of you, Katya," I assure her. "Even if your brother and father are."

"You're right. Staying here might keep your men from getting killed."

"Might teach you a thing or two about what it means to work with someone else instead of running people like Petr over."

"I don't run him over. I'm taking care of him, something you should've done in the first place!" The fire is in her gaze. She strides up to me, pausing in my space.

The beauty glaring up at me might be a turn on, if her tongue wasn't so fucking lethal.

"Maybe instead of telling him what he can't do, you can have him show you what he can do," I suggest.

"Maybe you should've been there for four months watching him heal instead of screwing him up and dropping him in my lap." That glint is in her eyes, the one that says she's about to slap me again.

"You got a freebie at Mikael's funeral," I warn her. "Slap me again, and things will go differently this time."

"What? You'll hit me back?"

"No, ma'am, I won't ever raise a hand to you. But you won't like what does happen," I assure her. "There will be consequences."

The taut silence that follows makes me think there's more than frustration between us, something I'll keep attributing to not getting laid in too long. She's small enough for me to lift with one arm, her flushed features and the challenge in her gaze warming me on the inside.

Someone like this would be wild in the sack.

"If we're done here, leave please, so I can change," I tell her with forced politeness.

Another pause, and then she stalks out, slamming the door behind her.

I release my breath, suddenly identifying what I feel. It's the sense I get before I walk into battle, the combination of roaring adrenaline, exhilaration and extreme focus.

Shaking tension from my shoulders, I know she's angry but can't quite write off everything she said.

Maybe you should've been there for four months watching him heal instead of screwing him up and dropping him in my lap.

There's some truth in that, a sense of guilt I experience whenever I think of Petr. I promised to be there when he woke but wasn't. I don't know exactly what goes into amputation and giving someone a new leg, but I can't imagine the experience is simple or remotely pleasant.

If there's one thing I know about Katya, it's that she didn't leave his side the entire time. Which means, I brought the war home to her, too. One dead, one crippled for life, and one scarred emotionally.

I fucked up her family, her world. She'll never forgive me.

That makes two of us.

I change quickly. The others are wearing jeans. After so long in uniform, I've lost some fashion sense, so I pull on dark jeans and don one of the polos, tucking it in. It irks me not to wear a belt; I end up using my uniform belt. I'm pulling on stiff hiking boots when someone knocks.

"Captain Mathis?" It's Petr's voice.

I cross to the door and open it. He's dressed similarly, wearing an assigned polo.

"Can I talk to you for a minute?"

Assuming Katya said something to him, I step aside and sit on my bunk, waiting.

"Just, uh … a request, sir," he starts with a smile. "Please don't trade Katya. I know she'll be a pain in the ass. She's never camped a day in her life. She's a good girl, though, and I'd feel safer knowing she's with you than anyone else."

Assuming he's thinking of the creep Harris, I nod. I owe him this, if nothing else.

"She'll be a challenge."

"I never back down from a challenge." *As much as I'd like to this time.*

"I think you're the only one here with the temperament to handle her, and …" Petr pauses. "I really want the man who saved my life and the woman who sat beside me for four months while I healed to be friends. Or maybe, at least not hate each other."

Understanding softens some of my anger. "You asked for us to be partners?"

"I might've recommended it to Zach when he was creating the teams." Petr gives a roguish grin.

"It's my pleasure," I reply with diplomacy I've learned as an officer.

He laughs. "No, it's really not, sir. But I appreciate it."

I can't turn down a request like this, especially from him. It's just a week and just an angry woman. It can't be that bad. After all, she's sexy as hell, even with the attitude.

"Your leg holding up okay?" I ask, glancing down at it.

"Awesome." He slaps it. "Can't wait to show the kids. I loved that shit when I was little."

Smiling, I motion to the door.

We exit the dorm into the humid, warm afternoon. I automatically take accountability whenever I walk into a room or situation involving my men. The others are there, and I'm not surprised to see Riley flirting with the brunette, Brianna. Katya is the only one missing, and I glance around.

"Horse stables, sir," Petr says before I can ask. "If you ever can't find her, she's there."

"I'll go get my partner," I say. Not about to show him how reluctant I am to be dealing with his sister, I strike off in the direction of the stables and follow the stone trail.

The trees rustle from a warm breeze while blue sky peeks through the canopy above. I breathe in the scent of forest deeply. I can't get the peppermint out of my nose, which makes me think there's a drop of it somewhere, maybe on my shoes. Being overseas, I've missed four seasons and vegetation such as this. The setting is serene, cheerful, and a little surreal.

Katya is at the corral near the stables, her arms draped over the railing as she watches the horses in the paddock. Her position has caused her shirt to hitch up, and my gaze lingers on the perky ass and long thighs clad in her snug leggings.

Not now. Not her. I remind myself. I go to the railing a few feet from her, eyes following the movement of the two horses. A glance at her makes my jaw clench. Her eyes are rimmed with red.

Fuck. "I did that, didn't I?" I ask quietly.

CHAPTER SIX: KATYA

THE ASSHOLE'S QUESTION MAKES ME look when I swore I would ignore him the rest of the week. His tone is soft for once. He's dressed in jeans fitted enough to reveal the long, lean lengths of his thighs and the narrow width of his swimmer's hips. The polo is snug across his broad shoulders and tight around his biceps. Even without his uniform, he's got the detached, commanding air that tells people he's something different.

"No," I lie.

Captain Mathis holds my gaze.

"I went too far," he continues in the same tone. "I apologize."

I'm not expecting an apology from the Iceman or the way my face feels warm under his direct look.

"I'll be at the reception center." He pushes away from the railing and walks away.

I turn to watch him, uncertain what to think.

He pauses, saying over his shoulder, "I'm a stickler for details. Your belt is on wrong. If you want help, let me know."

I look down at the camp-issued belt, irritated, and then back up at him. Confident and strong, he's got a quick gait and a nice ass. The man I think he is never would've apologized. Nor would I want him to. I want to hate him, because I don't know how else to deal with Mikael being gone.

After a moment, I receive a text from Zach saying he's waiting in the parking lot with my stuff. I go there instead of the reception center. He helps me carry everything to the lodge where I'll be staying with the jackass. I set up my side of the room, wash my face in the bathroom and leave.

The others are laughing and talking when I enter the reception center. Brianna is the center of attention from all the guys, even Harris. I want to throw something but sit down in my seat to look at the paperwork they've been going over when I was out.

First aid procedures. *Ugh.* Schedule with two days marked as being *offsite camping. Double ugh.* I'm not the kind of person who wants anything to do with living in a tent. I don't know any of this stuff, and everyone else seems a lot more comfortable with it.

"Ten minute break, then we'll get started again," calls Brianna. She's definitely relishing being in charge.

I tell myself not to give her an ounce of thought, but it's kind of hard. It doesn't help that I have an unpleasant history with her. I'm feeling raw again, a combination of being somewhere I've never been without Mikael and feeling out of place with the others here.

God, I miss him so much.

"Hey, Kat."

Dammit, Brianna. Leave me alone. I plaster on a fake smile and rise to talk to her.

"You've lost weight."

"Been taking care of my brother. Hospital food leaves much to be desired."

"Hmm." A shadow crosses through her features. "At least you're not up to your old antics anymore."

"Some things are more important than my personal life," I reply innocently.

That gets the response I want. Unable to provoke Captain Mathis, I know I haven't lost my touch by the flare of red that goes up Brianna's pretty face.

"We missed you at the hospital," I add, digging in deeper.

"It wasn't my place to be there," she snaps. "I'm sorry what happened to your brothers, but –"

"You came here," I point out. "You've always preferred the easy road, I guess."

"This coming from a trust fund baby who spends every night at the club and has done nothing with her life!"

"Wait a minute." I pretend to consider. "Weren't you sleeping with *both* my brothers when you agreed to marry Petr?"

"Ohhhhkay, ladies." It's Riley. He's looking between us. "Let's just step away and cool off." He plants a large hand on each of our shoulders and pushes us away from one another, moving his muscular frame between us. "Hey, Iceman, come get your partner before she tears mine apart."

At least he knows who'd win. I take some satisfaction out of the acknowledgment and whirl.

Captain Mathis is across the room, hands on hips, watching. Impossible to read as usual, though one eyebrow is up in either accusation or inquisition. He nods his head to the side in a silent command for me to join him.

I have no idea where this guy gets off thinking he can boss me around. It might work with his men, but not with me.

I go outside instead, feeling claustrophobic.

Maybe being here is a mistake. I want to think it's for Petr and Mikael – and it is – but there's another reason I feel compelled to stay. I think there's a piece of me that needs this, too, though I'm not sure why, when this is totally not my scene.

Tossing my head back, I gaze at the late afternoon sky, so blue and beautiful. The forest calms me, and I shake out my shoulders.

"Is there anyone here you don't have a problem with?" Captain Mathis asks from behind me.

"We'll find out, won't we?"

He's quiet. I have a feeling he's not entirely certain what to say in response.

After a minute, he circles and stops in front of me, reaching for my belt. Not expecting the sudden proximity, I freeze where I'd normally move or push him out of my space. He smells lightly of coconuts once more, and I find myself staring at the width of his chest and the shapely arms and shoulders. His brown eyes are the shade of dark chocolate, his skin rendered golden by the sun and his hair kept in a neat high-and-tight. His heated strength is different than that of my brother's.

I notice his body, how close he is to me, the way his roped forearm muscles shift with the movement of the long fingers unsnapping my belt. I've never paid any attention to my brothers like this.

"Grommets on the outside," he instructs me. He steps closer to pull the belt out and twist it before settling it again at my waist. Snapping it into place, he drops his hands but remains a little too close for my comfort.

"Thanks," I murmur.

In a manner of seconds, I've forgotten why I hate him and Brianna. It's uncanny, as if my senses overtake conscious thought when he's around.

"Your brother's old enough to fight his own battles."

Anger stirs, and I look up at him. "I know that!"

Captain Mathis is calm, always so calm. I wonder what it feels like not to experience emotions the way I do.

"So you're just picking fights today?" he asks.

"None of your damn business!"

"For this week, it is," he says firmly. "We're a team. If you're going to be picking fights all week, I'd like to know."

"Why? So you can trade me?" I challenge, crossing my arms. Being so close to him is a little too intense right now. I step back self-consciously.

"So I can make sure I have your back, if it elevates," he responds. "It's what teams do. Take care of their own."

"Except for Mikael." I can't help it. I'm feeling furious with the handsome man before me once more.

Captain Mathis doesn't even blink. If anything, he seems to grow colder. "Whatever you *think* you know about me, I will have your back, because that's the way this works."

It's not what I'm expecting to hear. He has a way of either infuriating me or deflating my anger. The weird tension stretches between us, the one that manages to replace thought with a physical awareness of his body.

We're evaluating each other.

"Hey, guys! We're starting again!" Harris calls from the porch.

I don't like the idea of backing down – ever – and Harris's shout is well timed.

Spinning, I retreat towards the reception center. Harris smiles at me, but I ignore him, returning to my assigned seat. Captain Mathis sits beside me a moment later, and I wait to see what new torture the counselors are about to be put through.

What the hell am I doing here? Really?

"This is a fun one!" Brianna is grinning. "Basically, an interview. You interview your partners then do a little verbal report to the group about what you've learned about your partner! Cool childhood memories, hobbies, favorite songs, anything."

Really? Are we in junior high? Or maybe hell?

"Ready, go!"

Captain Mathis and I face each other. I sense more than see he's uncomfortable with me. I suspect Mikael will always be between us. We stare at one another, neither speaking, until the silence gets so awkward, I shift in my seat. I can't read him, don't know how to take anything he says or how he looks at me. He's so calm, it's almost unnerving.

"This is what we call an interrogation in my line of work," he breaks the silence at last. "I'm not a fan."

I laugh at his dry humor, suspecting this is as bad for him as it is for me.

"Let's do the opposite," I suggest.

A curious smile tugs up one corner of his mouth. "Like what?"

"Instead of telling each other about ourselves" I roll my eyes "let's make up stories about each other. It'll be a lot more fun."

He shifts.

I lean forward. I've caught him off guard. Finally.

"Ah. So you're a total gingerbread man," I assess. "Cookie cutter, same as everyone else, no imagination or ability to think for yourself."

A spark of something lights in his gaze. Captain Mathis leans forward as well, elbows on knees. "You don't get to where I am by not thinking for yourself."

"Prove it," I challenge. "Tell me a story about me. Make it good." I'm almost curious about what he'll say but convinced he'll prove me right about being unable to think outside the box of discipline and nicely folded corners of his bedding.

Captain Mathis studies me for a moment, long enough for familiar heat to stir inside me, before he begins.

"Katya Khavalov is the kind of person who thinks throwing lemons at enemies is better than making lemonade. Fiercely independent, she learned at a young age how to use mind control on those around her. It worked on everyone but her dog, Sawyer, who was immune to the mind control and would chew on her shoes every night."

By the end, I'm laughing again. Captain Mathis has a wry, subtle sense of humor that catches me off guard and a deadpan delivery that makes me wonder if I'm supposed to laugh or not.

"Not what you thought?" he asks with another of the faint, half smiles.

"Okay, my turn." Composing myself, I spend a few seconds righting my story then share it. "Sawyer Mathis was born as a statue in a garden near a witch's cabin. One day, the witch made him human, and sent him out to win her battles with the garden gnomes that were invading her lands. Handsome, dashing and indestructible, Sawyer won every battle, until he came across the dragon Katya. She swallowed him whole one evening but he turned back into stone in her gut and was stuck there forever."

He's smiling more widely this time. Dimples form in his cheeks that turn his features from handsome to almost charming.

"Isn't this more fun?" I ask.

"I would've preferred to be a garden gnome to an orphan."

"Oh. You're an orphan? No family at all?"

"Not since I was two."

"That's sad," I murmur, studying him. "Is that why you're in the Marines?"

He raises an eyebrow. "I'm in the Marines because the man who set me straight was a Marine. He taught me a few things about life, and I decided I wanted to be like him."

"What do you mean set you straight?" I ask. "You had to have been born like this." I wave at him.

"Not exactly." He doesn't seem to want to answer for a minute but finally relents. "I was in a gang for a few years as a teen, on a life path that would've put me in jail, if he hadn't stepped in."

I don't want to, but I feel bad for Sawyer Mathis. I don't envision a dark upbringing when I look at him. My family is my world. I can't imagine what it would've been like to grow up without my brothers and parents, to resort to a gang life. He doesn't say it, but I'm pretty sure that means he grew up pretty poor, too.

We're nothing alike and even more of opposites than I initially thought.

"What about you?" he asks. "What's your story?"

I shrug. "Your story is interesting. Mine is kind of boring."

"I doubt that. You seem to cause trouble everywhere you go. I'm sure you've got some good stories."

"You heard Brianna," I reply. "Spoiled trust fund baby with no plans for the future who likes to club." The sarcasm in my words is heavy enough, I expect him to move on. He's easy to talk to and listens intently, but I'm ready to retreat into my shell once more. I'm not here to make friends, especially with him.

"I don't see any of that," he says.

Eyeing him, I lean back. "Not so detail oriented?"

The flare of anger is in his gaze but disappears quickly. I'm starting to think I can get more of a rise out of him than he wants to acknowledge.

"I imagine that's what you want people to think about you," he replies. "Katya Khavalov is passionate, a woman with a big heart that makes up for her complete lack of discipline in any area. She's creative and smart enough to do anything she wants with her life, loyal to the death, and beautiful. There might or might not be a sweet center beyond her crunchy exterior. Most people are too afraid of her to find out, which is the way she likes it."

Crunchy? My face is hot by the time he's done. Uncertain what to think about anything he's said, I clear my throat.

"Sawyer Mathis likes to hide behind an icy exterior, to replace emotion with discipline and routine. He knows he can't lose anyone or anything, if he doesn't get attached, and if he does lose someone, it won't hurt as much as it could. He's brave and strong but alone. Always alone."

We gaze at each other, neither speaking. The others are enjoying themselves around us. Every one of my interactions with Sawyer somehow skirts the shallow end of the pool and plunges into the middle of the ocean. I can't help wishing I hadn't proposed straying from the instructions. Maybe then I wouldn't have learned a thing or two about the man I need to hate that makes me think of him differently.

I have a feeling he won't be the first to break the thick tension this time. I rack my brain for a topic so benign, even we can't mess it up.

"So …" I say. "Do you have a speech for tonight?"

"Yes."

"That's good." *This is so awkward.* I'm not even certain why it is. Do we have a connection or did we piss each other off more? Shouldn't I know one way or the other?

He pulls out a folded piece of paper from his pocket and hands it to me. I unfold it and start to read. I'm not surprised he's gotten it down word for word. He's not the kind of person to wing it, the way I would.

Frowning, I reach the end. "This is awful."

"Really?" He eyes me, as if suspecting I'm picking a fight again. "Why?"

"This is so impersonal and … I don't know. Canned. Like a report or something. The Iceman thing might work in combat, but you're talking to a bunch of kids who lost a parent. You should try to connect to them more."

He's quiet. I wish I could read him, at least a little. Is he remotely open to what I'm saying?

Like I care. I tend to act then think about whether or not I should have.

I take a pen and flip the paper over. "Maybe you should start with your own background. You're an orphan. You know what it feels like." Hearing my words, I look up. "Sorry. I don't mean ..." My face flashes hot.

"I understood," he says with the half smile. Resting his elbows on the table beside me, he's too close again. I'm starting to like his scent more and more, the combination of pure male and coconuts.

Heady and sweet. It makes me hungry for chocolate dipped macaroons.

"Maybe you can talk about that a little and the guy who inspired you to join the Marines. I mean, these kids all understand military stuff." I make a few notes on the paper. "They probably need a bit more of warm and fuzzy."

"Because I'm the warm-fuzzy type."

I roll my eyes. "You can connect with normal people without going all gooey."

He chuckles.

"And without ordering them around," I add.

"It bothers you."

I glare at him. "Really? You're just now figuring that out?"

He doesn't answer, but there's amusement in his dark gaze that makes me think he's messing with me this time. I'm not sure what to think about him teasing me.

I finish making notes then hand it to him.

"Thanks," he says, reading it.

Whatever. "It's fine if you toss it."

"Why would I?"

"People don't like listening to me."

"Because your delivery sucks. Not because you don't have something worth listening to. If you stopped nagging and yelling, you might find people listen better."

My mouth drops open.

His attention is on the paper.

"You are such an ass," I manage, unable to come up with a better line.

"I'm an honest ass."

I lean back, too angry to respond. I'm not sure how else to show I care for Petr and help others, other than to nag. It's the only thing that works on people like my brothers and father. Crossing my arms, I turn my gaze to the ceiling.

Captain Mathis scribbles a few more notes into the outline I created for him. I'm sorta surprised he's considering it. He seems too … rigid to be open to change.

When he's finished, he replaces it in his pocket. We return to the weird quiet and thick tension, simply staring at each other.

I really hope the rest of today passes faster. I'm pretty sure these team-building exercises are going to kill me.

Chapter Seven: Sawyer

MY FIRST DAY AT THE CAMP probably couldn't be stranger. At least it's quick. After our exercises, the kids start to arrive. There's a big dinner with the families, and then my speech. By the time the evening reception is over, it's lights out for the kids.

I'm almost grateful when Katya goes to bed early, too, leaving me with the guys for a couple hours of poker and talking. I don't have to admit to her that she was right about the speech. Maybe she's right about me being too detached. I never thought of it that way, but there is a great deal of distance between me and pretty much everyone else.

I guess it's my comfort zone. I never really thought of it as an issue before she pointed out that I'm always alone. Is that really so bad, given my line of work? I'll never be able to forgive myself for the four guys I lost a few months back. If my guard was lower, how could I live with myself, if it happened again?

Like every other conversation with her, Katya somehow manages to make my head spin in a direction I'm not used to. I spend an hour with the guys before heading back to the barracks. Being with them leaves me relaxed, the opposite of Katya's effect on me. Being around her leaves me oddly energized yet also unusually drained, as if our mental grappling is taxing our bodies as well.

Stepping out of the warm night into the barracks, I'm pleased to see that the kids are out cold, and so is she. Silently, I prepare for bed, irked to discover her lotion on top of my dresser when she's got space on hers. Her shoes are in the middle of the floor, her suitcase open at the foot of her bed. She's taken over the bathroom, too. Everything I need is confined to one small bathroom bag.

Katya's shit spills over the tiny sink area, and there are fluffy pink towels hanging beside my military issued olive, sandpapery one. The bathtub is littered with no less than five bottles and one of those pink scrubby-loofa things.

One week, I remind myself. Seeing the disaster that is our room makes me itchy. Clean, neat and orderly – it's how I like to live. Battle is messy, a place where adapting is a matter of survival. Here, at home or wherever I'm sleeping at night, I can control my immediate surroundings, even if that's nothing more than keeping my weapon at my side or a canteen by my head.

"Civilians." I survey the bathroom again then decide that no, I really can't live like this.

Within five minutes, I've got her shit straightened or put away, the towels folded correctly, and the bottles in the shower corralled in the basket hanging over the showerhead. When it's neat once more, I automatically relax. I can pretend the rest of the room isn't an issue in the dark.

I go to bed mostly satisfied but also too aware of the woman sleeping six feet from me in her fluffy comforter. She's the kind of complicated I don't need in life. I'm not sure I want to know more about her, though I'm not sure I'll have the choice after a week with her.

If there's anyone I should keep distant from, it's her. That much I know, even if I'm not yet sure why.

My alarm goes off at five, an hour before sunrise. It's the time I always get up. From what I've read about kids, controlling them is dependent on managing their energy levels. Which means, before our day officially starts, we're going to do some drills.

I roll out of bed, refreshed and ready for the first full day of camp.

"Katya," I call quietly. "Lights on."

I give her a minute and go to the bathroom to change and get ready. When I return, I flip on the lights.

She hasn't moved.

"Katya," I say more loudly. "Time to get up!"

"What?" she replies sleepily, and pulls a pillow over her head. "What time is it?"

"Five."

"We don't have to be at breakfast until eight."

"Come on. We've got work to do."

"No way."

Why do I have a feeling she's going to be harder to manage than the six kids we're assigned?

Rather than arguing, I go out to wake up everyone else. The light going on wakes half the kids. Pulling out my phone, I flip through my music files, turn up the volume, and blast Reveille.

The piercing, quick-paced bugle song can wake a man from the dead. Its effect is immediate.

The kids bound up.

I hit pause. "Good morning, team," I start. "You have ten minutes to get ready and be outside in a line, tallest to shortest. Understood?"

They're staring at me. A few nod.

"Understood?" I repeat in sharper tone.

"Yes, Captain Mathis," two chirp. Their words are echoed by others.

The team gets up, grabbing their clothing and bathroom bags in varying degrees of urgency and head out of the barracks to the community bathrooms located at the center of the barracks.

Except one. We have a range of kids in our group, from the sixteen-year-old girl and boy, to the six-year-old girl still sitting in her bed. She's blinking back tears, and I wait.

"You, too, Jenna," I tell her firmly.

"I can't."

Clasping my hands behind my back, I approach her bed.

"Why can't – oh, Jesus." Her bed reeks of urine.

The tears start.

I sit down on the bed opposite her, frowning. "You're six. You're too old to be wetting the bed." At least according to my research she is.

"I d…didn't mean t…to." She sniffles pitifully.

"We may need to call your mother. I'm not sure this is going to work out," I say.

"My mother is … dead."

Fuck. I read the list of kids and their issues last night five times. I don't remember her mother being mentioned as the one killed in battle. In fact, I know it wasn't on the sheet. Her father died last year in Afghanistan.

Jenna's wail makes me jerk. I sit, frozen, debating how to handle her. I know how to deal with Marines who get scared in battle or those who have medical issues. But they're not six.

"Holy hell, Sawyer. What did you do?" Katya hurries into the bay. Blinking but awake, she's in a t-shirt and underwear, eyes on the screaming kid. Without waiting for a response, she crouches down in the space between me and the kid, her long, wild hair brushing my forearms. There's something insanely sexy about her mussed state.

Jenna points to the bed and keeps sobbing.

I grimace.

"C'mon. Let's get you cleaned up." Katya's voice is cheerful, and she stands, picking up Jenna. Immediately, the little girl starts to calm.

"Ten minutes," I call after her. "Workout attire."

Katya shoots me a dirty look over her shoulder but doesn't respond. She walks back towards our room, completely unaware of how fucking sexy she is in her underwear. My eyes travel down her body, lingering on the rounds of her ass, visible beneath the boy short-style underwear, and down her shapely thighs. She's toned in a way that says she does yoga or Pilates, definitely not in the way of a hardcore athlete.

She has a small limp, one I hadn't noticed before, either. I don't see anything wrong with her shapely legs but don't wonder about it too long, because I'm not the only one staring at her.

The sixteen-year-old boy, the oldest on our team, is frozen in the doorway of the barracks. His jaw is slack, his eyes wide as he stares at her ass.

"I forgot my ... my ..." He stops.

"Turn around, and go to the showers," I order.

He's still staring.

"Now," I bark.

The kid stumbles away from the door. I watch, understanding exactly what he's thinking at the moment.

Within about fifteen minutes, all five of them are outside, standing in a line as directed. A little antsy – or maybe cold – they don't seem to be capable of standing still.

Not that I care at this point. I don't need perfection from a bunch of untrained civilians, just effort. I walk around them and send in those who forgot water or in one case, meds, to retrieve them.

At the twenty-minute mark, Jenna dashes out of the barracks and assumes her spot at the end of the line. She's clean, dressed and carrying her water like she's supposed to.

"Where's Ms. Khavalov?" I ask her.

"She's not ready yet."

How does a bed wetting six-year-old show up a full-grown woman?

"Tanner, move out to the pit," I instruct the oldest boy. "Stay in a line. No one leaves the trail. Understood?"

More *yes, captain* and *yes, sir* mumbles. The kids turn and begin walking.

I trot inside. The door to our room is closed, so I knock. "You almost ready?"

"Yes!"

By her tone, I'm in for a hell of a morning. I can't help smiling at the amount of resentment I hear.

"We'll be at the pit. Don't forget your water. Grommets out," I respond. I don't stick around to learn how well she can throw shoes but join the kids and continue walking with them in the dark to the pit, a large area with a soft layer of woodchips. In the Corps, we use a place like this for any number of drills, from combat arms training to morning push-ups to accountability formations.

"We'll start with some jumping jacks," I tell the kids. "Ready? Start!"

"Starting them young and early, I see," a female voice teases from behind me.

I turn to see Captain Harper, dressed for a run. We've worked together for about six months, and she's never failed my team, no matter what I've asked of her. The opposite of Katya, she's disciplined and motivated. I always enjoy talking to her. It's easy to be around someone with similar priorities and values.

Something I didn't realize until trying to understand Katya more. The friction I feel dealing with Khav's sister isn't here, and it's kinda nice not to have it hanging over my head.

"You want me to give you a hand?" Captain Harper asks.

"Sure."

CHAPTER EIGHT: KATYA

HAVE I EVER VOLUNTARILY BEEN up this early? I stayed up with Petr for days straight in the hospital, but this is different. This is *camp.* I need coffee and a hot shower before I'm ready to start my day. I'm not sure why I'm staggering around the room getting dressed as quickly as possible. I'd like to think it's because the kids might need me.

But I'm pretty sure it's because my sleepy mind is listening to Captain Mathis' curt order.

With a sigh, I sweep my hair up into a ponytail and walk through the dorm, emerging into a chilly morning. In shorts and a long sleeve t-shirt, I'm shivering by the time I make it to the place he calls the pit.

The kids are doing laps. I slow and stare, surprised to see them running around the pit while Captain Mathis stands with someone else in the center. He's dressed similarly in short shorts that reveal the long, thick thighs of a swimmer.

He had to have nice thighs.

More irritated at him, I fold my arms across my chest and approach. The easy smile on his face fades when he catches sight of me. I can almost see him tense. The woman with him, who I recognize from yesterday, turns to face me.

"Good morning," Captain Harper says with a smile. Perky and alert, she looks the opposite of how I feel.

"Morning," I respond.

"Now that your partner's here, I'll take off," she says to Captain Mathis.

"Have fun!"

She leaves, taking with her the cheerful atmosphere.

Captain Mathis and I gaze at each other.

"Five o'clock," he begins.

"If you have coffee ready at that hour, I'll consider it."

His jaw clenches. "Do you have any self-defense training?"

"No. Baba said that's why I had two brothers."

"Everyone should know something," Captain Mathis replies. "I know you can slap. Punch?"

I almost smile but shake my head.

"This will be interesting," he states and beckons me towards him. "I want to teach the kids some basics."

"Train them to kill young?" I ask, glaring at him.

Captain Mathis watches the running kids. "Train them to take care of themselves. A sense of vulnerability often comes with the death of a loved one. It might help build confidence and ..." He faces me and stops.

The awkward silence is heavy. I'm trying to keep my face expressionless, but not emoting is not my forte. It's too early to hide the pain I feel at the reminder. Captain Mathis searches my face briefly with his brown eyes then takes a step towards me.

It's hard for me not to want to scream every time we stumble on even the most innocent inference to Mikael's death. I can't forget that my brother isn't coming home because of the man standing in front of me.

"It'll be good for you to learn," he says and rests his hands on my shoulders, shifting my body. He squares me to face him. "This is a good stance for you for our drills."

"Because somehow this will help me forget Mikael's death?" I challenge.

Every once in a while, something sparks in his eyes that makes me think I've hit some emotion. Just as quickly, it's gone.

"No, Katya," he says quietly. "Because everyone should know the basics." He drops his hands.

I watch him move away.

"Fall in!" he belts to the kids.

They scramble to face him, lining up from tallest to shortest.

"My god! They look like the Von Trapp kids," I say, shaking my head.

Captain Mathis ignores me. "Pair up and gather around," he instructs the six sleepy members of our team. "We're going to do some self-defense training."

Returning to me, he addresses the kids.

"First lesson of self-defense. Escape if you can. Don't fight someone bigger or stronger. Got it?"

The kids nod.

"Second, if you have to defend yourself, remember the parts of the body that work well as weapons: Meat of your palm. Fist. Elbow. Forehead. Hips. Knees. Heels." He raises or points to each as he speaks slowly. "Got it?" He repeats them, and the kids mirror his movement. "Now, put one of those in the part of a body where it hurts to get hit. Throat, eyes, groin, solar plexus, toes, fingers."

I assess him as I listen. The kids seem entranced.

He talks them through a few things, and I try to pay attention. But in truth, I'm feeling the lack of caffeine and having trouble concentrating. Jenna giving a shriek startles me, and I jerk out of my thoughts.

She's in a fighting stance, pretending to kick an invisible opponent. The other kids laugh, and Captain Mathis is smiling. He kneels down in front of her.

"See how balanced she is?" he asks, pushing her shoulder gently. "Something to remember. Always keep your feet on the ground and maintain your balance."

My goodness, she's adorable with her fierce scowl.

"Let's start with a few scenarios. Remember what I told you?" he asks, standing. "You're at the mall and someone grabs you."

He beckons to me, and I approach reluctantly, certain I'm about to become the crash test dummy. Captain Mathis circles me and wraps both arms around me. The move shocks me, as much from the sudden impact of our bodies, as the hardness and strength behind me. I was expecting a punch, not a full-body connection.

The strange sensations that overwhelm my thinking throw me into complete awareness without coffee. Touching him is like downing a shot of whiskey. My blood is on fire, my senses scattered. I'm no longer cold this early, not with his body heat finding its way through my clothing. It's hard not to want to melt against him, to relax in his arms and know without a doubt he's strong enough to support me.

Thank god he's talking to the kids. It takes me a minute to switch my focus from how solid he is to his low voice.

"...take a step forward."

I realize he's talking to me. I do what he says and feel his body weight shift to me.

"Kick him in the crunchies!" one of the kids cries.

"Crunchies?" I echo. Realizing what he means, I start to laugh.

"Not the best position to try that," Captain Mathis says, amused. "What else can she do?"

"Elbow!" someone says.

"Okay. Try to move your elbow."

I wriggle and pull, but he's got my arms pinned solidly against me.

"So that won't work. What next?" he asks.

"Stomp on his foot!"

"Try it," he tells me.

I do.

The kids clap.

Eventually, he gives the steps for how to get free. Not that I'll remember them. I'm a little too ... aware of him to recall anything. But for the next hour, his hands don't leave my body. He's more patient than I expect, walking the kids through scenarios over and over until they get it. As strong and detail oriented as he is, he's also gentle with me, positioning my body and shifting me around with absolutely none of the awkwardness that I feel.

In fact, I'd say he doesn't notice me any more than he would one of his men.

When the hour training is up, he moves away from me. My body is humming with uncomfortable warmth that makes me wish I had the guts to wear a t-shirt instead of a long sleeved shirt. I haven't worn anything but long sleeves out in public since I was thirteen, after the kids at school made fun of my scars.

The kids are being sent on a run around the pit once more. Captain Mathis watches them, hands on hips.

"This isn't boot camp," I remind him. I want to fan myself but know better than to give him any sort of sign I'm attracted to him.

"You'll thank me when they're in bed at eight while the other teams are up past midnight," he replies. "They'll be easier to manage throughout the day this way."

"Are we going to start every day this way?" I ask.

He glances at me then back. "If learning self-defense keeps you from biting my head off, we might."

I glare at him.

"Though, I wonder if you were so quiet because you wanted to learn how to take me out?" he asks, raising an eyebrow.

"Maybe." There's no way in hell I'd ever admit to him the real reason: that I was distracted by his body too much to say anything. "You are a half-decent instructor." Hoping mind reading isn't something he learned in the Marines, I follow the kids with my gaze, my face warm.

"If Harris ever gets too fresh, you know what to do."

There's an edge in his voice that's reflected in his gaze. I'm not sure what he's saying – or why he seems tense once more.

I spot movement through the trees and see Riley and Brianna walking with their kids through the camp, towards the dining hall.

Captain Mathis broke Petr's body, but that woman broke the hearts of both my brothers. Not to mention she likes to embarrass me. What the hell does any man in his right mind see in her?

"Is it safe to assume you know more than self-defense?" I ask thoughtfully.

"I can snap a man's neck in a few different ways. Is Harris that much of an issue?"

"What the hell?" I stare at him.

He's not joking.

"Harris is my business," I reply. "Why you and my brother are fixated on him ..." I shake my head. "No. I just ... no. How the hell did you get from knowing how to hit someone to snapping necks?"

He shrugs. "In my line of work, I never rule out the possibility."

"This is reality, Captain Mathis. There's no snapping necks here." I can't even imagine ...

My eyes go to his large hands, the same hands that were on my body not ten minutes before. That he can be so gentle and so lethal is really kind of freaky.

My brothers never told me what happened on their missions overseas, and I'm beginning to understand why. I can't fathom an existence where you might have to kill someone with your bare hands!

"Sometimes things escalate more quickly than you expect," he adds at my stunned silence.

Meeting his gaze again, I find myself wondering if he's talking strictly about war or something else.

Don't be an idiot.

As if feeling the weird tension between us, he clears his throat. "What do you want to know?" he asks, moving closer. "I thought you were a peace loving liberal."

"I am, but every once in a while you meet someone who needs a good punch," I reply and cross my arms.

"Someone like ... me?"

I look him up and down, already suspecting it'd be more trouble than it's worth to try. Though I might like it if he wrestled me down ...

Stop it, Katya!

"Not this time," I reply.

"You have someone in mind."

"None of your business. I need to know how to punch someone a couple of times," I answer.

He's eyeing me warily. "Who and why?"

"You said everyone needs to know the basics." I point out. "What do you care who I punch? And don't tell me because we're a team. I can wait until you're gone to do it!"

"The basics of self-defense are important for getting yourself out of trouble, not into it," he replies.

"So you won't show me?"

"Not until you tell me why."

I've never had to answer to anyone in my life, even my father. There's no way I'm answering to *him*. "Never mind. One of the other guys will show me."

Captain Mathis seems to debate silently, studying me. I'm not about to crack and tell him. As if sensing so, he relents. He steps close enough for me to feel his body heat and takes my wrist.

"I recommend not punching. You're just as likely to hurt yourself as someone else," he starts. "But if you insist, keep your wrist braced." He straightens mine and places his hand around it. "Completely straight. Make a tight fist."

I do.

"Thumb here. You want to hit with the first two knuckles." He taps the two he means.

I watch carefully, trying to take in everything from how it looks to how it feels.

"So I have to have a straight shot basically," I murmur. It seems more complicated than I thought. "You've hit real people?"

"Yeah." He meets my gaze. "It's not pretty, Katya. You can shatter your wrist or break a finger if you do it wrong."

Ugh.

"You're better off learning some solid self-defense skills."

"What if something escalates?" I ask. "Friendly chat one minute then everything explodes."

Holding my closed fist in both of his, he's gazing at me.

Heat flutters through me once more, and I realize what I've said. Or maybe, how it could be taken, if he's remotely affected by me the same way I am by him.

Which he can't be, because he'd have to be human first to have emotions.

"There's usually something to spark it," he responds quietly. "Explosions don't just happen."

What the hell are we talking about?

I'm not sure, but my stomach is turning over and my pulse is racing beneath his direct gaze. Uncertain how to respond, I tug my hand free and move away.

"It's getting close to breakfast, and we all need showers," I say, turning away.

Captain Mathis clasps his hands behind his back and moves towards the center of the pit.

"Fall in!" he orders.

The kids scramble into a line in front of him, panting.

"Tanner, lead them back to the barracks," he orders the tallest boy.

He walks beside the line of kids, while I trail, trying to get my head on straight once more. It doesn't help that I keep looking at his nice thighs and trying to remember when the last time I went out on a date was.

Before Mikael died.

Almost instantly, I'm sad again.

CHAPTER NINE: SAWYER

K ATYA TAKES THIRTY MINUTES to get ready. We're late to breakfast, and I'm silently wishing she was one of my Marines, so I could deal with her properly. But she's not, and I'm at a loss as to how to help her pull her head out of her ass and pay attention to what's going on around her.

As soon as we sit down at the table with blue flags, we're served by a staff of two smiling women in cooks' whites. I'm excited to see what kind of breakfast a kitchen this nice can make compared to the usual military fare and am secretly hoping for some sort of gourmet French toast, my favorite.

My tray is set before me, and I stare at it. There's no hot food here. No bacon, eggs, and pancakes like I'm used to eating every morning in the mess hall. I'm not sure what the fuck this is, but it's definitely not French toast.

A glance at the other tables shows that they *are* eating hot food that smells and looks insanely fresh and homemade, and I start to think we got the leftovers for being late.

"What is this?" the ten-year-old boy, Jacob, asks, peering into a bowl of what appears to be cream cheese. His older sister, Morgan, is seated beside him, equally confused.

"Greek yogurt and organic granola, honey and flax seeds. If you mix it all together, it's one of the healthiest breakfasts you can have," Katya says cheerfully. "It'll keep you full for hours."

I say nothing, wanting to be a better sport about her mentoring than she is about mine. *One week of this shit.* I stab the thick yogurt with a spoon then begin emptying the other fixings into it, doubting anything is going to make this taste like the bacon I crave.

"Dig in!" she says.

Jenna alone seems interested in our breakfast and starts throwing everything into the yogurt. The other kids glance at their food and then at me.

"You've got ten minutes to eat," I say.

The kids take their cue and begin eating quickly.

Katya slides onto the bench beside me. "I planned all our meals."

"For the whole week?" I ask.

"Yeah. I hope you like hippy food." She smiles sweetly. There's a gleam in her eye that makes me think she's still pissed about me yelling at her to get out of the shower.

"Is there any real food this week?"

"This *is* real food. No preservatives or chemicals, refined sugar or flour or anything else artificial that'll kill you. Petr has been eating like this for the past four months, and look how healthy he is."

"Is there any fake food this week?" I grumble.

"Nope."

She's trying to break me. If there's one thing people don't fuck with, it's a Marine's food, especially when he's home for a few days from Iraq. Does she know that, or is eating hippy food really the way she is?

"Physical activity isn't the only way to manage hyperactivity," she says. "I took a few psychology classes, nutrition and a bunch of other stuff. Chemicals in food are linked to behavioral issues. So, you rein in the kids your way, and I'll do it mine." Katya pours me coffee out of the slender metal carafe on our table.

I can't argue with her logic, even though I suspect she's more interested in torturing me than helping me tame the kids.

I dig in anyway. I'm surprised to find it doesn't taste as bad as I'm expecting. Sweet and tangy, the smooth yogurt is actually pretty good. It will never replace bacon in my life, but it's not bad.

Ten minutes later, we're leaving the mess hall and gathering around a rose garden nearby to hear morning announcements. Katya is texting on her phone and starts to wander off. Anticipating losing her several times today, I snag her belt, drawing her back to me.

"Stay with your team," I remind her.

She glares up at me. "You aren't my babysitter."

"I can be if you need one."

With a noisy snort, she tucks her phone away but doesn't try to leave again, staying where I put her in front of me, a little too close for my comfort. Not that I'm intimidated by her, but like this morning doing drills, I kind of like the idea of being close enough to touch her. Maybe it's because she smells like a woman – a mix of her own musk, fruity hair product, vanilla perfume and some sort of baby powder smell I think comes from helping Jenna get ready – or maybe it's because she is so completely feminine. Dressed in a fitted, long-sleeved camp polo and leggings that cling to her shape, she's sexy and fiery.

Whatever it is, standing this close almost makes up for her being a bitch most of the time. When she's quiet, I like being near her. When she's not, I know being too close might tempt me to strangle her. I'm feeling no animosity towards her now, despite the breakfast, instead interested in her scent and warmth.

We may get through this after all. I concentrate on Brianna, who is giving the line-up for the morning. I'm overly aware of how close Katya is and how perfectly her body fit against mine this morning during the drills. For the first time since we've met, she was semi-cooperative and quiet for all of an hour. If she was like that more often, I might be in real danger of starting to like her.

"Try not to kill anyone on our team this week, Captain Mathis," she whispers to me.

Thank god she's a bitch.

We listen to the announcements and go to our assigned activity. The first day of camp is an easy one filled with activities meant to familiarize the kids with everything and help build a sense of teamwork.

I'm optimistic about the physical activity and building a team. It's what I do in Iraq. We aren't in war, but the environment is familiar. Confident and eager, I'm starting to think even being stuck with Katya can't fuck today up.

Hours later, I know how wrong I was to underestimate her. The kids are better disciplined and easier to work with.

By the end of the first full day, I'm ready to drag Katya back to her brother and demand a trade. Never mind that she couldn't follow instructions to save her life or the fact she didn't wear the right shoes for the trail hike and outright refused to paddleboat or the way she rolls her eyes at me whenever I'm working with the kids.

It's the fact we can't interact without *something* hanging between us. Anger, tension, frustration ... I can't name what it is, but it taints every conversation we have. We aren't on the same page.

We aren't even in the same fucking library. I'm at a loss as to how to bridge that gap, though, which is something that never happens to me. I can learn to work with anyone – but her.

It's nine o'clock, and I'm in front of the barracks. The kids are in bed at eight like I predicted, completely zonked after their long day. I'm not sure where Katya is, another of my issues with her. She can't seem to understand the point of *teamwork* and communication. At all. How hard is it to tell me she's stepping out for ten minutes?

Right now, it's a good thing she's not around.

I try to tell myself she's got a merit or two. The kids *love* her, and she's great with them. She's as warm as I'm cold. They obey me and flock to her. With them, there's none of the tension or snarkiness she displays with me. The food she planned leaves me wishing for more, but is at least healthy and her intentions good. At the very least, she's not cooking.

But I can't recall ever working with someone this stubborn and oblivious.

I sit on the stairs of the barracks, comfortable with the warm evening air. Our team is the only one racked out, while lights glow in the windows of the other barracks.

"How's it going?" It's Riley, approaching from the direction of his assigned quarters.

"Definitely not boring," I reply.

He sits beside me. He's the muscle on the team with a Hollywood smile and the ability to charm any woman he crosses. While all the guys are strong, Riley is a bear.

"That's the way we like it," he says with one of his trademark grins. He's looking at the open door to his barracks. Light pours out of the front door and windows, and I can see kids dancing and milling around.

"You having issues getting them to sleep?" I ask.

"Nah. They'll wear themselves out." He's quiet for a minute.

"Hopefully. I didn't realize kids had this much energy."

I laugh.

"Got two of my own. No fucking clue," he quips.

With a nod, I don't pry. Riley had a problem keeping his dick in his pants the first few years in the military. I know his history only because I had to look over his admin paperwork a time or two. Two kids, two different mothers, neither of which he's married to. A diehard bachelor, he's learned a thing or two about not sleeping around as much, though I'm pretty sure the kids and child support aren't a total deterrent.

"You figure out why your partner wants to kill mine every time they cross paths?" he asks. "She won't say."

"I can't even begin to guess," I reply. "I have never met anyone so stubborn."

"Hey, at least she ain't hitting on you all day," Riley said ruefully. "I love a pretty girl, but Brianna … pretty sure Petr's got his eye on her. He lost his leg to save my ass. Not gonna take his girl."

"Pretty sure you can handle flirting."

"It's better than people shooting at you."

"I wish I could say the same about his sister."

Riley laughs.

"Great team we have here." Katya's cold voice comes from behind me.

Goddamn it. I checked our room and the bathroom before coming out. Assuming she'd gone wherever she fucking wanted, I didn't bother looking for her anywhere else. *I can't say anything right around her.*

"It's almost a compliment," Riley says, not missing a beat. "Captain Mathis loves a firefight."

We both twist to look at her. Standing in the doorway, she's glaring at me, dressed in shorts and a long sleeve t-shirt, her arms crossed.

"It was an inappropriate thing for me to say." No part of me wants to apologize, but I remind myself that I'm dealing with a civilian.

"You're welcome to find yourself a new team," she says. Stepping inside, she closes the door quietly.

I hear it lock and curse under my breath. I really didn't think today could get any worse.

Riley laughs.

"That woman …" I stand and pace. I grit my teeth to keep from saying more, in case she's standing at the door, listening. "Fucking A!"

"Never seen anyone get the drop on you, Captain Mathis." Riley stands and claps a hand on my shoulder. "Fuck her or leave her. Otherwise, she will drive you mental before this is over. I've got a lock pick set. Wait here." Grinning, he heads back to his barracks leaving me fuming in front of mine.

Fuck her or leave her. I honestly don't know which I'd prefer. Something tells me all this shit would be worth it for a night in her bed, if only for the sense of satisfaction in seeing her melt beneath me, but fuck. I'm not looking to get laid and especially not from a woman trying to make my world hell. It'd be easier to walk away. For good.

Except that Petr wants me to work with her. I don't fully understand why, unless he's hoping I can change her attitude enough that she no longer drives him crazy.

Don't think that's possible. I take a few deep breaths and do a couple mental relaxation exercises, like counting to ten and reciting the Marine Corps honor code. By the time I've regained my calm, Riley is on his way back.

He passes off his lock pick set. I use it to get in the front door then hand it back.

"Good luck," he whispers.

"You, too." I reply and motion to the two preteen boys that are darting out of his barracks and racing around the square.

Riley grimaces and starts towards them.

I close the door and wait a moment for my eyes to adjust to the dark. The whir of the air conditioners keeps any of the noise from outside from disturbing the sleeping kids. Walking quietly through the bunks, I approach the door to the room I share with Katya. The edges are outlined by the light from inside.

One day down. If I can handle back-to-back tours in Iraq, I can survive a week with her.

I open the door and walk in.

Katya drops something and whirls, staring at me. She's in shorts and a tank top for once, and if I'm not mistaken, she's not wearing a bra.

Not that I'm looking. She's got nice breasts, and it doesn't take a genius to notice.

"Figures," she snaps. "Couldn't knock?"

"It's my room," I reply calmly. Realizing I'm watching her, I close the door and enter the room fully.

She kneels to pick up the lotion she dropped, and I freeze.

I've seen a lot of wounds and scars in my time. I don't know that I've seen anything close to what's on her shoulder, peeking out of the tank top.

"What the fuck happened?" I crouch behind her and instinctively touch the knotted scars on the back of her shoulder.

She knocks my hand away. "None of your damn business." Katya starts to rise. I grip her arm, keeping her in place. My knees drop to either side of her thighs to aid my balance. Too interested in the old wound, for once I don't notice our bodies touching or how close I am to her.

"This is why you limp," I guess. I run my fingers down her back, following the feel of the scarring through her shirt. It stretches diagonally from her left shoulder to her right hip.

She's stiff, tense. "You noticed?"

"I notice everything. What the fuck did this?"

There's a brief hesitation then Katya tugs her arm free. She pulls the back of her tank top over her head, exposing the damage.

Speechless, I rest a palm on her back. The scar tissue is as wide as my extended hand, from the tip of my pinkie to the tip of my thump. It covers most of her back. The skin is warm and soft despite how ugly it looks.

"There was a fire in the family ski lodge when I was nine," she said tersely. "It's what killed our mother. I got trapped under a super heated steel beam. Cut right through me. Spent six months on my belly in the burn unit."

"And I thought getting shot was bad." Knowing this doesn't make up for her being a bitch. It's giving me a little more insight into why she's got this shell around her.

"I'm sure it is." Her voice has a slightly breathless quality in it, one I'm not expecting to hear. Almost like she's ... affected by my touch.

Which makes no sense. This woman hates me with a passion I've never reserved for anything. My gaze travels down her narrow, feminine shoulders to her shape. Trim torso, tucked waist, perfectly rounded hips. She smells more of her own scent and less of other products this evening, a smell I find myself leaning forward to breathe more of.

Shit. No. She's not remotely interested in me, and I'm not in her. At least, I will continue to tell myself this.

"I can't believe you noticed." She sounds upset.

"The scars? This is the worst shit I've ever seen."

Katya pulls her tank back on, pushing my hand off her back. She twists to glare at me, face red. "That is the rudest thing you've said yet!"

Civilians. I shift to make room as she turns to confront me, my hand falling automatically to the soft skin of her upper thigh. Our bodies are touching, her face a few inches from mine. I can see the different hues of blue and green in her eyes.

I can also see that her pupils are dilated, a second sign of physical arousal. I'm not sure what to think of that, especially when she's clearly angry with me once more. I don't seem like her type, and she's definitely not mine.

"I meant, I can't believe you noticed my limp," she snaps. "I've spent years fixing it!"

"I only noticed this morning when you were walking back with Jenna," I reply. "When people are tired, they aren't always able to regulate themselves like they do usually."

She's upset. I'm not sure if it's because I noticed her limp and scarring or because I've been too blunt with her again.

"If it helps, I'm more detail oriented than most others," I add. "Is the scarring why you don't wear bathing suits?"

Her flush deepens. She crosses her arms.

I don't know how she does this: infuriates me yet makes me sympathetic to her in the same breath. The idea a woman as beautiful as she is can be self-conscious is absurd, yet her blush confirms it. It's probably why she didn't want to get in the paddleboats when everyone stripped down to bathing suits this afternoon. I'm once again torn between reaching out to comfort her and getting away, before I say something that I can't take back.

"You shouldn't let the scarring deter you. You've got a great body," I tell her.

She rolls her eyes. "I assume you noticed that, too."

"Absolutely," I reply without hesitation.

"Whatever. You don't have to lie about it."

"Do I strike you as the kind of person who tells you anything but the truth?"

"I'm well aware you'd rather be in a firefight than deal with me!"

"I meant that, too."

She's staring at me like she either wants to kill me or figure out what kind of alien I am.

"I can't imagine it's the first time you've heard either of those things," I add, growing irritated by the tension between us.

"You are such a dick," she responds. "Pretty sure that's not the first time you've heard that, either, is it?"

Fuck her or leave her. Right now, I'm thinking there's a third option, one that makes me wish we were in the deserts of Iraq, where no one would find the body.

Every conversation ends this way between us. It's the reason we shouldn't be alone together. Ever.

I have the urge to breach the delicate space between us. She's breathing more quickly. I don't let myself consider that it might be because she's attracted to me and chalk it up to being anger. I do realize my hand is on her bare leg and my body is humming with adrenaline and anticipation, the way it does before a mission.

Or before I fuck a girl I'm insanely attracted to. This is like high school attraction: untamed, burning, and consuming. It's not like me to feel like I want to lose control with someone, to allow my calm control to be burned up in passion.

A knock at the door makes her jump and jars me.

Katya rises quickly and answers it.

My gaze follows her ass, and I shake my head, standing and moving away.

"I think there are spiders in my bed," Jenna whispers from outside the door. "Can I sleep with you?"

Oh, hell no.

Katya glances at me. I shake my head. Jenna is too old for this.

"Sure!" she says to Jenna.

Jenna smiles and enters.

Maybe this is a good thing. I don't say anything but go to the bathroom for a quick, cold shower. When I emerge, Jenna is wrapped in Katya's arms, and the two are buried under the comforter.

I turn off the lights and lay down. My blood is moving too quickly for me to sleep, and I stare at the ceiling. I don't know what to think about what passed between Katya and me this evening.

I'm starting to really wish I was back in Iraq, where life is much simpler.

Chapter Ten: Katya

I CAN STILL FEEL HIS HAND on my back the next morning when he all but drags me out of bed at five again. Jenna didn't pee in the bed, for which I'm grateful, and I bear through the morning drills. There's no self-defense this time. I'm not sure if I'm happy about that or not, especially when I join in the drills, running laps, circuit training, other shit I'm not a fan of. I can't help feeling too aware of my limp today. I spent years in physical rehabilitation and am careful not to give any sign of the accident that took away my mother.

The fact that Captain Mathis of all people noticed it …

It's too personal, like sitting with him on the floor last night, our bodies touching and his warm palm on my thigh. Not that he noticed anything, but I definitely did. It makes me fevered thinking about how close we were together.

Post-morning torture, we go to breakfast and then head to a couple of activities before we're sent back to our dorms to gather our gear.

Today is the day I've dreaded most. We're going off into the woods to spend the night. No dorms, though I guess there are outhouse style bathrooms. No showers, though.

Ugh. I straighten from packing. I've been very studiously ignoring him today, not engaging unless I have to. Self-conscious about my back or maybe in general, I have the urge to crawl inside my shell and stay there.

"You're taking all that for one night?" Captain Mathis asks from his side of the room.

"Just in case."

"Just in case *what?* The world ends?"

I shoot him a dirty look. Everything he's taking fits into one small pack. His sleeping bag is rolled tightly and attached to the military style bag. I've got a suitcase and a sleeping bag almost as big.

"You never know," I say defensively.

"You can't carry all that to the site."

"That's what your truck is for."

"We're hiking, Katya."

"What?" I face him, suspecting he's messing with me.

He's not.

I should've asked more questions. I don't know what the hell I'm doing out here, but everything I do or say is wrong. The others don't seem to be having issues adjusting like I am.

"You don't need a suitcase for one night."

"I don't have a pack like yours," I tell him.

His jaw clenches. I turn away, waiting for him to tell me tough luck and to lug my shit there. I'm itching for a fight with him. It might make me feel better after the weird intimacy of last night.

"Both of our stuff should fit in one pack," he says at last. "Pull out what's essential, and I'll put it with mine."

Hmm. Didn't think he'd say that. I want to refuse and hope they forbid me from going. But ... I still feel like I need to prove something to myself by making it through this week. I'm not sure what it is, and I pray that it's worth it by the end of this mess.

I push my suitcase on my bed and unzip it, considering its contents. I don't notice Captain Mathis looking over my shoulder until he speaks.

"First, you need to be wearing these."

I jump.

He leans around me, his forearm brushing mine and his chest at my back. Warmth spirals through me. I ignore it, more concerned with him destroying my clothing. Grabbing my hiking boots, he drops them on the bed.

"I figured I'd change into them once we get there," I rationalize.

"You don't need two pairs of shoes for one night."

I roll my eyes.

"One compete change of clothes, one small bathroom bag and rain gear," he rattles off.

"Rain gear? Really? You Marines have some sort of sixth sense that tells you when it's going to rain?"

"You don't have to be a Marine to tap the weather icon on your phone. It's common sense to check before you go camping," he replies evenly, gaze on my clothing. "What is all this shit?" He picks up a lace blouse I had packed in case there's some sort of formal affair.

I snatch it and push him back with my shoulder.

He moves away. "Bring extra socks and pajamas, if you want them. Anything else gets the axe."

"Pajamas if you want them? So you sleep naked or something when camping?" I snap. Too late, I hear what I said. What's worse, I'm already imagining him lying buck ass naked on his sleeping bag. If the rest of him is as nice as his thighs and biceps …

Stop it, Katya!

"We've got to be outside in five," he says.

"Yes, sir!" I say sarcastically. Thank god he didn't catch the naked comment.

He leaves me, and I shake my head. It takes me a few minutes, but I boil everything down to two changes of clothes, sandals, extra socks like he recommended, pajamas and one bathroom bag stuff to the gills.

His pack is half empty. I wonder if it's because he was expecting me not to be prepared or if he always travels light. I don't dwell on it too long but shove my clothes into it.

I emerge from the room dissatisfied, feeling as though I'm leaving behind everything I own. I guess, in a way, I am. That seems to be the purpose of camping: to get away from everyone and everything you've ever known.

I've never had that desire, though, so this is even more uncomfortable for me.

The skies are cloudy. There's no sign of rain, and I silently pray that the weather report is wrong. It's going to be rough enough without being miserable in the rain.

We all board a bus that takes us to another point in the forest where

Petr and Mikael set up the obstacle course. The kids are excited, and their enthusiasm puts me at ease. I sit with them on the bus while the other adults all congregate towards the front. Watching them makes me feel even more out of place. They all get along so well. Even Captain Mathis, who is tense around me, is relaxing and smiling with the others.

People don't relax around me. Can he be right? My delivery drives off people I'm trying to help? I've always been a bit socially awkward, more so after my mother died. My father and brothers became overprotective for a few years, and I barely left the house until I was in high school. Stuck in an elite, private school with kids who had grown up with one another, I really didn't have any motivation to make friends. I didn't have good friends until college, and I'm grateful that a bunch of them stuck around this area.

The others here are so much better adjusted than I am. I guess it helps that this is their scene, while mine is at home or in college or at the club.

I don't look too long, and pay attention to the girls I'm sitting with, needing the distraction from our destination.

When we arrive, everyone piles out of the bus. On the other side of the three-mile course is where we'll be camping. This afternoon is a familiarization round. Tomorrow, the kids will run the course, with the team with the best time winning.

The tree near the start of the course is where Petr and Mikael both carved their names and the date they finished building the course. They did everything together, from laying cement foundations where needed to chopping wood to testing and fortifying every rope, bridge, bar and anything else on the course. It took them a year to build the course. I used to come out with lunches and watch them, helping if and when they'd let me.

The world seems to fade as I gaze at the tree. The others are gathering around Brianna and Harris for a safety briefing. I go instead to the tree.

It's weird to see Mikael's name scratched into the bark. I didn't approve of them doing it, preferring they didn't harm some innocent tree. But now, I'm kind of glad they did. Seeing his sloppy handwriting is realer than a picture. He *touched* this, left a mark in a way only he could.

I'm hollow standing before the tree, almost able to imagine every detail about the day he carved his name here. Being in his forest is hard, but standing where he did two years before, looking at his name, is harder.

"Hey, Kitty-Khav." Petr's voice is soft. He stops and stands beside me, nudging me with his shoulder. "You doing okay?"

"Not really," I reply. "I shouldn't be out here with you guys, Petr. I'm totally out of place."

"Yeah you're no fan of camping."

I sigh.

"Mikael would be happy you're here."

"I hope so." Gazing up at him, I look into the face identical to Mikael's. I was always the only one who could tell them a part. Petr smiles and I see sadness in his features.

"He would be laughing his ass off if he heard you were here," he adds.

I roll my eyes, knowing as much. Mikael was the jokester. He used to tease me a lot about being too prissy.

"Baba says you dropped out of school last month."

I shrug. "No worries."

"Katya, if you did it because of the time you spent with me ..."

"You're my family."

"I know, but I'm fine and you've got a life to get back to," he reminds me. "I'm not going anywhere. You can go back and get your degree or take more classes or whatever it is you do."

I love him too much to feel burned by his words. If Brianna said something similar, this conversation would go very differently.

"Did you ever figure it out?" he prods. "What you want to be when you grow up?"

"An annoying little sister," I retort.

"Seriously." He nudges me again. "You've spent the past four months worrying about me. I'm worried about you now."

"You shouldn't be. I'm just ... me, Petr."

"You could go into child psychology or something. Kids are the only people you get along with."

I elbow him.

"You're good at health stuff, too," he suggests.

"Omigod. I don't need you telling me what to do!"

"Seriously, Kitty-Khav. There's got to be something out there you want to do aside from babysit me. You aren't going to waste your life watching over me," he says firmly.

"I'm not wasting anything," I respond. "I just never knew what I wanted to do. Still don't." It's not entirely true. I used to think I wanted to go into psychology, child or adult, until Mikael died. Now, I don't think I'll ever be able to help other people going through what I have. I can't dwell or see others dwell in the depths of despair and sadness that I have, even if I'm trying to help them.

It's too much, too personal, too dark for me. Nothing else really speaks to me in terms of a major to finish college. I've always thought my path is to help people somehow.

"Figure it out," he suggests.

"Don't be an ass!" I grumble.

"Gotta take care of my little sis!" He wraps his arms around me in a bear hug and lifts me off the ground.

"Stop, Petr!" I cry, wriggling in his arms. "You're going to knock your leg off!"

"Didn't I teach you how to get out of this hold?" Captain Mathis asks from behind us.

"I'm not going to hurt my brother!" I snap.

"We can snap his leg right back on," Riley says.

Petr laughs.

"There is something wrong with all of you!" I yell.

He sets me down and releases me. I push him.

The sight of his grin keeps me from being too cranky with him. I'm secretly happy that Petr is so chipper this week. He's in such good spirits, and I know it's because of having his friends around and being at the camp.

"All yours," he says, turning to Captain Mathis. Petr winks at me and joins his team.

Whatever.

Captain Mathis appears as enthused as I am about being stuck with each other for another day.

The teams leave in twenty-minute intervals to give everyone the chance to learn about the obstacles. I've walked through the course but never did the obstacles; I'm curious how much of a train wreck it'll be tomorrow, when the kids are racing through it.

Our team is last, and the kids sit on a log, waiting and talking quietly. I have to admit – Captain Mathis is right about them staying calm. The other teams are basically bouncing off the trees while our kids are seated and quiet.

"This one is huge!" Jacob is leaning over the side of the log.

I don't get too close. He's got a thing for bugs that I noticed yesterday. I'd rather not know what he's found. The guys gather around him while the three girls join me.

Though she's six, Jenna has a lot of mannerisms of someone much younger, which I suspect stems from regressing some while trying to cope with the loss of both parents. Her father died at battle and her mother from cancer.

She climbs in my lap and sits while the other two girls, sixteen-year-old Lexi and twelve-year-old Morgan, sit cross-legged in front of me.

Lexi is texting while Morgan seems content watching everyone else. She strikes me as shy and hasn't said more than two words since arriving.

"So gross." Lexi is staring at her brother, Jacob, who has the world's largest daddy long leg by one leg.

Morgan nods, and I shudder. I really am not the camping type.

"It's gonna rain," Lexi says, and shows me the weather forecast on her iPhone app. "You think they'll let us go back to the dorms?"

"Probably not," I reply. "Did you all bring rain coats?"

They nod, even Jenna.

"Captain Mathis made us," Lexi says.

Damn Marine. I know it's not Captain Mathis' fault that it's supposed to rain, but I don't mind blaming him for it, especially knowing I probably should've listened to him.

The skies are overcast but I don't smell rain yet, and I pray not to see any until we get back in tomorrow evening.

As usual, my luck doesn't hold long. We make it through the obstacle course, a quick lunch and then begin a hike to the private campground where we'll be spending the night.

It starts raining an hour before we get there. Not a drizzle – a downpour. I think I'm the only one without a raincoat or poncho. At least the kids and Petr are okay, even if my mood is tanking fast. Quickly soaked and cold, I keep one eye on the kids and another on the muddy trail beneath me. Captain Mathis was right about socks, too, and I'm almost glad I listened. My feet are soaked by the end of our march.

As the last team to go through the course, we're also the team that spent the most time in the rain.

I'm not sure what to expect when we get to the campground, but it's not a damn tent city. There's one that's acting as a cafeteria and a second one for the kids then four smaller ones, one on each side, that I assume are for the counselors. The bathrooms are modern, at least.

Twisting my hair into a bun, I see the youngest boy, Rory, as he slides in the mud and lands on his face in a puddle. His pack and sleeping bag go sailing and land in a puddle. I'm the last in the caravan, so I stop to help him.

"Gotcha," I say with a quick smile. My hands are almost numb from cold, and I haul him up.

Only to feel my feet slip in the mud.

We both crash down again. Wetness soaks through one side of me, and I resist the urge to curse in front of him.

Rory is giggling. Unconcerned with the mud, he pushes himself up to his knees and grins at me.

"You're enjoying this." I can't help but smile at the look on his face.

He nods. "Do you think they have cocoa?" he asks.

"I hope so," I reply, and carefully climb to my feet once more. Grounding myself more firmly, I offer him my hand and pull him up.

I hate being dirty. A glance down at my side shows me that I'm caked with mud. I'm already soaked through and looking forward to crawling into my sleeping bag, where it's warm.

I spot his sleeping bag in the middle of the puddle and groan internally.

Or maybe I'll sleep outside in the rain tonight.

"Rory, is this yours?" I ask, picking up one end.

"Yeah." He wraps his arms around it and carries it towards the tent.

"You can't sleep in that, honey," I tell him. I retrieve his backpack and follow.

"Okay."

I'm not sure what that means. I trail him into the kids' tent. It's warm, dry and buzzing with activity. The kids each have a cot with a trunk at the foot where they can put their bags and things. They're talking and excited, unaffected by the rain. Captain Mathis is with the team, helping them set up their sleeping bags then stowing their stuff away so as not to look messy.

I swear – he's got to be the most anal person I've ever met. Then again, he's dry and I'm soaked through. I might need to start listening to him about the weather, if nothing else.

Trailing Rory, I'm too miserable and tired to notice perky Brianna until she addresses me.

"Oh, did you fall, Kitty-Khav?" she asks in a syrupy voice. "You should've checked the weather." Unlike me, she's dry as a bone and smiling. Her team was the first to go through the obstacle course, which meant they probably caught about ten minutes of rain, as opposed to our hour or so.

Fuck off. I don't say it, because of the kids, but I'm definitely thinking it. I glance at her and keep walking. I've been practicing punching my pillow in anticipation of the day I get some alone time with her.

"Katya, I hope it's okay, but Riley and I are going to stay with the kids tonight just to make sure there are no issues," she calls after me.

"Sounds good," I reply, not surprised to be exiled to the pup tents outside.

"I heard Jenna's a bed wetter, so I'll come get you if she has any problems."

I stop, surprised she'd say something like that so loudly. Doesn't she know how sensitive a kid is to something like that? I was ridiculed as a preteen for my scars; I know how cruel kids can be. Half the tent had to have heard her.

My eyes find Jenna. She's staring at her feet, her face red. A few of the other kids snicker.

Glancing at Brianna, I see her smirk before she turns away.

Oh, hell no. I shake off my sleeping bag and start towards her, only to be stopped short when someone's arm wraps around me. I'm pulled back against a hard body I instantly recognize.

"Not the time or place," Captain Mathis says softly.

"You don't fuck with a little kid like that!" I whisper and strain against him. It's one thing for her to pick on me, but on a sweet six year old? Who does that?

He holds me tight against him. "Stop, Katya. We'll handle it a different way."

With a frustrated growl, I stop struggling and rest my head back on his shoulder, craning my neck to look up at him. His chiseled jaw is clenched, his brown gaze on Brianna as she walks away.

"Jenna needs a hug, and Marines don't do that shit," he adds, nodding his head towards the little girl.

Jenna's eyes are watering, her chin trembling.

Seeing her like that crushes me. I can't stand to see someone hurting. I sigh. "Let me go."

He complies, and I leave him to kneel on the floor beside Jenna. I'm too wet to sit on her bed, so I take her hands. She crawls into my lap, not caring that I'm cold and drenched. She's warm and smells like a child, her soft hair tickling my nose.

"You're doing good, sweetie," I whisper. "Okay? Trust me."

"Ms. Khav, do you think this will dry before bedtime?" Rory asks, tapping me on the shoulder.

I manage to stand with Jenna in my arms and turn. His cot is the one beside hers, and he's stretched out the sleeping bag.

It's completely soaked. There's no way that thing will be dry in time. It'd take a few cycles in a dryer, which I'm guessing isn't an option.

This is why camping sucks. "Probably not. You can use mine," I say without hesitation. "Can you grab it? I left it in the aisle."

He nods and goes to fetch it.

"If you want to change, I can take care of Jenna."

Of all the kids on the team, I'm not expecting the tall but skinny Tanner to volunteer.

"I've got a little sister," he adds. He's staring at me in mild awe, like a teen with a crush.

Amused despite my condition, I decide I'd rather duck out and change socks at least before going to dinner.

"Sure." I hand off Jenna to him. "You all get ready for dinner, okay?"

He nods and hefts Jenna onto one hip.

"You're not holding her right," Lexi complains and takes Jenna from him.

I turn away, content to let them figure out what to do while I find some dry socks. Rory is spreading out my sleeping bag on his cot.

"Ms. Khav, I need someplace to put them." Jacob appears before me, holding out a huge spider.

"You scared that hell out of me, Jacob! Don't dangle that thing in front of my face," I shriek and push his hand aside gently. "Why don't you let it go? Be free?"

His face falls. "He's a friend." He sets the arachnid in his palm and gazes at it.

I have no idea what some of these kids have been through but I'm not about to take away the friend of someone who lost a parent recently, even if that friend horrifies me.

"I'll go find you a … box. Or something," I say. "Hang onto him until I get back. Is that cool?"

Jacob smiles and nods.

Maybe it's a good thing I'm not sleeping in here tonight after all. I'm not sure how many little friends he has hanging around.

With an involuntary shudder, I step out of the tent into the cold, rainy night, intent on locating a container for a damn spider. Assuming the kitchen staff will likely be the only people to have one in the middle of the forest, I head there first.

"Hey, Katya."

I'm not in the mood for Harris. I face him, hoping the rain keeps this quick.

"Hi, Harris. What's up?"

He draws near, and I'm irked to see he, too, has a raincoat. I hug myself, shivering.

"Thought you might be up for a chat," he replies.

"Um, not in the rain. Maybe tomorrow when we get back," I say and start away.

He snags my arm. "You always do this, Katya." He sighs.

I tug loose from him and look up at him again.

"You always say later. I thought we were friends."

"We are, Harris," I say with some impatience. "The past few months have been really rough."

"You couldn't make the time for one phone call?"

I groan. "Is now the best time to do this?"

"I can't get your attention any other time."

There are days when I adore Harris and days when he's so damn moody, I can't stand him. He's in a mood now, one I don't want to deal with. It's times like these when he makes me uneasy, and I start to humor Petr's insistence that there's something off about Harris.

"Look, Harris, let's just talk tomorrow. We'll both be at camp. Okay?" I say.

"We've got time now."

"Fine. What do you want to say?" I ask through clenched teeth. "Make it quick, because I'm soaked."

"It's always about you, isn't it?"

Oh, god, not one of these kinds of conversations … I'd rather be arguing with Captain Mathis than dealing with Harris.

Chapter Eleven: Sawyer

I'M FINDING IT HARD not to pity Katya. She's clearly miserable, though I warned her about the rain. If she were one of my Marines, I'd call this a lesson. But she's not. She's a clueless civilian who gave up her sleeping bag to one kid after almost taking out a fellow counselor for hurting the feelings of another kid.

She really is a contradiction. So oblivious in some ways, worse than a child, yet capable of purposely needling me to try to piss me off. There's an instinct that's been building whenever I'm around her, one I wasn't able to define until this evening. I'm beginning to think her problem is that she doesn't have someone who takes care of her the way she tries to everyone else. Petr watches over her from a distance but even he won't get too close, knowing she'll give him hell if he does.

Someone like Katya needs an occasional ass kicking and someone to hand her a jacket every time she gives someone the shirt off her back. She's both completely selfless about taking care of others and a selfish bitch when it comes to how she's viewed everything involving me. I'm not sure how someone can be both.

So frustrating. I want her to simply be a mega-bitch, so I don't feel concerned about what she'll do without a sleeping bag. As wrong as it is, I don't want to feel compelled to take care of her. It's a slippery slope. If she were anyone else, anyone who hadn't managed to creep beneath my guard and get an emotional reaction out of me, then it wouldn't matter.

But I'm feeling the need to maintain some distance – physical and emotional – between us. I'm starting to realize why, and I don't like it. It's something more than basic attraction, which is what I've been trying to tell myself it is.

She exits the front of the tent after talking to Jacob. As usual, she doesn't bother telling me where she's going or for how long. Maybe it's a civilian thing. I'm used to a lot better communication than this.

"Don't forget," I tell the kids firmly. "Team first. Always."

They nod. Lexi is holding Jenna while Tanner helps Rory.

With a glance at my watch, I add, "Dinner in ten. Be ready."

I pull up the hood of my Gortex jacket and go out the second entrance, headed towards the tent Brianna said was ours. I reach it and stop.

It's in a puddle, partially collapsed.

I'm beginning to wonder which girl is the bigger bitch.

"You can have ours," Riley says, joining me. He points to the one on the north side of the camp. "We're sleeping with the kids."

"Great, thanks," I reply.

We walk towards the other pup tent. These aren't basic military issued canvas. These are lightweight, professional, high-end camping tents, another sign that the Khavalovs spent money all over the place.

"I never thought I'd like cooler weather like this. I'm tempted to sleep outside," I say wryly.

"It's a nice break," he agrees. "Sorry about Brianna." Riley clears his throat. "You ever wish they were service members, so we could just deal with this problem the easy way?"

I laugh and glance around to make sure Katya doesn't get the drop on me again. "Every fucking day."

"I'll run interference. Is Jenna really a bed wetter?"

"Yeah."

"I don't even know how to deal with that."

I smile. There's always an easy air with other members of the team. Most were hand selected for my team, and I trust them completely, know them better than anyone else. It's relaxing being around Riley, even when we're quietly standing in a steady stream of rain for a few minutes, each of us lost in our own thoughts.

"Mikael would like this," Riley says.

"Yeah, he would." It's hard to forget the reason we're out here. I have to tolerate Katya for Mikael's sake, as well as Petr's.

"Captain Mathis, Rory hid my shoes."

Riley laughs. We give each other a look then turn to face Morgan. She's wearing her raincoat – and is bare foot.

"See you at dinner," Riley says with a snort and starts towards the mess tent.

"All right, come on," I say to Morgan.

She takes my hand, and I bite my tongue, wanting to remind her that Marines don't hold hands. Seeing her feet sink into the mud, I take pity on the girl and swing her up into my arms and over my shoulder. She's slender and weighs about what my pack today did after Katya stuffed it full of clothes and god knows what else. I didn't double check before slinging it onto my back.

Morgan is giggling. I take her inside the tent and deposit her near her rack. Her shoes are sitting on top of her sleeping bag, and she whirls, glaring at Rory, who looks guilty.

"I told you I was getting Captain Mathis!" she yells.

"No yelling at team members," I chide. "And no stealing shoes." This I direct towards Rory.

He mumbles something. I'm not sure if it's an apology or excuse, but I won't humor either.

"Dinnertime. Line up!" I order them.

The kids scramble into a line, with Morgan falling in last. We're getting looks from the other teams. Unconcerned, I critically evaluate my little team.

"Water?"

They go down the line saying *check.*

"Meds, Jenna and Rory?"

"Check!" They chorus together.

I glance around without seeing my fellow camp counselor. Not surprised, I march the kids out of the tent, into the rain, and next door to the mess hall. We're the first there, for once, and the scents of barbecue are thick in the air. My mouth waters at the thought of pulled pork sliders and cornbread.

And then I remember Katya's healthy meal plan. With some reluctance, I go to the food table designated for our team by a blue flag and take in today's surprise. A smiling cook is waiting to scoop whatever this shit is onto our plates.

"This is what?" I ask, indicating the main dish, which looks like barbecue, if meat came in cubes.

"Tofu-cue!" the cook says cheerfully. "Homemade tamales, refried chickpeas, organic cornbread and almond-soy custard for dessert."

"Fucking A." First my bacon, now my barbecue. If Katya is using food to wear me down, it's working too fucking well. Trained to lead by example, I present my plate anyway. "Load me up."

The cook fixes up everyone a plate. I'm pretty sure the cornbread is all that I'll be able to choke down. Like usual, the food isn't bad. It's not what I want right now, and it doesn't taste like real food, even if the consistencies and coloring are similar.

The kids don't complain, even though almost all of them avoid what the cook called *tofu-cue*. I don't even know what tofu is, except that it can't be anything that grows naturally. It's definitely nothing I've seen served in a mess hall.

Too occupied trying to understand what I'm eating, I don't notice that Katya isn't there to enjoy the menu she picked out until I'm done. I finish before the kids, who aren't used to eating quickly like I do in the field.

Bet she's secretly eating a pulled pork sandwich and laughing. Twisting around, I assess Katya isn't at dinner at all. I don't think even she would wander off from this place, especially in the rain. It's not like her to be absent. She may not like it, but thus far, she's gone everywhere the team has.

Brianna is here, which makes me relax some, until I start to think maybe Brianna won their face off and buried her in the forest. Katya has heart, but I spent an hour with her teaching basic self-defense. If Brianna has an ounce of training, Katya isn't going to win.

Harris isn't here. The hair on the back of my neck rises the way it does when I've walked into a surveillance web. I tell myself it's nothing. He may be in his tent or something. *This isn't a war zone, Sawyer. We aren't surrounded by people trying to kill us.*

Sometimes, it's difficult to take your mind out of the war zone, even if your body already is. Shaking away my unease, I go back for another piece of cornbread.

Half an hour later, I march the kids back to their tent and turn them over to Riley. I imagine it'll be more comfortable in the big tent and wish Katya could stay there instead of a pup tent. I'm sure Riley would gladly give up his cot, if the two women weren't on the verge of killing one another.

Tomorrow will be an early day. We're starting at six instead of eight. Our team, however, will get to sleep in an hour. I head back to the pup tent and unzip the opening. Stripping quickly out of my wet clothing, I roll everything tightly and enter the tent, which has a lit lantern hanging from the low ceiling. There's enough room for two people and a few feet of space for packs at the other end. By military standards, this is luxurious.

Katya isn't here. Irked, I pull out my phone and text her to ask where she is, not for the first time in the past two days.

Her response is quick. *With the kids. Don't wait up.*

"Sometimes …" I stare at the phone. I'm not going to let her rattle me tonight.

I hang up my wet rain gear at the other end and set my shoes there, too. The patter of rain on the top of the tent promises to lull me into sleep. Stripping off my layered shirts and pants, I change quickly into sweats and sit on my sleeping bag.

Thunder grumbles. It's far off and reminds me of the sound of a distant battle. I listen to it, recalling when the last time was that I heard a thunderstorm. It was the night before that horrible day four months ago when I lost four men.

My thoughts return to that night, and I close my eyes. I can almost smell blood and sulfur, feel the scorching heat of the explosion that took off Petr's leg, hear the shouts of my team as they struggle to accomplish the mission while rescuing their fallen friends.

Worst night of my life. Yet, it led me here, to the peaceful forest helping children who are a lot like me. It's one of those paradoxes I'm not certain what to do with. When I was sixteen, I mugged a Marine, a man who then became my mentor and the reason I joined the Corps.

If I hadn't been involved in a life of crime, would I be here now? If I hadn't walked into an ambush four months ago, would I be able to touch lives of orphans like me and perhaps inspire them, too, to join a service one day?

These are the kinds of thoughts that sweep me away when I'm completely alone like this. I'm used to being around people twenty four seven, and I've never noticed how lonely it is in a pup tent a few meters from everyone else. As much as she irritates me, sleeping in the same room as Katya keeps these thoughts from plaguing me.

Not wanting to dwell on the past or the emotions percolating, I turn off the lantern and crawl into my bag.

Folding my hands behind my head, I stare into the darkness. There are some days when I think I have a problem that runs a little deeper than the occasional nightmare. I hardly sleep anymore and when I do, it's not well.

I'm beginning to think I'll have to hunt Katya down when the door to the tent rustles and unzips. A gust of wet wind enters.

"Just me," she says. "You awake?"

"Yep."

"Oh." She sounds disappointed and seals us back in. "Nice and warm in here."

I ignore my anger. "You missed a fantastic dinner."

There's a pause, and then she chuckles.

"I assume you're trying to torture or kill me with this food."

"Hmm. Why would I want to ... oh, yeah. Something about you killing my brother."

Walked into that one.

She settles on the other side of the tent. If the constant tap of some body part against the floor is any indication, she's shivering.

"Where you been?" I ask.

"Around." Her teeth are chattering.

Be cold, Iceman. "All right. Sleep well."

It's too dark to see in the tent. I can hear her rustling for a moment then sense her stretch out on the ground beside me.

I'm not going to do it. Not going to fall for it. Not going to get drawn in.

Not going to take mercy on her because she gave her sleeping bag to a nine-year-old orphan.

I know it's a losing battle before I grate my teeth and sigh deeply.

"I'll share," I say reluctantly. "Shoes, socks and rain gear off. You can hop in with me."

I am going to regret this. The last thing I want is to be so close to her, we're touching the whole night.

Chapter Twelve: Katya

"I'M FINE." WOW. Can he be anymore insincere? *What an ass.*

I can't feel any of my exposed skin, and my fingers are too numb to work right. Even so, I'd rather sit here and shake all night and risk freezing to death than trespass in his sleeping bag after such a forced offer.

"It's not a request," he says in the tone he uses with the kids.

I laugh. "Whatever. Like that shit works on me!"

He says nothing. *Jesus, I'm cold!*

"Come on, I'm serious," he says.

"Yeah, you sound really eager to share. I'm fine."

"Katya, you would make a terrible, terrible Marine. That said, you gave up your sleeping bag so Rory had one, which was a very sweet thing to do. The least I can do is share," he says in a softer tone. "I don't mind too much."

There are times when he eggs me on and those when he says something I don't expect. I touch my cheek. It's hot, the only part of me that is, after my little tiff with Harris. No one's ever slapped me before. It hurts more than I expected.

Then again, my hand does as well. Captain Mathis was right about the dangers of punching someone. My wrist feels swollen. It's not the first time things got weird with Harris, but it's the first that he actually hit me.

I'm not sure what to think about that.

"I'm okay here," I respond, drawing myself out of my thoughts. "I appreciate it."

"One."

I raise my head.

"Two."

"You are not counting down like I'm –" I snap, anger warming me from the inside out.

"Three."

"Son of a bitch. Fine!" I sit.

"Shoes, socks, rain gear off," he repeats.

I didn't wear raingear, remember? I keep quiet. I'm too soaked to get in fully clothed. After fumbling with my shoes and socks, I pause, considering. He really doesn't want me in there if I'm drenched and muddy. As reluctant as he is to share, I decide I'd rather be warm than anything else, like remain in these cold clothes. Besides, this might be a good chance to mess with him a little for his snide remarks about the menu I picked out this week.

Peeling off my clothes down to my bra and underwear, I sit, shivering. "Okay."

He rustles around, making room I assume, and I scoot towards him. One foot finds the sleeping bag, and I slide it in. My god, it's warm from his body heat and the insulation. I can't wait to melt into it.

Captain Mathis' hand finds my thigh, and I stop moving, struck by the heat and weight of his hand.

"What the ... are you *naked?*" he demands quietly, the amount of surprise in his voice making me smile.

"Not naked," I reply calmly. "I didn't have raingear and was soaked to the bone. Move."

For the first time since we've met, I'm pretty sure I just shocked the shit out of him. And I'm proud.

He shifts around again and I wriggle my way into the warm sleeping bag, my back at his solid one. A trickle of surprise and desire go through me. He's naked to the waist, and his warm skin is pressed to mine.

"Oh, god, this feels good," I groan. "I hate being cold."

He says nothing. I can't begin to imagine what's going through his head right now. I do think that I've finally won a round between us. Warmth sinks into me, and I relax.

"Thanks," I murmur.

"No problem."

The words are forced, like his offer.

This guy really hates me. It's kind of odd. I guess I'm not surprised, given our conversations. Yet there are times when I think the opposite, that there's a part of him interested or at least, human. Maybe he only hates me part-time.

If that was the case, I don't think he'd be freaked out about me being in my bra and underwear.

I'm not sure why that amuses me. Snug, warm and satisfied about surprising Captain Mathis, I drift off quickly, listening to the sounds of the rain and the distant rumble of thunder.

Some time later, I wrench out of deep sleep, alarmed. Lightning lights up the pup tent as bright as day. The smash of thunder immediately follows, strong enough to make the ground shake. My heart is flying, my adrenaline racing through my blood.

But it's not the storm that woke me.

Captain Mathis is thrashing, struggling in the sleeping bag, mumbling names and shouting words I can't understand. He managed to roll over me, and the sensation of being temporarily unable to breathe is what scared me out of sleep.

Night terrors. Like Petr used to get.

I prop myself up on my arm, twisted up in the sleeping bag with him. Our legs are tangled, and I'm lying half on top of him.

"Hey," I whisper, resting a hand on his arm. "Wake up, Sawyer."

He calms at my touch without waking. His head goes back and forth, and I recall what Petr told me about the dreams. He said it was like being trapped in a nightmare that was too real, one based on something terrible that happened. For him, he wasn't able to get past the night Mikael died. Over and over, he watched our brother die, every night for weeks.

I can't think about it without wanting to cry and focus on Captain Mathis. The night terrors scare me, remind me how deep the unseen wounds of battle really run. Petr's body is almost healed, but I have a feeling he's still having bad dreams.

"You're safe, Sawyer," I say. "Wake up. It's okay - you're safe."

They're the same words I used to repeat to Petr every night when his screams awoke me.

I rest a hand on Captain Mathis' forehead and murmur to him over and over, knowing that eventually, he'll snap out of it. His body is trembling, his brow clammy. I take everything in, not sure why it bothers me so much to see him like this. It doesn't seem like anything affects Iceman.

He wrenches awake and sits. My hand drops, and I sit with him the best I can, one of my legs caught between his.

"You're safe, Sawyer," I say again. I reach for him instinctively, wanting to help him the way I did Petr.

He pulls away.

I do it again, though, accustomed to this reaction from Petr. He used to tell me he didn't always know where he was when he woke up and me speaking to him helped him realize he wasn't in the middle of the battle anymore. Gently, I clasp my hands loosely around Sawyer's upper body the best I can at the awkward angle and lean into him, resting my head on his shoulder while tugging him towards me. I'm still murmuring, waiting for him to register where he is once more.

There's a hesitation before his arms wrap around me, and he buries his face into the nape of my neck. He's stronger than Petr was those first few weeks, his muscular arms pinning me against him. I relax into him, understanding what he needs right now. My voice helps, but it's my body that grounds him in reality. He's hanging on like he's afraid to fall again into the dream world.

His breathing is ragged, his skin covered in a sheen of sweat. His body trembles in my arms. It alarms me, a stark reminder that he was in the same firefight that killed one of my brothers and injured another. I want so bad to forget, to blame the cold man who let my brothers get hurt.

Any other time, I can. Right now, it's impossible to remain angry with him, when I'm starting to realize that he's as broken inside as Petr was. He simply hides it better.

"You're safe."

He rests his cheek against mine, his breathing growing steadier and the quaking gradually receding. I hold him and wait, uncertain what is stronger within me: remembering the pain I experienced seeing Petr like this or the desire spiraling through me at the feel of our bodies pressed together.

I shouldn't feel that way. I don't know why I do. It's confusing me when I need to be strong.

"I keep thinking of that night," Sawyer says hoarsely. "The ambush. The night Mikael died. Over and over ..." He grips me tighter, as if afraid that night is coming back to get him.

I suck in a breath, torn between walking out now and knowing he needs me here.

"It's okay," I manage. "Just try to relax."

"Petr was point, the first into the village. I swear, the two of them had some sort of psychic connection. All our intel said it was clear, but Mikael –
"

"Stop, please," I beg him. "I can't hear about that night!"

Captain Mathis lifts his head but doesn't release me.

My insides are churning. I had pieced together what happened listening to Petr's ramblings when he woke me from sleeping. I can't bear the thought of reliving those first moments from the time period after his return. The hollow pain that's been present since I arrived at the forest feels rawer tonight, closer to the surface. It's not the time to reminisce.

I can't bear the thought of holding Captain Mathis knowing what he's done to my family, but I can't let him go, either, not when he's as fragile as my brother was those first few weeks.

"Relax ... lie back," I whisper. My throat is tight, and I can feel the tears on my cheeks already. "You're safe. You can sleep."

Captain Mathis releases me enough to slide down into the sleeping bag again. He takes me with him, and I wriggle and shift until I'm comfortable on my side. His arms tighten around me, keeping me pressed against him. My cheek rests on one of his thick biceps, and I'm far too aware of the muscular expanse of his chest to be comfortable. One of his thighs is slung over mine, ensuring our hips are together. I'm fevered from the intimate embrace.

I'm starting to think it was a mistake not to climb into the bag with him in my muddy, wet clothing.

Tremors go through him again, and I listen to his heartbeat. It's been a while since I've been held by anyone, even longer since I've had sex. I'm self-conscious about my back, and then there's the issue with Petr. I tend to not have very serious relationships. Most last a few weeks at most. Captain Mathis doesn't strike me as the kind who has fleeting relationships like I do. We aren't compatible by any stretch of the imagination.

Why the hell am I thinking about that now?

"I feel like you should know what happened," Sawyer says. I can hear the strain in his voice that comes from fighting a dream battle.

"No," I reply. "It's fine."

"Katya, I have to. I don't want you hating me for the wrong reason. I don't want you thinking Mikael died in vain," he begins. "I made the decision to send them in. I was as certain as possible that there was no danger, but in the end, it's my responsibility as their commander. Petr went in first and tripped the first IED. As soon as he went down –"

"Stop!" I say more firmly. Captain Mathis is calming. This time, it's me who's starting to panic.

"- stranded in the middle of the street. We were taking heavy fire. Riley went to grab him and got shot. The other SEAL on our team pulled both to safety before he was gunned down, and that's when our scouts told us how bad it was."

"Sawyer." I pull my head back, eyes blurring with tears. "I can't hear this." I take his face with my hands. "Please." I place a hand over his mouth to try to keep him quiet.

He lifts his head away. "We had one way out," he continues. "One of us had to volunteer never to come home. Mikael-"

My chest seizes. I'm envisioning everything as he speaks, reliving the agony in the hospital when I was sitting two floors up from my dead brother and two doors down from a brother they didn't expect to pull through his surgeries. Reliving the horror of being nine again and trying to reach my mother as she screamed in the fire, only to be crushed by a steel beam.

I wanted to die the day they brought Mikael back. I wanted to die the day they said Petr wasn't going to make it. I wanted to die every time Petr wept with pain after a surgery or when he was trying to recover. I wanted so badly to trade places with him and spare him the pain.

I can't go back to those moments, to the pain. I barely survived it, and it's too much to experience again. My cheeks are wet with tears, my body shaking.

Sawyer is determined. The night terrors are slowly releasing him, and he wants me to relive the night I can't forget.

I can't do it again.

Trapped in his arms, I do the only thing I can really think of to get him to shut up. I take his face in my hands and kiss him lightly.

He stops talking. I'm not even sure he's breathing. He's gone rigid. Is he surprised or offended? Either way, I have his attention.

"No more." I say against his lips and then lean away, drawing an unsteady breath. "Okay? We -"

His lips claim mine. His kiss isn't the tap I gave him but something more primal, demanding and passionate. It's not the kiss of a man who has no emotions. His warm lips press hard to mine, his velvety tongue sliding between my lips. He tastes slightly minty and of his own elusive flavor. Fire bursts into life at the base of my belly, tearing through me with intensity mirrored by Sawyer's hunger.

He deepens the kiss. Not one to be outdone, I match his passion with my own, my hands sliding behind his neck to pull him more into me. It's then I start to understand the strange tension always between us. It might be partially hatred, but there's a great deal of lust as well.

He nudges my thighs apart, and pushes me onto my back, settling between them. My body melts beneath his. Any thought I might've had about who I'm about to fuck is gone, lost in yearning and pure desire.

I can't help the small moan as I feel his thick arousal pressed to the inside of one of my thighs. I wrap my legs around his narrow hips, my heels settling on those perfect thighs of his, and the hot, aching core of my body wet with desire. The clash of our bodies together, the feeling of his hot skin pressed to mine, the most incredible, strong body resting on top of me ... have I ever experienced need this hot and consuming?

One of his palms is moving down my side. I want his hands to touch me everywhere, all at once, to brand me and claim me in a way I have a feeling only he can. I wonder what it'll be like to let him control my body, to surrender to him the way I can't anyone else. Something tells me if anyone can handle a night of wild sex with me, it's this man.

My hands skim the thick, firm muscles of his back and chest in awe and fascination.

My god, he's so strong, so sexy, so perfect.

At the moment, I don't give two shits about why I should hate Sawyer Mathis. Someone who kisses like this is going to be worth a lot more than a night in bed.

His hand reaches my hip and traces the length of one thigh while he keeps me pressed to the ground with his upper body.

Suddenly, he breaks off the kiss and curses. "Fuck!"

Dazed and breathless, I wait a second, not understanding. When he seems to tense, I cup his face. "What is it?" I ask.

Captain Mathis relaxes once more. He rests his head beside mine, his breath tickling the nape of my neck. Taking my wrists, he pins them loosely by my head. His breathing is fast like mine.

"I can't do this," he whispers at last, his lips moving against my ear.

"Can't do what?" I tug at my arms.

He holds them in place, not moving.

"Fuck you."

A thrill spirals through me at his blunt words. Our bodies are pressed together, complete intimacy prevented by the thin fabric of his sweatpants. His arousal presses against my tender nether lips. So close ...

"I shouldn't have done that," he adds. "Shouldn't have kissed you."

My body burns for him, my blood humming. My senses are scattered to the four winds, and I breathe in his scent, letting it intoxicate me. I'm an emotional, sensual person, and the sensations of his body – the combination of soft skin and hard muscle, of his rough passion and cool control – is killing me. I *need* him.

I've never needed anyone.

There's a small voice warning me that Captain Mathis isn't the kind of person who does a one night stand, and I'm not looking for a relationship with the man who killed my brother. It's rare when I feel overwhelmed by someone the way I do him. I'm a split second from begging him, and I never beg. My will power is pretty much Swiss cheese.

Maybe it's a good thing he's backing out. God knows I won't. I'm a slave to my emotions, no matter what the consequences.

We lay together quietly, both so beyond turned on, it's insane that we aren't going through with it. Maybe that's why he's holding my wrists, because he knows I don't have an ounce of restraint. The amount of passion in his kiss tells me sleeping with him will be the best night of my life. He's too observant not to be an attentive lover, too proud not to be the best a woman's ever had, too controlled and patient not to give me as much as I can take before he gets off.

This is killing me! I try to rein in my hormones and focus on something other than fucking Sawyer Mathis. Recalling the nightmares that got us to this point helps cool my ardor some.

"I just wanted to help you," I whisper. "Petr had the night terrors every night for a few weeks. I was the only one to help him. I used to crawl into bed with him the way my mom did me when I had nightmares."

He's listening quietly, his grip on my wrists secure while his body remains atop mine. If dealing with Captain Mathis baffled me before, I'm not sure what to think now.

I want him, and I know he wants me. He's saying no, but his body is indicating the opposite. His erection is long and thick, and it shows no signs of abating as the minutes pass. I don't know how long I've been lying beneath him.

"You did help me," he says finally. "Thank you."

"Whatever it takes. If you need me …" I clear my throat. "I didn't quite mean it that way, unless …" *Shit. I totally meant it that way.*

"I have too much respect for you and your brothers, Katya," he replies. "Though I'm glad to see I was right. There's a very sweet side to you."

"It's hard to hate you when I know you're broken like Petr," I say. Minutes before, he was in my arms, shaking from the power of nightmares.

His breath hitches, as if he's surprised. I'm not sure why. He *is* human. He has to know he's got issues.

"I didn't know you were hurting, too," I continue. "If I can help you, ask me now. I'm going to go back to hating you in the morning." I mean it as a joke to lighten up the tension, but it's kind of true. Now that I've sampled what he's got, I feel the need to run far, far away, because a man like this isn't the kind of person you walk away from.

"That's probably a good idea," he agrees with a husky chuckle that makes me shiver. "It's easier when you're pissed at me."

Easier? I'm not sure what he's saying. A few times, we've come close to something only to backpedal. The sense that this … thing between us is more than opportunistic lust returns. I assumed the attraction was one way, given how terse he normally is around me.

He releases one of my wrists and brushes the back of his fingers against one cheek. I'm embarrassed by my tears and wipe them away quickly.

"You're hurting, aren't you? I upset you?" he whispers, his tone gentle.

"I haven't stopped since you brought Mikael back in a coffin," I reply hoarsely.

"You are terrible at taking care of yourself, even if you are great at helping others."

I have no comeback for the too accurate observation.

"You can help me. Let me hold you."

"Shouldn't I be holding you?" I ask, confused.

"I know I've caused you so much pain. I live with that reality daily. It will help me to bring you a little comfort, Katya."

More tears squeeze from my eyes at his tender words, and my throat grows too tight to speak. I never thought I'd hear such a sentiment from a man like him. Or anyone, for that matter.

"Okay." My response is barely audible.

He eases off me and nudges me to roll onto my side, my back towards him. I do so, unmoving as he wraps one arm beneath my neck and the other around my midsection. One of his legs drapes over mine, and he pulls me into his body. His erection is hard against my backside, and I shift against him.

"Stop," he hisses. "I'm trying to be honorable."

I relax, tension flowing out of my body. I don't think it's possible to sleep when I'm so turned on. My trembling stops in his embrace, and he holds me silently. Safely tucked in his arms, the hollow pain fades and is replaced by warmth. It feels a little too natural being in his arms and a whole lot scary to be lowering my guard the way I have tonight.

As good as fucking would've been, I start to think this is better, in a different way. With his broad chest at my back and thick arms and leg around me, my body melts in his strength and warmth in a deeper relaxation than I've ever experienced before. Comfortable, protected, home.

I like this way too much to be normal.

CHAPTER THIRTEEN: SAWYER

I WAKE UP BEFORE MY ALARM goes off. After my ... issue last night, I slept like a baby, better than I have in a year at least. I'm pretty sure it has to do with the woman whose body is part of the reason why I'm considering the snooze button. One of her thighs is between mine, half her body draped over mine with her head on my shoulder. Katya's breath tickles the skin on my chest. She's soft, firm and feminine, an appealing package.

God, she's the fucking sexiest woman I've ever known. She doesn't know or care to curb her passion the way I normally do. I value self-control over everything else, but Katya ... fuck! To complicate matters, I now know there really is a sweet girl buried beneath the shell, one who didn't run or freak out when I had one of my episodes. She stuck with me, talking me down.

It's getting harder to write her off.

Instinctively, I wrap an arm around her and lay still for a long moment, pensive and a little too comfortable with her in my arms. The scars on her back are pressed to my forearm, their knotted texture deepening my consternation. My scars aren't visible, but we share the same pain, hidden deep but still present. She's a lot like me in that regard, and I don't like knowing how much she's hurting. Any resistance she gives me during the day melted when I held her.

It's hard to hate you when I know you're broken like Petr.

I hate being vulnerable, hate feeling weak, especially in front of someone else. Emotions, self-doubt, and lack of discipline have no place in my world. Last night, I went through all three in front of the woman I am struggling to keep my distance from.

Am I broken? I really don't know. I was in counseling for all of a month after losing the four guys on my team. My response to pain is to create more distance between me and it, so I can function. If I admit to being broken, I could have my command taken. Even if temporarily, it's not something I want to risk. The Corps is my life and the guys I lead my family.

I can't lose any of that. Not even the psychologist assigned to the forward operating base where my team works out of was able to convince me to stay in counseling beyond the mandatory thirty days.

How is it that Katya makes me reconsider?

I want to let my hands travel her body but don't. Last night was wrong in so many ways. Kissing her, almost losing control.

Not fucking her when I had the chance.

You're an idiot, Sawyer. I know stopping was the right thing to do. I'm not ready for a relationship. Katya isn't the kind who wants anything to do with a military boyfriend – or the military. She deserves more than a one-night stand, and I'm not about to disrespect her brothers by sleeping with their sister.

Sometimes being honorable sucks.

I can't get over how different she was with me. Sweet, caring, gentle. Talking and holding me when I know she hates me.

Restless and frustrated by the thoughts, I ease out from under her. She's a deep sleeper, hard to wake up from what I've learned the past couple of days. I get dressed then shake her gently.

"Katya, time to get up."

She grumbles and rolls away.

"Katya!"

We've got half an hour before breakfast. I know how long it takes her to get ready and gaze at her, debating.

She's adorable, her hair everywhere and a sleepy frown on her face. In the grainy light of dawn seeping into the tent, her cheek appears bruised. I lean forward, hoping I didn't hit her in my sleep.

Definitely bruised. Fuck me. I'm gonna love explaining to Petr why his sister was in my sleeping bag.

"I'll give you five minutes," I tell her and stand.

It's chilly and cloudy outside the tent. After a quick trip to the restroom, I'm intercepted by Carson, the other Green Beret on my team. He's got a country twang and the polite manners to match. A lot of people underestimate him, because he comes across as a simple farm boy. Close to Riley's size, he's over six feet tall with a shaved head and dark eyes.

He holds out a mug wordlessly.

"Thanks."

"Think they'll let us take the tent back with us?" he asks.

"I wish."

He's the quietest on the team, so I'm not surprised that he doesn't feel the need to chat the way Riley likes to. I stand with him, gazing into the quiet forest. The coffee warms me from the inside out, and I let myself enjoy the peaceful morning. It smells like rain and …

Katya. Her scent is all over me. It both arouses and irritates me.

"Captain Mathis?" Jacob and Morgan circle us. They're up and dressed, for which I credit Riley. Jacob has his collection of spiders in a clear food storage dish.

"Can we have bacon?" Morgan asks.

It's the first time I've heard her talk. I shouldn't be surprised it's about the food. They've obediently eaten everything Katya planned.

"Please?" Jacob added. "It's French toast day!"

Carson chuckles. "Heard about your health food." He bends down to see Jacob's collection. "You got some good ones."

I don't mind spiders. I don't particularly care for them either. Jacob passes them over to Carson while I consider what to do.

"I was taking them out to go to the bathroom," Jacob explained.

"Spiders pee?" Carson asks.

"Yeah. Why wouldn't they?"

I snort, amused. I've never thought twice about spiders peeing.

"Bacon," Morgan prompts me. She looks desperate, the way I feel whenever we go to the mess hall.

A glance at the tent assures me that Katya hasn't gotten up yet. "I'll make you a deal," I start.

They wait expectantly. Carson hands back the container of spiders.

"Jacob, go show Ms. Khavalov your friends and have her help you walk them for their morning run to the head. Morgan, round up the team and line them up out here. If you both can do that within ninety seconds, you can have bacon."

Jacob sprints towards the pup tent while Morgan dashes into the larger one.

"Why do I suspect Khav's sister doesn't like spiders?" Carson asks.

I shrug and sip my coffee. It's a relatively easy way to put Katya and me back at odds, where I'm more comfortable being with her. If I let myself think too much about how much good she's hiding beneath the anger ...

Less than a minute later, her shriek rings out.

Carson gives a low, rumbling laugh.

I smile.

The tent looks ready to implode from the thrashing going on inside. Katya dashes out, still wearing underwear and bra. She bends over and frantically paws at her hair.

So fucking sexy. Whether or not I should feel regret, I do as I look over her body. I could have spent the night fucking her ...

But didn't. Because I'm a fucking good guy.

Jacob exits the tent, distraught. I wave him over, not wanting him to get yelled at for something I put him up to.

"This is good," Carson says, drinking his coffee as he watches the mostly naked Katya try to get spiders out of her hair.

"I could wake up to that every day," Riley agrees, approaching.

I eye him. I know how Riley is with women, more flirting than anything. His comment still annoys me.

His attention is on Katya.

"I lost a couple," Jacob reports mournfully when he reaches us.

"We'll find you more," I assure him. "Put them away and fall in with the others."

He perks and heads into the kids' tent.

"Katya! Put on some clothes!" Petr shouts, emerging from his tent. "What the hell are you doing?"

Shaking out her hair one last time, she straightens and stares at us. Carson continues to laugh. I meet her gaze and raise my coffee mug.

"Time to get up," I call.

"You put him up to that?" She flushes. I'm not sure if it's anger or in memory of last night. Either way, it's sexy as hell.

"Friendly reminder. You guys are within –" before Petr can finish, a shoe is flying at us.

It's a damn good throw, aimed at my head. I duck, and it sails over me. The second catches Riley in the chest.

He laughs.

Furious, Katya disappears into the tent.

"Show's over," Petr says with the gruffness of a protective brother. "Go inside before she starts throwing something that can do damage."

I turn away from the tent, warm for more reasons than because I just drank coffee. Morgan has the team lined up and waiting anxiously. Word about bacon and French toast must've spread, because they're unable to stand still more than usual.

Satisfied with my morning thus far, I walk them over to the mess tent then let them loose. Knowing what our day will be like, I load up on French toast and sit with the team.

It's *fantastic*. Vanilla, cinnamon, bread so fresh I almost groan … Why the fuck have I been eating yogurt for three days?

Katya. Trying to be an honorable guy and respect her. Because of that, I missed out on incredible food and getting laid.

She's absent again from breakfast. I'm not sure if she's pissed at me or what's up with her, but she missed dinner last night as well.

"You get in a fight with a bear?" Riley calls over to Harris, who walks in beside Harper.

"Allergies," Harris mumbles and ducks his head. He's got a swollen eye.

Riley catches my gaze and nods towards the civilian, amused. I shake my head. The guy clearly had a run in with someone. All the members of my team have had black eyes, whether from fighting enemies or sparring among themselves. We know what one looks like.

The creep probably deserved it.

I'm starting to consider taking Katya a plate of food to make sure she eats. I don't know that being alone with her is a good idea. Then again, when have I ever backed down from a challenge? After a moment of arguing with myself, I finish eating and stand.

She twists me into knots, and I *hate* that. Ordering the internal dialogue silent, I duck out of the mess tent. The kids aren't even halfway done, so I have time to check in on her and return for them.

Approaching the tent, I pause outside it. "Katya?"

No answer.

I know she's up. I push aside the tent opening and find the tent empty.

"Goddamn it, Katya." With a sigh, I pull out my phone and text her. Pressing send, there's a pause before I hear a chime behind me.

I turn to see her coming from the direction of the bathrooms, bag in hand. For a moment, I'm caught by her gorgeous eyes and perfect features. She's dressed in snug pants and a long sleeved polo. The bruise on her cheek is yellowish, and guilt trickles through me.

She glances from the phone to me with annoyance. "Right here," she answers.

"Are you ever going to try to be a team player?" I ask.

"Oh, you're going there?" Katya arches an eyebrow and stops before me. "Who sent a nine year old in to dump spiders on my head?"

I smile. I shouldn't. It's too damn funny not to. "I tried to wake you up three times. He had better luck."

The familiar tension is between us again. This time, I have a better idea of what I'm missing, of how incredible her body is beneath the clothes and how natural it felt against mine. I understand what this tension is, even if I don't like it one bit.

As if thinking similar thoughts, her cheeks turn pink.

For the first time since I've met her, Katya backs down. She moves around me and flings open the entrance to the tent.

"You missed dinner last night," I say. "Are you coming to breakfast?"

"I'm fine."

I go from being aroused around her to wanting to kill her in a flash. I'm not sure how she does that to me. But her welfare, whether or not either of us likes it, is my concern for this week. It's how teams work, even if she never figures that out on her own.

"It's going to be a long day. You need to eat something." I somehow manage to keep my tone level.

"I don't want to go in there!" she snaps.

Interesting choice of words. I frown. She didn't say anything about me and I know the kids aren't a deterrent. This conversation is reminding me of when she asked me to teach her to punch someone. She's hiding something. I can't even guess as to what.

"Should I bring you something?" I ask.

"No."

"You just can't ..." I swallow the rest of my sentence. Bitching won't help anyone.

"What?" She re-emerges from the tent with a sweatshirt on.

"Nothing. I'll get the team ready."

Katya rolls her eyes and starts towards the kids' tent.

There's so much hanging between us. I feel like I should say something, but god help me, I have no fucking clue what. Drawing a breath, I decide to approach it the way I would anything else. Directly.

"About last night."

She freezes.

I approach her, stopping close enough for her body heat to reach me. I don't want anything I'm about to say to be overheard, and well … I like being this close to the woman I can't stand half the time.

"Thank you," I manage. It doesn't seem like enough, and yet, it's too much. I'm acknowledging being weak to the one person who won't hesitate to throw it in my face.

She says nothing.

"And I'm sorry about your cheek. When I'm stuck in the nightmare, I'm not always -"

"You didn't do that." She turns and gazes up at me, too close and not close enough. "You wouldn't. Even by accident. You're wound too tight."

What the fuck do I say to that? And why do I have the urge to touch her? Nothing happened between us. We're not in a relationship. Just a few awesome kisses and a hint of what a night with her would be like … and that tension that makes my body flood with adrenaline and anticipation, preparing to charge into battle.

"You're sure?" I ask, eyes on her cheek. "Something happened."

"*You* didn't hit me. Trust me. I know." She starts away.

My emotions immediately slam silent. "Whoa." I take her arm. "Someone *hit* you?"

She shrugs. "Stuff happens."

"No, stuff *doesn't* randomly happen. After last night, you should know that," I snap.

She averts her gaze.

"Who? And don't tell me it's none of my business. I swear if you use that line one more time this week …" *Wrong approach.* Too late, I realize it.

"You'll *what?*" She challenges, a flash of fire crossing her gaze as she glares up at me.

Kiss you. Finish what we started last night. There's no safe answer. "If one of my guys laid a hand on you, I will take care of it," I tell her resolutely.

Katya shakes her head. "It wasn't them, and I took care of it myself." She holds up her right hand. "You're right about punching someone. It hurts. Totally worth it."

If this conversation weren't so serious, I'd laugh at her surprised look. I take her wrist without dropping her gaze.

"Who, Katya?" I demand. "Is that why you don't want to go to the mess hall? You're afraid?"

"Of course not." She sighs. "I don't want to get in trouble for hitting him."

"What the fuck? Someone here hits you, and you're worried about defending yourself?"

Then what she says clicks. *Him.* Not a member of my team, which leaves every male kid here and …

Harris, the man sporting a swollen eye.

"Let's pretend I'm not an idiot for a minute." She's getting pissed at *me.* "Some men don't like being showed up by a girl. It makes them more aggressive, especially if they're prone to being abusive already. I read about it in my classes. So, I took care of the issue. He won't bother me again, but I'm not about to make things worse by being around him."

I'm trying to digest her reasoning, because where I come from, it makes no sense whatsoever. Fighting with Brianna is one thing. With Harris, it's a complete no-go. I'm old-fashioned when it comes to women. I don't kill them in battle unless they're holding a weapon, firing at me, and I don't tolerate anyone hurting them outside of war.

"I give as good as I get. Maybe better," she adds sweetly. "You wouldn't know, though, would you?" She pulls at her wrist.

I tighten my grip without looking away. My goal isn't to stare her down, but I'm struggling to maintain my precious self-control, especially knowing Harris is all of twenty feet from me. I can't recall being this *furious* at anything in recent history.

"You're freaking me out," she says a little less confidently, searching my face.

My body is tense enough to hurt at the idea of someone hitting Katya. Taking a deep breath, I glance down at her wrist. "Where does it hurt?"

She shows me. The outside of her wrist is tender and a little swollen. "I'll get a wrap," I say and release her. "You can ice it when we get back this evening. Wait here."

Ducking into the tent, I release a long, slow breath, my insides twisting. *Why didn't she come to me?* I shouldn't be angry with her, but I can't help thinking that she's surrounded by four members of the Special Forces – and she didn't tell anyone, even her brother, or Harris would probably be dead. It's beyond absurd. Not only does she have no sense, she's absolutely, completely the most frustrating, difficult, stubborn, sweet, sexiest ...

Stop. Breathe, think, let it go. I want to give her a piece of my mind about not telling anyone she had that big of a problem with Harris.

The urge to protect her is stronger, to fold her into my arms and drag her back to the safety of the sleeping bag, where we can both let down our guards again.

After I kill Harris. "This isn't helping," I tell myself. *She's not mine. She wouldn't want to be. I don't need someone like her in my life.* I have a feeling Petr won't be happy, if I handle this on my own. Out of respect for him, I should let him deal with Harris.

Even if I want to rip that son of a bitch's head off.

I count to ten and repeat the Marine Corps code. Searching through my ruck, I grab an Ace bandage out of the emergency kit. By the time I emerge, I've decided two things: I need to keep more distance between Katya and me, and I'm going to make sure Harris understands exactly how many pieces he'll be in if he ever touches her again.

I wrap her wrist in silence. She definitely got in a better hit than Harris did, which I'd like to take credit for, if I didn't feel like shit ignoring this issue when every instinct in my body tells me to take control of this situation now.

"You've got five minutes to get breakfast," I tell her when I'm done with her wrist. "No one will say anything to you about Harris."

For once, she listens without smarting off. Katya goes to the mess tent.

I remain outside, needing to cool off before I see her or Harris again.

CHAPTER FOURTEEN: KATYA

C APTAIN MATHIS IS PISSED AT ME. It's the only explanation as to why he doesn't talk to me the rest of the miserable day on the obstacle course. My aching wrist keeps me from noticing the chill in the air. As long as I'm dry, I'm okay.

The kids love the mud. I'm surprised even the girls get into the course. Our obstacles are marked with blue flags, so I run with them between the obstacles, lifting, pushing, pulling and picking them up out of the mud.

Captain Mathis stays with me, present but checked out. We work together for the kids without ever interacting. I'm not sure why I'm disappointed, but I really am.

Despite his distance, I find myself laughing a few times at the kids. The little ones trying to tackle obstacles too big for them, the big ones being over-confident and landing in the mud. They're a great group. Captain Mathis manages them well, in charge and aware at every point, always calm and quick to resolve any issues. They're skills I don't possess, so I sit back and ride along, helping him when needed and the kids the rest of the time.

It's not until the next to the last obstacle that I swerve off course and ignore his directions. Jenna tugs on my hand. It's about six, and we've spent the fun yet grueling day on the course.

"I need to potty," she tells me.

"Can you wait? The finish line is there." I point. It's about a quarter of a mile away.

She shakes her head.

Shit. I'm so not into peeing anywhere except a proper bathroom. "Okay. Do you want to go in the forest?"

She nods.

I glance up to see Captain Mathis with the rest of the kids a good ten yards ahead. He's smiling and occupied. My eyes linger on his grin. His dimples are visible. He's stunning when he's relaxed and happy. I can't imagine what it'd take for him to smile at me. We've always been too … intense.

It's a good thing. I think I'd fall all over myself if he gave me one of the dazzling smiles he reserves for the kids.

Shaking my head, I take Jenna's hand and lead her into the forest. When we're out of sight of the others, I stop and gaze around. The ground is soft here, and there's a drop off ahead, a ravine beyond a line of trees. There are a few large bushes she can go behind.

"Okay, this should be good. Do you have toilet paper or something?" I ask with a grimace.

"Captain Mathis made us bring some."

That man is so freaking anal. It's moments like these that I can't imagine being with him long term.

Not that I'm considering it. Where the hell did that thought come from?

Jenna moves into the bushes.

"Careful, Jenna. Not so close to the ravine," I call, remembering the safety briefing warning about mudslides.

The rustling stops, and I wait. Five minutes pass. I pull out my phone to check the time. This really isn't the place for doing something other than peeing, but that's just me.

Another minutes passes.

"Jenna? You almost done?" I ask.

No answer.

"Jenna?"

Concerned, I push through the brush and frown. She's not there.

I hear some kind of sound, a squeak or muffled cry. Starting forward, I freeze. The mud here is even softer, giving out beneath my feet, sliding towards the edge of the ravine. I snatch a tree branch and haul myself back.

Panic stirs. I can't see Jenna anywhere. I circle around the tree and test the mud on the other side. It's loose but not as slippery. Stepping away from the trunk, I inch forward cautiously, freezing whenever the ground starts to give.

"I'm coming, Jenna," I cry. "Hang in there!"

No response. *Please, please be okay!* Desperate for a sign that she's alive, I risk moving away from the trees. Almost immediately, the mud beneath me begins to shift towards the ravine. I fall flat on my belly, and the shifting stops. Cold wetness sinks through my clothing. Carefully, I rise up to my knees and inch forward. A downed, rotted out tree has roots sticking out over the edge of the ravine, and I slide as close as I dare, hanging onto one.

"Jenna?" I lean over the edge.

She's a good ten feet below, hanging onto a tree root, sobbing and covered in mud.

"Oh, Jesus, Jenna!"

I'm feeling overwhelmed. The drop down the steep hill into the ravine is a good thirty feet of mud and branches. Seeing it makes me want to cry, because there's no easy way to get to her.

"Hang on, honey. I'll figure this out." I stretch back and grab my phone out of my back pocket. My hands are trembling. I pull up the contact information for the first person I can think of and text quickly. *Need help. In the forest with Jenna. Mudslide.*

Pushing send, I replace it.

"Can't ... hang on." Jenna is crying.

"Yes, you can!" I can hear the hysteria entering my voice. I move closer. There are branches and roots between her and me that I can use to climb down to her. I stretch for the first and test it. It's a little too flexible for my liking. My hurt wrist aches, and I ease myself onto another one.

"Katya!" Captain Mathis' shout reaches me no more than two minutes after the text I sent him.

"Here!" I yell.

"Stay where you are!"

Nope. Not when Jenna is about to let go. "Hurry!"

The branch beneath me snaps, and I drop. My wrist burns at the sudden weight. I quickly plant my feet on another branch. I trained as a ballerina for years under my mother and take yoga and Pilates now. My muscles are trained for tiny, isolated movements like these. Like a cat, I can balance on a pinhead if I need to. I never thought that skill would come in handy outside of the studio.

With one leg, I stretch behind me and test another branch before carefully shifting my weight. It's excruciatingly slow, but I'm making my way to Jenna. I concentrate on moving one branch at a time and not on how precarious my position is.

"Katya?" His voice is closer.

"Down here. Careful! The mud is really loose!"

"Are you all right?"

"Yeah. Jenna's stuck. I'm almost to her."

I hear him curse. I'm not sure this is the time or place to remind him not to say such things in front of the kids. I'm more worried about my balance at this point.

"I've got rope. Keep talking, so I can tell where you are," he orders me.

"I'm right here. Rescuing Jenna, who is not going to let go, right, sweetie?" I try to keep my tone upbeat. It's trembling, along with my insides. "Captain Mathis is here, Jenna. If you let go, he'll make you run extra laps."

"Nice." Captain Mathis doesn't sound amused. "Tell me if you see the rope."

I shift one branch lower and look up. A rope is snaking down from the branches of a tree nearby. It's a good three feet away.

"I don't think I can reach it and Jenna."

"Petr's here. Give me thirty seconds."

I have no clue what he's planning. His calm voice helps me focus, and I maneuver my way down through more roots and branches, closer to Jenna.

"You okay, sweetie?" I ask softly. "I'm almost there. Then Captain Mathis will help us up. Okay?"

Jenna nods, crying.

Another careful step down, and I reach out to her, taking her forearm. Unaware of how delicate my position is, she grabs me. One of the branches beneath me sags dangerously, and I shift to drape a leg over a sturdier branch and haul her warm body into my arms. She curls against me. I hiss through clenched teeth, struggling to balance us.

We're too heavy. Both branches begin to move beneath my weight, and I start to panic. "Jenna, honey, I need you to put your feet on this branch."

She's clinging to me, crying and shaking.

"Jenna, please! Just … try to stay calm and … focus on this branch." I can't keep my tone steady, and I'm losing my grip on one of the branches overhead. With one of my arms around her, I'm not in a position to move more than my legs.

The scuff of boots against wood draws my eyes upwards. With effortless ease I don't think I've ever felt for physical exertion, Captain Mathis is scaling downwards quickly. He reaches us and pauses a couple of feet up, where the branches are thicker and sturdier, then loosens one of the ropes around him, using the second to secure himself into place.

"Pass her up," he says quietly, holding out one hand. I take in his roped forearm and the bulging biceps and decide he's got a much better chance of getting Jenna to safety than I do.

My position is far from steady. My abs and thighs are screaming from remaining in place at the odd angle. I shift the best I can and tighten my grip on the branch above then carefully draw one knee towards my chest to push Jenna's bottom up.

"Jenna, hon, you need to help me," I say, straining. Cold fear is expanding within me, and I'm both terrified I'll lose my grip on her and certain if I stretch too much farther to push her up to him, I'll fall.

"Jenna, give me your hand." Captain Mathis' voice is firm and calm.

The girl in my arms unfolds, and I struggle to counterbalance us with her movements. She meets my gaze briefly before looking up.

"C…captain Mathis, I want bacon again," she says, eyes welling with more tears.

Again? It wasn't on the menu at all. Not that this is the right time to discuss breakfast.

"I'll see what I can do," he replies. "On the count of three, place your foot on that branch at your knee and climb towards me. This is like the wall you climbed over earlier today. Piece of cake. Right?"

Jenna doesn't answer, but she's stopped crying and is listening.

"One."

She shifts, and I grunt. I don't need to look down to know the branch under my right foot is getting ready to snap.

"Two."

She pushes at me with one hand to maneuver her foot.

Instinctively, I press Jenna against the muddy wall. She dangles dangerously. A split second later, my hurt wrist gives out the same time the branch snaps. Fear tears through me as my balance is thrown.

"Gotcha." Captain Mathis snatches my forearm.

"Holy fuck!" I breathe.

"Three, Jenna." Secured by a rope, he's got two hands free, one holding me while the other stretches towards her. "Katya, move your right foot up about six inches. That should hold you."

I'll never understand how he can sound so calm when I'm two seconds from plunging to my death. There are tears on my face, and I want to break down and sob. His steadiness helps me, and I shift my foot until it finds the rock jutting from the side of the ravine.

Jenna glances at me fearfully before shakily pushing herself up and reaching out to Captain Mathis. He grabs her. With my other hand free, I rebalance myself and tug my arm out of his grip. When I'm stable, I watch him quickly and expertly secure the rope around her in a way that she can't possible fall out of it.

"Petr!" He calls when he's done. "Sixty five pounds."

"Got it!"

Seconds later, Jenna starts upward slowly.

As soon as she leaves his arms, Captain Mathis motions to me. My muscles are burning and I force them to cooperate. He takes my wrist again and pulls me upward with strength I know he possesses but which surprises me nonetheless. It takes a minute or two before he can reach me well enough for his arm to circle my midsection and draw me against him. I find a sturdy branch for my feet and he leans into me, pressing me between his warm body and the cold, muddy wall.

"You okay?" he whispers, his breath tickling my ear.

"Sorta." I'm shaking from exertion and cold.

He wraps his other arm around me. "Relax for a minute."

I think you mean – go ahead and collapse. I keep my trap closed and listen to him, comfortable in his arms once more. My muscles are burning.

"I've got you, Katya," he says in the gentle tone he used last night. "Catch your breath then we'll move."

"Did I mention that I hate camping?" I mumble.

"You're doing fine, Katya."

I close my eyes. "I'm so sorry. If I was better at this shit or if I bothered to look before she walked off, maybe -"

"Focus on your breathing, Katya. Let's get through this first."

"You may be invincible, but I'm not!"

"Not the time or place," he says. The cold bastard has the balls to be amused, like we're not dangling off the side of a ravine. "Though if you feel like talking, how about telling me about Harris and that bruise on your cheek."

"Talk about not the time or place!" I saw the look on his face earlier. It scared the hell out of me. I'm pissed at Harris, but I don't want his neck snapped.

"Was he the one who hit you?"

"Really? That's what you're thinking about right at this very moment?"

"Yes or no."

"Why?"

"Yes or no."

Beyond stressed out, I don't want to think about Harris. "Yes. Now back off."

Captain Mathis shifts me in his grip and rests his chin against my temple. I don't want to know what's going through his mind, if he's recalling how he held me last night. Because Harris aside, I am definitely thinking about what almost happened. My body is fevered on the inside and chilled on the outside, and I'm far too aware of where his hands are, considering our dangerous situation. His strong, solid frame is at my back, the only thing standing between me and the ravine.

I like being this close to him a little too much.

He's too quiet.

"You aren't going to do something to him, are you?" I ask.

"Why do you care?"

"Because you're going to make things worse then go away, and I'll have to deal with him. I can handle it."

"I'll make sure you don't have to."

I sigh and sag into his body. He supports my weight with ease, and I rest my head against his shoulder. "Please don't."

"Someone's got to take care of you. You won't let your brother, and I'm not asking for permission," he replies.

"I'm fine. I don't need anyone taking care of me in any way!"

There's a pause before he responds. "The Harris issue aside … You won't let anyone else take care of you, so I'll say what no one else will. You haven't given yourself time to heal from Mikael's death. It's why you have these aggression issues and an unhealthy way of expressing yourself and why you are strangling Petr to death with mothering him."

This really isn't the time and place to hear him talk about something like this. I listen. His words hit harder than I expect, maybe because I'm in his arms. *Or maybe because it's true.* I've been running from the pain of Mikael's death, throwing myself into caring for Petr, because I don't know what else to do.

Maybe that's why this week is so important to me. I need to prove that I'm alive when I feel so dead inside. Petr is getting better. I know it. I see it.

It scares me, too, because when he gets to the point where he doesn't need me, when he goes back to viewing me as the annoying little sister he always has, I'll be alone with my pain.

"So you're saying I'm broken," I whisper. "Like you."

"Yeah. Maybe." There's a quiet note in his voice that makes me want to see his face. "Sometimes it takes someone you don't expect to point it out."

Captain Mathis is doing a damn good job of making this experience hell. He has a way of speaking the truth I would really like to avoid. I feel like my whole world is tumbling out of control and swallow tears.

"Speaking of last night …" I say, needing my anger. I let the words hang in the tension between us.

"You sure you want to go there?" he asks quietly.

With his heat at my back and muscular arms around me, I'm not sure how to answer. I'm an emotional wreck right now, more so than usual. Last night was even more intense than our normal exchanges. The potential for something incredible is there, but it's not what I'm looking for. And …

… he scares me. Sawyer has this way of seeing straight through me, of turning my world on its head and pushing aside my shell to reach the part of me I'm doing my damnedest to hide. I don't want that. It's too intimate to give someone like him access to me like that.

"No," I whisper.

"When you're ready, let me know."

What the hell does that mean? Does he want to talk about it, or does he want something more?

I hear my breath catch, and my lower belly begins burning. Last night was an utter mistake. If I could continue pretending there was nothing between us but Mikael, this would be so much easier.

"Maybe we can talk about something that doesn't make me cry," I manage.

"Okay … how about … I keep reaching for my good luck charm and realizing it's not there. I'm not happy about losing it. Had it for ten years, but I reach for it every day."

Grateful for the change of subject, I latch onto the innocuous statement. "Where did you lose it?"

"Somewhere in Iraq."

"Oh." *Keep talking about shit that doesn't matter!* I'm going to cry if I don't. I wrack my brain for what to say next. "What does it look like?"

"Ever heard of a Ruptured Duck?"

"No."

"It was a pin given to vets at discharge after World War One. Small little thing. Beat up and worthless to everyone but me. I took it everywhere from the time I was sixteen until a few months ago."

I smile to myself. This friendly Captain Mathis I really like. It strikes me that we never really have small talk. We tend to be too busy circling and poking each other to talk about the weather or something as simple as a good luck charm.

I bet he'd be nice to talk to, if we could talk like normal people. I know he's a good listener, and he seems observant and smart, if quiet.

"Got her!" Petr's shout breaks the tension.

"Our turn." Captain Mathis moves behind me.

I twist to see. He's unwrapping the rope from his body. He secures it around me and eases away.

"I'll go up then signal you to follow," he says, back to business. "Do me a favor and listen to instructions for once."

Asshole. I say nothing but grip the branches nearest me and wait.

Captain Mathis gives another display of effortless power, pulling himself up the rope with strength that makes me tremble inside for a reason other than fear. The sense I experienced last night – that he's got the most perfect body in the world – is returning, along with awe and respect I don't want to feel for him.

He reaches the top in seconds and releases the rope. Disappearing from view for a moment, I hear him talking to Petr without being able to make out either of their voices.

"Hel-*lo!*" I shout finally. "Waiting!"

His head appears, and his dark eyes hold mine briefly. Unreadable as usual, Captain Mathis pauses before taking the rope once more.

"Ready?" he calls.

I nod.

He pulls me up in another display of strength. I weigh one twenty five, enough that he should be struggling. But he's not.

Man that's so sexy. Whatever fear I should have about dangling over a ravine is gone as I sneak glances at his biceps between finding new branches and footholds.

In under a minute, I'm up. He wraps an arm around me once more and pulls me out of the air to the tree where he's got a second rope tied to. We balance on the tree roots. The muscles of my lower body are shaky, my wrist killing me. I melt into Captain Mathis, leery of the ravine a few inches away. He's got one arm wrapped around the second rope.

Petr is waiting on the other side of a few boards they laid across the mud. Riley is there as well, holding the other end of the rope attached to me, while the man I think is named Carson is holding a crying, shaking Jenna.

Petr appears relieved the moment he spots me and offers a tight smile. "You doing okay, Kitty-Khav?"

"Company could be better," I reply.

A surprised look crosses my brother's face before he belts a laugh.

"Cold. Captain Mathis saves your life and you still won't cut him slack." Riley lets a smile slip as well.

I can't see Captain Mathis' face, for which I'm glad. He doesn't drop me, so I assume he's not too pissed. After our unnerving exchange, though, I kind of hope he is, so we can go back to hating each other. Whenever we're alone together, I learn too much about him and me that makes me want to leave camp and never look back.

"Come on across," Petr tells me. "Slowly." He holds out a hand.

Captain Mathis loosens his grip, and I shift around him, stretching one leg until my foot finds the first board. It's not entirely steady, and Sawyer doesn't release me immediately. Resting my full weight on the board, I take a tentative step.

He lets go, and I make my way across them and fling myself into Petr's arms.

"Good Kitty-Khav," Petr grunts, catching me and squeezing me tight.

"What the fuck made you leave the path?"

"Language," I mutter.

"None of that shit, Katya." He takes my arms and pushes me away, blue eyes piercing. "You know better!"

"Don't yell!" I snap. I'm on the verge of crying again and give him puppy dog eyes.

He sighs. "Don't scare me like that." He bear hugs me once more.

I breathe in his familiar scent, comfortable in his arms.

"Is Jenna okay?" I mumble into his chest.

"Yeah. Scared. We'll have a medic look her over."

Guilt works its way through me. Petr is right; I'm an idiot. All I had to do was stay on the course, and everything would be okay. I didn't listen, and Jenna might be hurt.

Exhausted after the long day, I'm ready to crawl into a real bed and cry myself to sleep.

Petr takes my hand and leads me away. I don't dare look at Captain Mathis, embarrassed that he of all people had to rescue me. It doesn't help that I'm replaying our conversation in my head.

I'm not broken. At least, I don't want to be. I don't know what's what anymore. I'm too tired to think straight.

When you're ready, let me know.

Of everything that happened today, I can't stop the thrill that goes through me as I dwell on his words or the tiny voice in my head that can't stop hoping maybe, he meant something more than talking.

Not that I want that. I don't have a clue what I do want.

There's too much for me to think about, and my body is toast after the long day. Carson hands Jenna over to me.

"You okay, sweetie?" I whisper, hugging her close.

She nods and wraps her arms around my neck.

I teeter back and lean against a tree. My arms are shaky, my wrist killing me. I'm afraid I'll drop her and let the tree support my weight. With a sigh, I rest my head against hers and close my eyes.

"I'm so sorry, baby," I murmur. "I should've been more careful."

She's calming in my arms.

"I'll take her." Captain Mathis says quietly.

I look up at him. Normally, I'd argue, but right now, I'm feeling weak.

"Marines don't hug," Jenna replies.

"I'll make one exception," he replies without hesitation.

She goes to him and wraps her arms around his neck. "Can we have bacon again?"

Sawyer meets my gaze, his dark eyes taking in my features. I wipe my cheeks free of tears self-consciously. He's standing close enough to make my blood race, his scent and warmth tickling my senses.

"You good to go?" he asks.

"Great." I straighten, embarrassed by the intensity of his look, especially in front of Petr, who has on eyebrow raised. "By the way, when did you give them bacon?"

Sawyer starts to smile. A real smile, like he gives everyone else. He's holding my gaze, and my face is getting warm.

"Do you know how processed bacon is? There's nothing natural about it by the time they're done making it," I add. I can't summon the normal amount of anger I should, not after what we just went through. If he doesn't stop looking at me like that, I'm going to start begging him for bacon, too.

"But I love bacon," Jenna says mournfully. She rests her head on Sawyer's shoulder.

"Bacon should be its own food group," Riley seconds.

"Whatever." I move around Sawyer and start walking back towards the course. One look from him, and I'm having trouble thinking and don't even notice how soaked and cold my clothing is.

The warmth he creates lasts until I start to think about what he said when we were clinging to the ravine wall.

You haven't given yourself time to heal from Mikael's death.

I hate that he's right. It's the same reason I don't want to take down Mikael's pictures, because I'm afraid if I let go, I'll lose what part of him I still have.

By the time we're back to the dorms, I'm close to tears again.

CHAPTER FIFTEEN: SAWYER

KATYA DOESN'T SPEAK ALL the way back to the barracks. We arrive around eight, which is bedtime for the beat kids. She disappears inside. I don't bother trying to talk to her and accompany Jenna to the medic's.

After twenty minutes, we return. Jenna is bruised up but otherwise healthy. She's almost out, and I'm carrying her. I'm not at all anxious to get back to the room I share with Katya, so I wait on the porch while Jenna drags her feet to the community head for a shower.

I watch the other teams settling in for the night. Riley's got the wild kids, and his barracks is the only one active still. Petr flips off lights in his barracks and closes the door behind him, heading towards me.

Coated in mud, I'm content on the porch, trying to get my head straight after the past twenty-four hours. It has nothing to do with the ravine incident and everything to do with the woman I can't seem to dismiss the way I want to.

"Hey, sir." Petr reaches the porch and sits beside me. "Interesting day."

I snort.

"You ready to kill my sister yet?"

"She's something else," I allow. I'm not sure if I want to kill her or fuck her. I've never met anyone who provokes that kind of mixed reaction out of me. Usually, those sentiments are as far apart as they can get.

"Thanks for helping her out today." Petr's smile fades. A shadow crosses his features. "I can't lose another sibling."

"You won't," I reply firmly. I can see his pain briefly, the same that Katya expresses in those moments when her guard is down. It's a sobering reminder of the lives affected by a decision I made months ago, one that frustrates me. There's nothing I can do to help. "She keeps me on my toes. It's a good thing."

Petr laughs. "You couldn't sound any less eager!"

"She's not that bad." Today was unexpectedly rough. I learned a little too much about Katya, and it's made me uncertain how to handle that knowledge and how I feel about her.

He glances at me, as if to see if I'm joking. "Really?"

"Really."

"Interesting." A smile pulls up the corners of his lips. His eyes are twinkling. "Not many people give her a chance to show how sweet she is beneath that temper."

"She's got more depth than I thought at first. I didn't know she was hurt when your mother died in the fire."

"Yeah. When the alarms went off, Kitty ran the opposite way she was supposed to. Towards the fire to help us instead of escaping. The beam almost crushed her. Baba lifted it off her, but the damage was done. Our mother was dead and Katya close to it. Most of the muscular structure of her back and one hip was basically melted. It took her years in rehab to learn to walk right again."

The images his words create disturb me, more so because I can see her running into a fire to save someone she cared about. The woman I wrote off as a superficial bitch when we first met has incredible courage and loyalty to those she loves that puts a lot of Marines I know to shame. I get the sense she doesn't let many people near her, but those she does, she keeps, defends, and loves to her last breath.

This knowledge is what makes me so uneasy. Temper aside, she's an incredible woman.

"She's a lot like you and Mikael," I say, recalling how Mikael didn't even blink before sacrificing himself to clear a path for the rest of us to escape.

"Except I can't throw as well." Petr chuckles.

I smile. The more I learn about Katya, the more troubled I feel. I can't exactly pinpoint why Petr's explanation bothers me so much.

I don't want to care for her. I don't want our attraction to mean or become something more than physical lust.

"The guys said you went from cold to ice after the incident," Petr says softly. "Slightly suicidal, I hear, too. Taking risks no one else would dream of."

I don't respond.

"You, uh, know it's not your fault, don't you?"

"That can't be farther from the truth," I say in a hushed voice. "I sent the team in." I don't want to talk about this with anyone. I feel … obligated with Petr, though, given everything that happened that night.

"You didn't know. We all thought it was clear."

"Doesn't matter." I shake my head. "Your lives are my responsibility."

"You're a good man, Captain Mathis, but you're as fucking stubborn as Katya. What happened that night, what happens any night when things go wrong, is just the way war is. Sometimes no matter what choice you make, something's going to go wrong."

I listen.

"Mikael understood that, too," he continues. "We all knew what we signed up for and that we might not come back one day. It doesn't make it easier to lose someone, but his death is not your burden."

"I tend to agree with your sister on this one," I try to joke. It falls flat.

"She knows it, too. If she hated you, truly hated you, she wouldn't be near you. I think some part of her wants to understand you. Mikael chose to save you as much as me, and you are the only reason any of us made it out. Whether or not she will admit it, that means something to her. *You* mean something to her, because Mikael gave his life for yours."

I stare into the night. First Katya says I'm broken, and now Petr seems to be agreeing. I don't want to be broken. I don't want to admit that maybe my inability to sleep is an issue, that my actions in battle since that night have been more risky than usual.

I don't want to think about the idea that one day, I might have to return from Iraq, and there's nothing waiting for me, because I'm pretty sure I've decided to die in battle at some point. Leaving the war gives me time to think, which is why I've been avoiding taking the leave that my commander recommended. If not for this week at camp, I wouldn't have come back to the States unless I was ordered to or in a box.

If I were listening to one of my guys tell me this, I'd have to refer him to counseling.

"I can see my wounds." Petr slaps his metal leg. "I think yours are just as important to take care of."

"Maybe you're right," I reply. I'm not sure what to do about it. It's not in me to take a break from leading the team to nurse my wounds. The Corps and my missions are all that have ever meant anything to me. I'd rather keep active and find another way to address my issues. "Between us, I think Katya needs to be in counseling."

"She does. Baba and I have talked about it recently. She might listen to you better than us," Petr says ruefully.

"I wouldn't be so sure about that."

"I am. If you're brave enough to tell her."

I think I did earlier. "I'll handle it." I don't know why it makes me smile, but it does. "Three tours in Iraq, Petr, and you can't manage your sister."

He chuckles. "I'll leave that to the experts. I'm not sure how to handle her sometimes. There are days when I think she needs a babysitter and those when she's all that's standing between me and the pain."

I listen, not surprised to hear his views on his sister. My thoughts return to Harris. As much as I want to bury him in the forest, I'm thinking more than ever that Petr is the one who should handle him.

"Petr." I stop, hesitating. "I want to tell you something, but I want you not to react to it without some thought."

"This can't be good." His curious blue eyes are on me.

"It's Harris. I think he's gotten a little … aggressive with your sister."

All humor fades from Petr's features, replaced by the stony expression he gets before a fight. I can feel him tense beside me.

"She thinks she can handle it. I think she shouldn't ever be alone with him again," I add.

"What do you mean *aggressive*?" The lethal tone tells me he's not going to take this too well.

"Just keep an eye out." I have a feeling if he knew, he'd show none of the restraint I'm compelled to and will beat the shit out of Harris. Harris deserves it, and I'm tempted to say more.

"Sawyer …"

"That's all I'm saying."

He studies me and then looks out at the dark forest. "I always knew he was a predator."

"You'd be right. You're right about her needing someone to take care of her, too. I thought about handling it on my own, but ..."

"I need to do it." The firmness in Petr's voice is an indication I was right. "I've been medicated and treated like an invalid for the past few weeks. It's fucking frustrating. If he thinks he can roll over my family because I'm twenty five percent metal ..." He shakes his head, face hard. "I appreciate you letting me handle it."

"Not a problem." I feel better knowing he's aware now. Petr isn't going to let anything happen to his sister.

I'm still going to have what my guys refer to as a *wall-to-wall counseling session* with Harris before I leave. If he ever comes near Katya again, Petr can handle him first, and I'll finish him off.

"I can't believe she said something to you and not me." He's scrutinizing me now. "Something else you want to tell me?"

Jenna emerges from the head, dressed and dragging her towel behind her.

"It's bedtime," I say with a half-smile.

"That's it?"

"Nothing else to tell." I stand.

Jenna glances up but doesn't stop, going into the barracks silently.

"Poor girl had a rough day." Petr is watching her with a grin. He waits until the door closes behind her before standing to face me. "I love you like a brother, but Katya ..."

"I wouldn't dishonor her, you or Mikael," I reply.

"I trust you, Sawyer." He studies me briefly. "See you tomorrow."

"Night."

He walks back to his barracks. I wait, feeling even more determined to put up a barricade between my emotions and Katya.

Walking into the barracks, I see Jenna climbing into bed. I lock the door before heading back to the room I share with Katya. Fortunately, she's in the break room. I slide into our room, grab a pair of boxers and sweats and go to the bathroom. I miss the way women smell, the mix of bathing and hair products.

I just wish they weren't so damn messy.

"Damn civilians." Her stuff is everywhere again. I can't stand the disorder and straighten up before hopping in for a quick, hot shower.

When I emerge, she's seated on the edge of her bed, concentrating hard on wrapping her right wrist with her non-dominant hand. It's instinctive for me to help out younger Marines or distressed civilians. Tossing my t-shirt on the bed, I automatically cross to her side of the room and kneel in front of her.

"Did you ice it?" I ask, taking her wrist in one hand and the bandage in the other.

"Yeah."

Her smooth, toned legs are on either side of me, and she's in a long-sleeved t-shirt again, as if I hadn't already seen the scars on her back.

I unwrap her wrist and start over. "You want to alternate so it creates more stability," I explain and slowly begin wrapping.

She's unusually quiet.

I glance up at her face and pause. Her eyes are rimmed with red. Her wet hair is in a braid down her back, her gorgeous hazel gaze on her wrist.

"Does it hurt?" I ask.

"A little."

"What's wrong?" Too late, I debated whether or not I should ask.

She shrugs.

I hate that response, little less than the *none of your business* answer she gives me. Choosing to ignore it and the stir of my blood at being so close to her, I focus on wrapping her wrist.

"Jenna's fine," I say.

"The medic called to tell me. I'm glad." She sighs.

"Is that what's bothering you?"

"Does it matter?"

The testy answer is confirmation. For once, I'm not in the mood for a fight. "You did good today, Katya."

"No, I didn't! It's my fault she fell." Her voice trembles.

"You saved her."

She tries to yank her arm away. I keep it tight.

"Sometimes shit happens, even if you do everything right," I say firmly. "You can't always control all the circumstances. You go off your best judgment and then make a call."

She's silent.

Another look at her face stops me once more. Katya is the worst person I've ever met at hiding emotions, and those swimming in her gaze are more intense than usual. She's gazing at me a little too openly for my comfort.

Petr's shared insight has me thinking I know why she's looking at me this way, like she's both waiting for more and uncertain she wants me to continue.

"Sometimes even if you're ninety nine percent certain of an outcome, something else happens," I add. "You do what you did today: react as intelligently as you can. But it's not your fault she fell, Katya." Those words are the hardest to say, because I feel responsible for the decision that cost Mikael his life.

"I still feel guilty."

"I understand." *I don't think that ever goes away.* Clearing my throat, I finish her wrist. I've never met anyone who wears their emotions on their sleeves like she does. I'm not sure what to say to help or even if I can.

I release her hand.

"You feel this way about Mikael, don't you?" she asks.

"Yeah, I do." We're at eye level with me kneeling in front of her. Meeting her brown-green gaze, I try not to think about how close her body is. The tension is between us again, almost unbearable when we're alone in the emotionally charged environment that follows us wherever we go. My fingers are twitching with the need to touch her, my body heated from the inside out.

We simply gaze at each other for a long time.

"Do you ever wish we could have a normal conversation?" she asks out of the blue. "Like other people do?"

I snort. "I hadn't thought about it that way, but yeah."

"Do you think it's possible?"

"I don't know, Katya."

She nods and wipes her cheeks.

I hate seeing her sad.

The protective instinct I don't want to feel is only getting stronger, compelling me to act when I'd rather walk away. Rarely do I do anything without a great deal of planning or control, but something about this woman touches the primal side of me that doesn't feel constrained by deliberate thought.

I cup her cheeks with my hands and kiss her. I'm expecting her to freeze, to react negatively somehow.

Instead, she responds with the same unbridled passion she did last night. I shift to lean against the bed between her thighs, and her arms go around my neck. Her kisses are hot and deep, driven by emotion that makes my blood race and my adrenaline spike. Any thought of restraint melts under her fire, replaced by the need to feel her soft skin against mine and her body beneath me, to wear her scent and taste every inch of her body.

Just when I start to think we're in some serious trouble, she breaks off the kiss and hugs me hard. Her breathing is rough in my ear, her large breasts pressed to my chest and her natural scent covered by shower smells.

My arms go around her, and I squeeze her into me, my resistance surprisingly low, even considering what I know about the risks of getting involved with her. I'm not usually one for hugs, but from her, I'm starting to enjoy them. Her knees part and I pull her more solidly into my body, recalling too well how we fit together as if made for one another.

A tap at our door prevents anything more from happening. I don't know whether I'm relieved or frustrated. What's clear: we've started something. I don't know what the fuck it is exactly, but it's much more than I arrived here with.

"I'll get it," I say and withdraw reluctantly from her warm body.

Crossing to the door, I open it and see Jenna standing in the hallway.

"I can't sleep," she says.

"You can stay with me, hon," Katya says.

I say nothing. It's probably a good idea, even if every part of my body wants me to crawl in bed with Katya in the six-year-old's place.

Disappearing into the bathroom, I take a cold, cold shower. The more I'm around Katya, the more I want to be around her.

It can't happen. We can't ever be anything. I chant the words mentally, resolved to the fact that nothing could ever work out between us, not with the circumstances that brought us together to begin with.

The kids sleep in the next morning, their reward for the grueling, muddy obstacle course. I get up early and go for a run then a swim to try to get rid of the sexual frustration that's making me too wired to think straight.

When I return to the room, I see Jenna asleep in Katya's bed. Katya, however, is nowhere to be found. We have a seven o'clock counselors meeting at the pool. Not daring to assume where she'll be, I text her the same thing I've sent her at least twice a day since arriving.

Where are you?

Not expecting a quick answer, I take a shower and check the message awaiting me.

Pool.

Impressed that she's ahead of me for once, I dress and head that way. With Petr on alert about Harris, I'm not as worried about her running into the shitbag who hit her. It'd shock me if Petr didn't have a talk with Harris last night or if Harris didn't show up black and blue today.

"Morning," Riley greets me, trotting to join me.

"Morning."

"First decent night of sleep here. No kids fucking around in the middle of the night." He sighs.

"You outta try running them through drills first thing. Seems to work."

"Brianna doesn't get up before six."

"Drag her ass out of bed. If I can get Katya up, you can wake up Brianna," I say with some amusement.

"Spiders?"

I laugh, recalling the look on Katya's face. "Not my most creative method of motivation."

Riley grins.

Before we reach the pool, I hear the raised voices: two females arguing. There's no mystery as to who it might be. Riley and I exchange a look and trot towards the pool area.

"Never seen anyone who needed more of a kick in the ass than these two," he mumbles.

"Agreed."

We reach the pool area in time to see Katya punch Brianna. Teetering dangerously, Brianna nonetheless has the sense to snatch Katya before she topples backwards into the pool. They splash into it. Seconds later, they surface and continue fighting.

I never should've taught her to punch. This girl has some serious issues, and I'm not at all certain she'll listen to anyone about going to counseling.

Riley and I pause poolside. He squats and watches the two trying to kill each other.

"Thirty seconds?" he asks, glancing up at me.

"Should be enough to wear them down." We've been through drown proofing a million times, so we know about how far we can push ourselves as well as newbies, before there's a real danger of death.

Katya, can you let anything go? Though I'm starting to think there might be a reason for her anger towards Brianna. The comment the first day about scars and short-sleeved polos makes more sense, given what I know of how self-conscious Katya is about her back. Still, it seems really … childish to be fighting over something like that.

With Katya, there's no real way of knowing.

"You want help?" Carson asks as he joins us.

"Nah. We got it," Riley responds.

Coughing, cursing and thrashing, the two women are a little more determined than I expect two civilians with no sense to act. They slow as they struggle, the drag of the water taking a toll on both. Both have tried to drag each other under.

I glance at my watch.

"Thirty," I report.

Riley dives in, and I push off my shoes before following his lead. As the token Marine and SEAL on the team, we're more accustomed to water drills than the others. A swimmer by birth, I feel in my natural state in the water and can hold my breath long enough to outlast everyone in any class I've been in.

I open my eyes underwater and swim the few strokes between Katya and me then emerge behind her.

Riley is waiting behind Brianna. At my nod, he snatches her while I grab Katya haul her away.

Katya shoves at me.

"Stop!" I snap.

She mutters something but goes limp. I drag her to the side of the pool and haul myself out before I pull her out with me. She's panting and rests back against my chest. I raise one leg to help prop her up. Brianna is pushing Riley away across the pool. She staggers to her feet, shoots a furious glare in our direction and marches away.

"Bitch," Katya whispers.

"That's all you got?" I respond.

"I won. I think."

I shake my head and lift her wrist. It's still bandaged. I have a feeling it's going to need a medic before the end of camp, if she continues to agitate it.

"What happened this time?" I ask.

Katya twists her head to meet my gaze. "None of your business." And then she smiles, tired but satisfied.

"What happens later is on you. Remember that," I warn her.

She rolls her eyes. "What? You gonna kiss me again?"

Is she daring me? There's a gleam in her eyes that makes me think she is. We hold each other's gazes, the intensity of our mutual attraction undeniable. I start to think we won't make it through camp without fucking, even though I really think it'd be a huge, huge mistake.

"Was this about the Jenna incident?" Riley crouches down near us. "She was going off about it last night."

She looks towards him, releasing me from the spell that settles between us whenever we're together. "It was about a ... few things," Katya says vaguely. "She had that coming."

"Civilians," Riley mutters.

"Go get cleaned up." I nudge her with my knee.

Riley stands and offers her a hand, pulling her up.

With a lingering glance at me, Katya leaves. I watch her until she disappears behind the door leading out of the pool area.

"Petr know you're fucking his sister?" Riley asks with his normal bluntness, confirming the instinct that's telling me what's between us is getting stronger.

"I'm not," I reply.

"Coulda fooled me."

I eye him.

"Not prying." He holds up his hands, grinning. "She's hot. With a temper like that, she'll be a wild fuck. Just saying ... she's Petr's sister."

Carson nears, as if interested in my response. I climb to my feet.

"Because she's his sister is why I'm not," I say carefully. "That's all I'll say about it."

Riley nods. Carson is smiling. They know my tone well enough to know they need to drop it.

"Hey, guys. What'd I miss?" It's Harris.

I face him, my mind growing quiet the way it does before I punch someone. It takes me a minute to remember that Petr gets to deal with this shitbag.

But that doesn't mean we can't have a little talk.

"You got a minute, Harris?" I ask casually with a smile.

"Yeah, sure."

"Come on. Let's walk and talk." I start towards the gate. "We'll be back in five, Riley."

CHAPTER SIXTEEN: KATYA

MY WRIST IS KILLING ME AS I walk back to the dorms. It's not the pain that's at the forefront of my thoughts. It's the way Captain Mathis looked at me after I asked him if he's going to kiss me again later.

Because I really want that to happen, whether or not I should. I can't get over the way he kissed me last night and hugged me. Almost like he was concerned and definitely like he's attracted. I know we both feel what's between us, even if we don't talk about it. I'm not sure how to handle it, given that we sit on opposite ends of the spectrum in pretty much everything.

For the first time since meeting him, I think I understand better what he's been through. Why he's so cold. What surprises me: how right I was the first day here during our team building exercises when I guessed he was always alone. I can't blame him, really, not when I think of Jenna almost dying. It'd kill me if she did.

The guilt of knowing I should've been more aware is killing me now. She's so sweet and innocent ... and she trusted me to take care of her.

How does Sawyer make it through the day with four deaths on his conscience? By staying numb to the world? What kind of life is that?

Why didn't I stop to think about what he's going through at any point over the past four months? How can he take the time for something like wrapping my wrist when I've been blaming him for Mikael's death?

I haven't been able to stop these thoughts since last night, when I fell asleep with Jenna in my arms.

Sawyer is human, someone hurting as much as I do. And that disturbs me for too many reasons. I want to help him and hate him, melt into his arms and run away.

I don't know what to think about him anymore.

"You swim in your clothes?" Petr calls as I enter the quad area.

I wave him away.

"Hey, Baba wants you home this morning."

"What?" I face him, not expecting this news. "Why?"

"Not sure. He called last night and said he needs you back."

I frown. "Is he okay?"

"I think so." Petr is hiding something. He has a little tell, a crunching of the corner of his right eye. I learned it when he was lying to doctors about his pain level, because he's too stubborn to admit when he needs help. "Zach is on his way to get you. I'll pack up your stuff and bring it by this afternoon."

"Now?" I ask. *Before I see if Sawyer is serious about kissing me later?* I feel like a teen who's never had a boyfriend. Why does the idea of him holding me excite me so much?

"Yeah."

"Oh. Well, I need to say goodbye to Sawyer. Captain Mathis. I mean, the kids," I stammer. "Just the kids."

Petr's eyebrow rises. He considers me for a minute. "The guys are coming by Saturday before they ship out."

Ship out. Any excitement I experience about seeing Captain Mathis dissipates instantly. It's not possible for me to forget who and what he is, but for a short while … I don't know. I forgot that his reality is so far different from mine. Maybe I really am not thinking straight. I've never considered dating someone who spends his life overseas. I don't even know if there's anything between us that would survive a deployment, considering we know nothing about one another. I lost track of my own brothers when they were gone. How can two people who barely know one another even consider something like this?

How can I see this as anything other than what it is: a potential one-night stand, however incredible it might be? He's got to resent me for how I've acted towards him, even if he does want to sleep with me.

You're an idiot, Katya.

"Never mind," I murmur. "Let me grab my purse and I'll go out front."

"I'll walk with you."

My spirits are sinking. They shouldn't be. I came here determined to hate Captain Mathis and am leaving doubting everything from why I bothered to come to the camp in the first place to who I should really blame for Mikael's death.

"Captain Mathis won't have a partner," I murmur. He's more than capable of taking care of the kids on his own, but I kind of want to stay. And run. And cry because I'm so freaking confused.

"Harris is leaving this morning," Petr says. "We'll combine the two teams."

"Harris?" I echo.

"Family emergency or something."

Petr isn't usually vague or moody like he is now. I'm not sure what's wrong with him.

"Your leg okay?" I ask.

"Great! Can't wait to tell the doc how many of his rules I broke."

"Petr!"

He grins, his dark mood vanishing. He's not usually clingy either. He doesn't leave my side, even following me into my room. I'd normally yell at him, but I appreciate the company this morning. I'm feeling hollow again. He walks me through the dorm, where the kids are still sleeping, and along the trail leading to the front of camp.

I feel kind of like I'm giving up. Or that I failed Mikael this week by leaving early. I don't say anything to Petr, knowing Mikael is never far from his thoughts, either. We wait quietly for Zach. When he comes, I hug Petr and go home.

In a way, I'm glad I'm leaving early. I'm not sure what would've happened between Sawyer and me, had I stayed. I can't quite understand my own feelings or why I suddenly need space, even from Petr, even if that means not watching over him to make sure he's okay.

There's too much stimulus here. I'm drowning in emotions and struggling to hang on to my anger about Mikael being gone, because it's the only thing that helps me through the day.

As we pull into the driveway of my home, I realize I can no longer summon the emotion to blame Sawyer Mathis. I'm angry with him, but it's tempered by the knowledge that both of us are suffering, and neither of us has healed from my brother's death. It's hard to blame someone that I innately want to help, someone broken like me.

I go to my room without saying hello to my father. I need to be alone right now. I need to sort through everything in my head.

A day passes and then a second and a third. Baba never does tell me why he pulled me out of camp. I wonder if it's the Brianna issue. If so, it's absolutely my fault for not being more mature about seeing her.

Petr sends pics, and I smile when I see them and save them, so I don't ever forget this week.

Captain Mathis, however, never bothers to text again. Not even one of his annoying *Where are you* messages that drove me crazy. I'm not sure what to think about his silence, except that maybe everything we went through this week was a matter of circumstances rather than any real attraction.

For him maybe. I end the week rawer than when I started it. The only good thing about this all: I don't have to be in the rain that started the day I left and continues to storm through Saturday. It washes out the barbecue the guys on Petr's team were supposed to have today. It's left them confined to the house and me avoiding the common areas downstairs, so I don't accidentally run into anyone.

I don't feel up to it, especially since I'm pretty sure Brianna was invited. Every time I mess up, she rags on me, and I'm sick of it. I tell myself this is the reason I don't go downstairs, but I'm pretty sure it's to avoid Sawyer Mathis and the complicated mess of emotions surrounding every interaction with him.

Baba taps on my door in a familiar rhythm. I close the browser on my laptop and lean back from the office corner of my large bedroom.

"Kitty-Khav?" He opens the door. His large face breaks into a smile. "Why are you hiding?"

"I'm not *hiding*. I don't want to be around anyone," I reply curtly.

"You've been up here for days."

"Just thinking, Baba."

He enters my room and closes the door behind him. My father goes to the couch facing a fireplace and sits, patting the spot beside him.

Reluctantly, I join him. He wraps an arm around me the way he always does and kisses my forehead.

I sigh and sink into his warmth. He smells of his spicy aftershave, and his bushy beard tickles my temple.

"What is bothering you, *kotyonik*?" he asks. "It is not like you to hide."

I debate what to tell him. "It was a rough week," I say finally. "Being in the forest made me miss Mikael too much."

"He loved the forest."

"Yeah, I know."

We sit in silence.

"Petr and the boys will miss you, if you do not come down."

"I don't want to see anyone." *Especially not Captain Mathis.* I want to erase him from my life and curl up in his arms simultaneously. I can't really handle those emotions. I've been in deep thought for days and my head remains a disaster area.

"What is this?" Baba leans down to the coffee table to grab a jewelry box I forgot about.

"Nothing." I reach for it.

"We love secrets." He chuckles and plays keep away, finally flicking it open with his thumb. "I have not seen one of these in a very long time."

My face is hot. I take the box and close it.

"Ruptured Duck," he continues. "Mint condition. You looked hard for it?"

"No. Just ... whatever."

"Who is it for?"

"No one, Baba."

I bought it the day after I came back with express shipping, wanting to give it to Captain Mathis, so he'd have his lucky charm when he returns to Iraq. I then decided it wasn't a good idea. He's not the kind of man I need in my life, and I don't want him thinking there's something between us, when there can't be.

He's a career military man. I'm a trust fund baby who can't figure out what to do with her life, but I'm pretty sure it's not wait around for a deployed boyfriend to come back from Iraq. I will never stop opposing the war and violence, and he will never stop being involved in them.

Even if the war is fought by good men like him and my brothers.

I've never been so conflicted in my life.

Fingering the box, I open it and stare at the little gold lapel pin I spent hours hunting down. I still wonder where he got his, since he's an orphan. Was his charm the last piece of family history he had? He said it mattered to him and had for ten years.

If so, and I give him another one ...

It's way, *way* too complicated and intimate a gesture for someone I need to forget. I've given myself a headache debating what to do about the stupid duck pin.

"Baba, I think I need to go into counseling again," I murmur, closing the gift that will never leave my room. "This week really ... really brought a few things to light." My voice is trembling.

"I think, this is good."

My father has a talent for dramatic understatement. The words sound simple, but it's his way of saying it's a damn good idea.

"Katya *moya* has not been happy since she was nine. Always trying to protect her father and brothers to make sure she doesn't lose them," he says. "You need to be Kitty-Khav and let go of us all. I promise. We can land on our feet like my kitten can."

I rest my head on his shoulder, listening to his gruff, soft voice. "I feel so lost without him, Baba," I whisper.

"We all do, *devoshka moya.*"

"I don't know what there is outside of you guys. I've never really been interested in what I took in school."

"You are interested in the camp?"

"Yeah, that was cool."

"I had thought to create a new charity to help military families and put the camp under it. It will need someone to help manage it. You have always wanted to help people."

I run my thumb over the seam in the box. It doesn't slip past me that I can help people like the kids I met this week and Captain Mathis, who was also an orphan. I can help others like me, too, who are hurting from losing a family member. The camp was an incredible idea, and I imagine there are other positive ways to help others that also ease my pain.

"I might like that," I murmur.

"Petr will help you."

"I thought he wanted to go back to the military." I lift my head.

"We talked about it. We think you need us now, *devoshka moya.* You have taken care of us long enough. Now it is our turn." My father gazes at me tenderly.

Tears spill down my face. I'm too touched to speak. I know they love me. I've never felt broken before, never really thought I needed them as much as they do me. Dealing with Captain Mathis made me confront the reality that I'm not ready to let go of Mikael or accept his death.

"So he will stay for a while, until you are ready to send him back."

I give a startled laugh that quickly turns into sobs. Baba wraps his arms around me and holds me. I cry into his expensive sweater, and he murmurs to me in Russian.

The time I spent with Sawyer was frustrating, infuriating, crippling. He managed to pry me out of my shell and hold a mirror in front of me, so I could see how damaged I am. Like him, I'm broken by Mikael's death.

Am I fixable? Is he? Why do I hope we both are and that one day, we can sit down for coffee and have a normal conversation?

I don't think I'll ever see him again.

The idea crushes me. I'm too upset to know why exactly.

Chapter Seventeen: Sawyer

S *HE DIDN'T EVEN SAY GOODBYE.* The last thing I need to be thinking about in a war zone is Katya Khavalov. Maybe it's the abrupt manner of her ditching camp or the fact she didn't come down to see us that Saturday, but I can't get her out of my mind.

Thinking about her stirs my blood like a triple espresso, even when I've spent the past forty-eight hours awake on mission. I don't know if it's desire or anger. She has that affect on me and leaves me wired when I need sleep. A month after camp ended, and every conversation we ever had continues to haunt me.

Sweating and tired, I'm the last of the team to enter the isolated, abandoned house we've been using as a base of operations in the Iraqi desert for the past two weeks. No one was hurt and we found our target. It was a successful day.

Lowering my ruck to the ground, I glance over at the skinny Ranger who's in charge of our communications.

"We up?" I ask.

"For an hour."

"I gotta get my report in." I crouch at the station where the single laptop connected to the outside world that we always take on a mission is hooked up. Internet is hit or miss. We rely on satellite connections rather than ground lines, and most days, they're shoddy at best.

Duty always comes first when the mission is over. Reporting to my commander, taking accountability of the team's health and mental awareness, assessing the condition of our equipment, setting up the duty roster for the night, cleaning my own gear, food and then, if there's time, sleep. Thank god I type fast, or I'd never have time to sleep.

Hunkering over the laptop, I have the report done and out before the connection goes down. I check on the guys and equipment then take care of my gear. The two-room house has an antiquated bathroom and a main room that serves as our living and sleeping quarters. The guys are cleaning their weapons by lantern light, and I join them, claiming my spot between Riley and Carson.

Taking apart my weapon is second nature. I go through the motions without registering them. The token Air Force spec-ops guy, Ian, is racked out already while the others are either eating MREs or cleaning weapons and gear.

"You've been quiet," Riley says, glancing at me.

"Not him. Everyone," Carson replies. "The Khavs always had the stories."

"Yeah, they did."

It's odd that five months later, we still can't go a day without mentioning Mikael.

"You hear from Petr, sir?" Carson asks me.

"Not since we've been out here," I reply.

"Katya?" Riley questions with a small smile.

"No," I respond emphatically. "Pretty sure I won't."

"I kinda liked her," Carson says. "She made life ... interesting."

I smile, and Riley laughs. He's too polite to say what Riley or I might: that she was the frustrating combination of an ambush and a puppy rolled into one.

"Will be good to be back tomorrow for a few days," Riley says. "I need some real fucking food."

I agree silently. I finish up, eat what I'm willing to, and lie down to stare at the ceiling. There's a good chance I won't sleep more than an hour, and if I do, I'll dream about the night I woke up with night terrors and Katya was there.

It's been three weeks, and I can't stop thinking about her. I'd like to say my thoughts are positive, but a lot of them really aren't. I swing between thinking she really was a superficial bitch and knowing that I had just begun to scratch the surface of something incredible.

Not that it matters. With Petr out of the picture, the chances of us meeting up again are completely gone. I don't even have her email address and am pretty sure she'd delete anything I sent her, even if I did.

Why the hell does that make me want to email her even more?

"Sir, you going to Petr's Christmas party?" Carson asks me.

Then there's that. The holidays are four months away. Petr already invited us back to Massachusetts. I guess his family gives some sort of insane party over the holidays. Riley even found it on gossip websites as being an exclusive event apparently everyone in New England tries to get an invite to. Celebrities, supermodels, socialites and other people of that caliber attend the three-day event.

I can't understand that kind of wealth, and I'm not at all impressed by people who are famous for being rich or on TV. It's one more reason to keep my distance from Katya, a reminder we're nothing alike. I grew up on the streets of Chicago before joining the Corps. I'm good with my money, more so because I don't spend shit when I'm deployed. I paid for what little I own, mainly my truck, in cash.

But I'll never be anything close to what the Khavalov's are in terms of money, and it's not like I have family Stateside I visit on leave. Going all the way home for a party seems stupid.

Unless I'd see Katya.

All the more reason to avoid it.

"Probably not," I reply. "I usually stay behind so you guys can take a break."

"You going, Riley?" Carson asks.

"Fuck yeah. Supermodels? Petr promised to hook me up with anyone I want."

"I want to go, too," Carson says. "Mainly so I can send pics of me with celebrities home to my mom."

"How's she doing?" I ask. Carson's mom has been in the hospital for a year with stage four cancer.

"Still won't die," he jokes. He smiles, affection crossing his face. "Too stubborn."

I return my gaze to the ceiling. The guys are quiet for a few minutes before Riley speaks again.

"I found something the other day when we went back to the village where the Khavs got hurt. Some shitbag in the bazaar was trying to sell it."

My good humor flees. For all of two seconds, I was able to think of something other than that night. I hear him dig around his ruck.

Sitting up, I wait to see what it is.

He tugs free a set of dog tags, each of which has black rubber around its edges to keep them from jingling.

"Mikael's," he supplies and hands them over.

Surprised, I take them. "How the fuck did these make it?" I read the name to confirm. They're dirty, and the rust color indicates dried blood is what clogs a few imprinted letters.

"I thought you might want them."

"We should send them to Petr," I reply, studying the tags.

"Or take them back at Christmas," Carson adds. "Might be a nice gesture."

How would Katya react to having them back? I'm not sure at all. Would it infuriate her or would she appreciate it?

I read Mikael's name over and over on the tags, touched more deeply than I should be by holding them. That something so small can mean so much …

"Great work, Riley," I say.

He nods, smiling. "Mikael's still with us."

"Hey, sir," the Ranger calls from his corner, where he's messing with the comms equipment. "Captain Jacobson says we need to move. Someone picked up on our position. She's saying to head back along our planned route, and she'll send someone to pick us up."

"Roger." I rise instantly. The guys don't need to be told it's time to move – quickly. I pull on Mikael's dog tags and tuck them with mine beneath my shirt.

We pack up and are leaving the covert base within ten minutes, headed stealthily along the route of egress we planned. Alert and wary, we walk the five clicks towards the rendezvous point, where the security detachment she sent is waiting as promised.

An hour later, we're back at the FOB. It's a small compound in the middle of nowhere, heavily fortified, but it's got real beds and decent food.

I'm not surprised to see Harper in the command center when I arrive. I nod as I walk by then go to the barracks area my team usually occupies when we're in from a mission. After depositing my gear, I return to the center to check in and let my commander know we're back.

"Good mission?" Harper asks from her spot in front of a computer.

"Always."

"Your guys all right?"

"Yep."

I slide into the seat beside her, ignoring the looks of the night shift in the center. I look and smell like I've been in the field for two weeks. Harper is used to dealing with us, even if the others manning the intelligence and operations forward operating base tend to regard the secretive spec-ops guys like mythical animals.

"How long you in for this time?" she asks.

"Four days."

"Any plans while you're here?"

"None."

"Your team need anything?"

"Nope."

"Riley's right. You're different, Sawyer. Are you okay?"

I pause, realizing I've been responding on autopilot. I get in mission mode sometimes, too focused to pay attention to much else around me. Lately, I've felt stuck there, and Petr's words about me distancing myself too much from others returns to me. If Riley noticed and said something to Harper, it's got to be obvious to everyone.

Sitting back in the chair, I meet her brown gaze. Captain Jacobson is a gorgeous woman, strong, disciplined and smart.

"Been a long few months," I reply and draw a deep breath. "Thanks for the tip. I appreciate you watching our backs."

"It's my job," she says with a smile. "You're welcome."

I study her. I'm beat and have no clue what else I should be saying to prevent people from assuming something's wrong.

"If you ever need to talk, let me know."

Talk? What the fuck … Do they think I'm that bad?

"Yeah, thanks," I force myself to say.

"If you ever need anything else, let me know that, too. Sometimes it helps." She smiles. "Not looking for a relationship, just … you know. Stress relief."

I'm pretty sure she's not joking. Sex is officially forbidden in the war zone, though it doesn't stop a lot of people. I understand what she's saying. I've had a few situational flings with women like me who needed the release or companionship after so long away from home.

"Thanks," I reply. "You all must think I'm pretty bad off."

"We notice. But it's not just you. I lost one of the new kids yesterday. Nineteen, walked over an IED dropping off supplies. Spent the day picking up his pieces." Her gaze grows haunted, and her smile fades. "Makes you realize how quickly everything can end or change or whatever."

I feel her pain and know there's nothing I can say to soothe the guilt and fear that comes with seeing someone die before your eyes. I squeeze her hand instead, understanding better where she's coming from. Sex, or maybe intimacy, has a way of grounding me, reminding me that I'm human when the world feels like it's about to end. It's no surprise that it does the same with others.

There would be no complicated emotions with Harper like there would've been with Katya, had I slept with her. This would be physical, purely stress relief and companionship.

"Thanks. I'll keep it in mind," I respond and face the computer once more.

"Get some rest," Harper says and stands.

I nod and check my email, ready to shoot off a note to my commander, who is stationed around Baghdad.

There's an email from Katya in my inbox. I blink and hit refresh. I've been tired enough to hallucinate before.

It's really there.

Leaning forward, my exhaustion slides away, replaced by intense curiosity about hearing from her when I never expected to again. I don't know why I hesitate to open it, but I do.

Finally clicking, I see her note is short and there's an attachment.

Hey-

Assignment I did in counseling. Probably not supposed to send it. Figured I had nothing to lose.

KK

I'm not getting a warm fuzzies about this. My gaze lingers on the first sentence. I'm guessing Petr and their father convinced her to go into counseling, and I'm impressed she did it.

My stomach churns when I open her attachment.

To the man who let my brother die.

I find myself pushing away physically from the computer, as if it will put distance between the issue and me. Realizing how ridiculous that is, I force myself to read.

The letter is pure Katya, filled with emotion, passion, honesty and directness. If I thought she was candid at camp, this letter takes it to a whole new level. Anguish, rage, sorrow ... all are expressed clearly in such a raw manner that I struggle to close the door on my own reeling feelings. The sense of being stripped to the soul and twisted inside out, the same I experienced standing at Mikael's funeral, return. It's stronger this time, crippling, because the emotions aren't mine alone. They're hers, too. I don't want to ... I *can't* see the depth of the pain I've inadvertently caused others. I can't live with myself if I do, can't function as a leader the way I need to. The hour or two to sleep I get a night will turn into minutes if I let myself dwell on how much I hurt for others.

I finish the first page before I close the document, blinded by both fury and pain. I've written letters like this in counseling, letters that are never meant to be sent but are used as an exercise to express the emotions of the person writing them.

Fuck you, Katya.

My body is so tense, it aches, and my emotions boil over for a moment, paralyzing my ability to think. I stare at the screen, wanting to delete her email and erase her words, her very existence, from my mind.

How the fuck can she affect me when I'm halfway around the world? I haven't seen or spoken to her since she left midweek at camp. She has the power to reach out and obliterate the barrier I keep between my emotions and the rest of the world with a single email.

"Fuck!" My curse draws the eyes of half the center. I log out and rise, slamming my chair back under the desk before striding out.

It's hard to hate you when I know you're broken like Petr. The words have stayed with me. She may be right about me being broken, but she's wrong about hating me.

It's clear she does. Always has.

Why does that shred me as much as anything else I've been through?

"Hey, you okay?"

I don't realize I'm standing in the hallway, leaning my forehead against the wall, until I hear Harper's voice. Straightening, I gaze at her. She appears alarmed and concerned.

"You need to talk about something?"

There's no way to explain what's in my head, especially since I have no fucking clue how to sort out my thinking about Katya.

I just ... Want. Her. Gone.

So I can think, function ... fuck – so I can *breathe* right whenever her name comes up! My body and my mind react to her in a way I can't control.

"I don't want to talk," I tell Harper, refocusing on my surroundings. "If your other offer is on the table ..." *Something has to fix this.*

Harper nods, studying me.

"I'll get cleaned up." I stride away, towards the showers. I try to tell myself this has nothing to do with trying to forget Katya.

But it does. She's physically out of my life. I need to get her out of my head.

After a quick shower, I sit down in the closet-sized tiny quarters that are mine. I don't share with anyone, because of my rank. My head hurts, and my body is sore. I'm exhausted and wired, a sign I won't be able to sleep, if I don't take Harper up on her offer.

Assuming she'll be by when her shift is over, I sit on my bed and lean against the wall, unable to purge my mind of the letter Katya sent. It was four pages. I barely made it through the first.

Do I owe her? Should I finish reading it before I delete?

I'm too tired and emotionally drained to know how to handle it. My gaze settles on the pad of paper and pen on the Pelican case I use as a suitcase in a corner. It acts as a table in the tiny room. I have a few student pen pals who sent letters over for class assignments that I keep in touch with every once in a while. It's normally easier to handwrite responses, since my computer time is dedicated to work.

If I could say anything to Katya, without consequence, what would it be? She has no qualms about destroying me, no concerns about consequences. What if I took the same approach, just once in my life? What if I told her exactly what I feel and think?

We've never even had a friendship. The brittle relationship we do have isn't going to survive her letter – that much I know. So does it really matter what I tell her?

I stretch and grab the pad and pen. I start writing and stop after her name. I'm drawing a blank, despite the amount of things going through my head. It's probably my detail-oriented nature, but something tells me I need to read all four pages before I start. She has a way of surprising me, and part of me hopes there's something less poisonous in the letter.

Someone knocks at my door.

"Come in," I call.

Harper enters. "Good time?" she asks.

"Always."

I set the paper aside, warmth stirring within me for a different reason than anger this time.

Fuck you, Katya. I can't help thinking of her even now, when I'm about to spend the night with another woman.

I stand and strip off my shirt. Harper sits and unties her boots.

"Is Colonel Lawrence still here?" I ask casually.

"No. His replacement is here. A civilian named Petra." She looks up at me. "You want to talk to her?"

I debate responding. On a base this size, everyone will soon know if I show up on the doorstep of the psychologist assigned to the FOB to help monitor the mental health of those assigned here. Anyone can talk to her, but a lot of people avoid the shrinks for fear of looking bad or weak in front of everyone else.

I need to get rid of this shit in my head. The guilt, self-doubt, fear.

Thinking of Katya reminds me of all of that, of the night when four men died under my command.

"Yeah," I say with effort.

"I think that's a good idea, Sawyer," Harper says warmly.

Not really. It's probably a bad career choice, because I'll have to tell my commander, who can choose to take me off missions. It's a fear I've had for a long time, about losing what matters most to me.

But I can't function like this. The emotions aren't going away. They're getting worse. If I don't get a handle on them now, what happens if I'm on a mission and lose my focus? What if I had read Katya's note before going out on a mission?

I won't let anyone else die because I can't get one fucking woman out of my head.

It's hard to hate you when I know you're broken like Petr.

"Goddammit," I mutter. I need her voice out of my thoughts. So she's right. So I need to go back to the shrink.

If I can reconcile what happened that night and my destructive emotions, will it help me get her out of my head as well?

CHAPTER EIGHTEEN: KATYA

I NEVER EXPECTED CAPTAIN MATHIS to respond to my note. I pulled his email address off a card he gave Baba. I don't even know if it made it to him and wouldn't blame him if he deleted it on sight. Imagine my surprise when I receive a letter from him a few weeks after sending the email that my therapist told me was a pretty bad idea.

The envelope is thick, and I open it in the privacy of my room with some apprehension, not wanting to guess what he has to say. His handwriting is neat and small, covering both sides of four pages of plain, lined paper.

My hands are trembling already. I bared my soul to him in my letter, whether or not I should've sent it. I felt like I owed it to him to say what's inside me to his face. Or at least as directly as possible, given our locations.

Sinking onto my couch, I start to read.

Katya,
I read your letter all the way through a few times. It took a lot of courage for you to write what you did, which I respect. It means I need to respond.

"That doesn't sound good." My stomach is churning already.

I don't know exactly where I should start, so I'll start at the beginning.

I devour the first two pages, not expecting him to tell me his life story. From being born to a druggie mother who died when he was two and never knowing his father, to leaving a foster family to live on the streets when he was twelve, to meeting the Marine who helped him leave a gang when he was sixteen and finish high school and college. Sawyer explains his life in a way that reminds me of how my father communicates. Both have a knack for understating the importance of the information they're conveying. It leaves me stressed out, because I tend to do the opposite: put my emotions first then the story second. If I have to fill in the emotional blanks, I usually overreact.

He writes much like he speaks – with brevity and a general lack of emotion. I'm uncannily fascinated by his history, because I've always been curious about the side of him he hides, what made him the way he is, even if I don't want anything to do with him.

Mikael and Petr respect and admire him. I want to see him the way they do, the way I've never been able to, because of Mikael's death.

Page three makes me stop reading. At camp, he tried to tell me what happened the night Mikael died, and I wasn't able to hear it.

In writing, I guess he assumes I can't stop him. He tells me what happened and then goes on to talk about the four men whose lives were lost.

I set the letter aside a few times, because I can't read through my tears. I don't know how he can write this horrible event the way he does – with even less emotion than the first two pages.

When I finally make it through, I turn over the fourth page, expecting more of the same storytelling. Instead, there's only one paragraph more.

Katya, your letter destroyed me. It served its purpose in a way, because I started counseling the day after I received it. There have been so many times I wanted to reach out to you, but I chose not to. It doesn't mean that I don't feel what you do or that I don't think about your brother's death every day. If I could take Mikael's place that night and spare you your pain, I would gladly do it. If I could make your pain go away, I would. But I can't. All I can say is that I'm sorry and I hope you one day find peace. It won't happen with me in your life, so I'll wish you well and will remove myself from your life.

> *Take care,*
> *Sawyer*

I set the letter down and stare at the blue sky visible out my bay window. I'm crushed and frozen and so confused by the emotions, I don't know how to react.

Sawyer Mathis wants nothing to do with me. I expected that, but to see it written … to know I hurt him enough to drive him off …

I do that to so many people. I didn't realize until now that I didn't want him to be one of them.

As usual, I've reacted without thinking about the consequences. His farewell cuts so deep, I can't cry. I don't know why it hurts, not when I've been alternating between wanting to hate him and hoping he comes to the Christmas party. Before I left camp, we were on the verge of something I instinctively know could only have one of two outcomes: ecstasy or devastation.

There can be nothing in-between, not with how deep we both dive into one another. Is this how whatever it is between us ends?

Definitely not ecstasy.

I fold the letter carefully and replace it in its envelope then put it in my desk. The jewelry box with the Ruptured Duck is on top of my desk, and I pick it up once more. I've debated sending it to him every day since I got it.

It doesn't matter now.

"You're stuck with me, duck," I whisper.

I stare into space for a moment before shaking my head. I put it in the same drawer and slide my feet into flip-flops for a trip out back.

Whenever I feel like this, I go out back to talk to Mikael.

The October weather is a mix of warm and cool. The trees hedging our property are starting to turn, and I breathe in the fresh air deeply. When I open the gate to the peaceful space, I'm surprised to see Petr there, standing in front of Mikael's grave.

He glances up at my approach and smiles. There's sadness in his strong features. When I'm close enough, he wraps an arm around my shoulders and pulls me into his solid frame. He has no idea how much I need the hug right now.

We stand in silence for a few minutes, gazing at Mikael's tombstone.

"Bet he's built an obstacle course in heaven by now," Petr says.

"Probably."

"It'll suck without my help."

I giggle. My brothers were best friends but also super competitive.

"I invited all the guys back for the Christmas party. I think everyone is coming, except Captain Mathis. He doesn't really take leave."

"I'm not surprised." I'm not sure how, but my heart feels like it's breaking even more. It's in so many pieces, it has to be dust by now.

"No? I figured you'd want him here."

"Why?"

"You guys got along well." Petr laughs.

I roll my eyes.

"He's got time to change his mind."

"He won't," I say softly.

"Does that bother you?"

"None of your damn business!"

"Oh, shit. One of those. I thought you were dating the neighbor. What's his name? Oliver?"

"Yeah. Nothing serious," I reply. My therapist thought it was a good idea for me to get out more. Oliver asked and I said yes. We've kissed a few times, and he's a nice guy.

He doesn't move me the way Sawyer did. I don't think anyone ever will. I'm really good at messing up friendships and relationships. I shouldn't be hurting about him, considering we didn't have anything going on at all.

"You didn't invite Harris, did you?" I ask, eyeing my brother.

"No." A flash of something goes through his gaze. For a split second, I almost suspect he knows about Harris slapping me.

"Good. Take Brianna off the list. You deserve so much better," I tell him. "And I won't have to beat her up again."

"Brave little Kitty-Khav." He squeezes me closer. "You like your new job?"

"A lot." I perk up. "Baba even sends me official checks."

He chuckles. "What do you have planned for next year?"

"Tons of stuff!" I thought I'd enjoy helping manage the charity organization my father set up. I had no idea I'd love it. "Fleecing everyone in the state at fundraising dinners, a race, four iterations of camp next summer, one for each age group and a scholarship fund for military kids. I've been talking to the governor's office and two huge sponsors." It doesn't hurt that my father opens his checkbook to fund whatever I want.

"You're definitely going to improve lives."

"Yeah." My eyes return to Mikael's grave. "It helps. And Brianna can't say I haven't done anything with my life."

"She won't be around anymore, so you don't have to worry about showing her up."

"You break up for good?"

"We did. You may have been right about her all along," he allowed.

"Oh, really? It only took you four years to figure that out?" I slap his chest lightly. "Maybe next time you'll listen to me!"

He laughs, his blue eyes sparkling. "I always listen, Kitty-Khav. I just do whatever I want. Kind of like you."

I glare at him.

"Am I wrong?" he challenges. "I think that's why Captain Mathis liked you. You're so passionate and strong."

"Liked me?" I shake my head. As much as the idea thrills me, I know for a fact it's not true. "He was being nice to me because he killed Mikael."

"Jesus, Katya." He laughs. "Okay, never mind."

He doesn't know that talking about Sawyer hurts me. It's not his fault, but I'll be happy when he stops bringing him up.

"Come on. Let's get some ice cream." Petr loops his arm through mine and starts walking back towards the gate and the house.

This, too, has become a daily tradition of ours. We meet up in the afternoons for ice cream or cookies. Petr spends a couple hours a day at the gym on our property, so I'm pretty sure he can eat them and be fine. I've had to start walking in addition to my usual yoga routine to make sure my weight stays where I want it.

We're finishing our treat when Oliver is led in by the butler. Tall with curly dark hair and a quick smile, he's the son of the family that lives about ten miles down the road in the exclusive estates where we live.

"Hi Katya, Petr. Am I interrupting?" Oliver asks.

"Not at all," Petr says. "Go have fun." He leaves the kitchen.

I hop off the stool at the breakfast bar and gaze up at Oliver. He's the opposite of Sawyer in pretty much every way. He's open, friendly and so laid back, even I can't get a rise out of him. He lets me call the shots and seems content hanging out. He's a great listener, too, though I rarely tell him anything private.

I should like him more than I do, but I don't feel the same compelling pull towards him that I did Sawyer. I don't think a pull like that is healthy, given how things turned out between us. I'd still prefer to have something more than the comfortable yet unenthused response my body has to Oliver.

It'll never be serious between us. I want to be burned up with fire for whomever I date next. Oliver barely causes a spark.

"Movie day?" he asks with a charming smile.

"Sure. I've got a conference call at five."

"Not a problem."

I need something to take my mind off Sawyer's letter and the good luck charm I don't know what to do with.

If I could take Mikael's place that night and spare you your pain, I would gladly do it. Sawyer's words kill me. I knew he was broken by the event that destroyed our lives, but I didn't understand how deeply he felt.

I don't want him hurt, and I definitely don't want him dead. I'm not entirely certain what I want, except that I find myself wishing I'd sat down with him and just … talked. Like normal people. Learned more about him, how he thinks, why the hell he was so nice to me when I was determined to hate him.

Too late. I messed that up beyond repair.

There's always Oliver, I guess. And the duck.

CHAPTER NINETEEN: SAWYER

DECEMBER
IRAQ

"YOU SHOULD GO HOME for the holidays, Marine."

I stand and go to attention when my commander comes into the command center for his walk through. Colonel Howard is lean and half a foot smaller than me with large blue eyes. I used to think he'd make a good Marine Corps promotional doll with those eyes.

Not that I'd ever tell him that.

"This is my home, sir," I reply.

"Leave it to the Marines to hold down the fort."

He's looking around at the empty center. He's been here every month to visit, the only one above the rank of captain to venture out here routinely. We're far enough away from Baghdad that even the brass who like to brag about being associated to spec-ops don't want the hassle of traveling to our base to hang out with us.

"At ease, Marine," he tells me.

I relax.

He motions to the chair at the computer where I was sitting and takes the rolling chair beside it.

"Fuck the food here," he grunts.

I smile. What tastes like shit to those stationed on bigger bases is gourmet compared to what we eat on operations and at the FOB.

"How's life?" he asks gruffly.

I know what he's asking. Even less of a warm, fuzzy type than I am, Colonel Howard rarely talks about anything aside from missions and duty.

"Maintaining mission readiness and taking care of the personal thing," I reply.

"Good. Dr. Gomez seems satisfied with your progress."

"It helps being able to stay active in command."

"She says the same. Routine and discipline make for a quiet mind."

"They do, sir."

"Whatever it takes to keep you out there. You make my life easier," he says with a rare smile. "You're always on target and ahead of schedule. Doesn't hurt that you can string a sentence together with proper grammar. I'm not embarrassed to send out your reports like those from some of my captains. Can't ask for more."

I snort. "Thank you, sir."

"Excuse me, gentlemen. Package, Captain Mathis."

I glance up at the Army specialist holding a few boxes in his arms. He sets them down on the desk nearest the door.

"Santa's late this year," Colonel Howard says. "Give that shit to Marines, and we'll make sure it's on time with a pretty fucking bow."

"Yes, sir. Sorry, sir." The specialist tosses me a small box.

I catch it, not recognizing the return address. "Why the fuck does it take so long to get here?" The postmark is four weeks ago. I set it on the table and return my attention to the boss.

"Because you're in the middle of nowhere," Colonel Howard replies. "Too small to be cookies."

"Yeah." I glance at it again, not sure who would've sent me anything. I keep in contact with one of my foster families and the widow of the Marine who mentored me when I was a teenager. No one else, outside of military channels, sends me boxes. "Thanks, Smith."

The specialist gathers his boxes and leaves.

"Dr. Gomez recommended a couple weeks off at some point," Colonel Howard continues.

"Staffing is low over the holidays," I reply. "I can wait, sir."

"Don't wait too long, or I'll have to order you to take it."

"Understood, sir."

"Last convoy to Baghdad leaves in two hours, if you change your mind."
He rises. "Happy holidays, Marine." He claps me on the shoulder.

"You, too, sir."

I wait until he's gone to pick up the box again. I'm not exactly excited
about the idea of taking time off. Dr. Gomez has been telling me I should
for a month. Guess she got tired of me brushing her off and went to my
boss.

Damn civilians. I pull the knife on my belt out of its sheath and slice the
tape on the box. Not sure what to expect, I replace the blade and open the
package. A ring-sized jewelry box is inside, and my brow furrows. *Did
someone send me the wrong thing?* Sometimes, we get care packages
shipped to us by charity or volunteer organizations Stateside that collect
donations and send everything from candy to socks to deployed service
members.

Every once in a while, one of us will get something odd, possibly
shipped by mistake.

I'm convinced this is the case, until I open the box.

For a moment, I stare at the golden Ruptured Duck nestled in the black
velvet interior. There are only two people in the world who know the
significance of this little pin to me, and one of them is deceased.

It doesn't seem likely that Katya sent this, not after the exchange of
letters we had weeks ago. It seems even less likely that a dead man sent it,
though.

I pluck it out of the box and study it. The one given to me ten years ago
was beat up and worn with a colorful patina, an heirloom in every sense.
This one is in mint condition, polished to a soft shine. I'm not a collector by
any means, but I can assess that finding a flawless, nearly one hundred year
old gold Ruptured Duck probably wasn't cheap.

Its light weight is familiar. I missed my good luck charm. My mentor
gave it to me as a reminder for me to stay on the straight and narrow. I was
not happy with myself for losing it. I always treasured it for what it
symbolized – selfless, honorable, brave service. I understand the concepts
better now after losing men and having my own command for close to a
year. I think, somehow, it means more to me now than it did before that
night that changed my life in so many ways.

There's only one person I know capable of the level of thoughtfulness
it'd take to track one of these down and pay what I would consider to be a

small fortune to buy it. Katya is many things; superficial will never be one. Even if I want to deny it's her, I'll always know it is.

Don't let her get to you.

It's too late. My insides are already growing warm, the hot emotions I feel any time I think of her trickling into my thoughts. In a blink, she takes away the quietness in my mind.

"Fuck, Katya." I can't help saying the words aloud. The tiny gift stirs me in ways I don't know if I'll ever be able to get over. It's not only what I feel for her but the newfound appreciation I have for those men like her brother, who didn't even flinch when he volunteered to sacrifice himself for others.

This pin represents everything I've learned and gone through since that night.

Katya has a way of provoking emotions when I want to be numb. I set the golden duck on the desk.

There's still something there between us, something more than the emotions both of us feel surrounding Mikael's death. I don't know what it is or how deep it might run, but it's not going away. Neither is it to the point where I can determine if and what either of us actually feels towards one another. It's like walking blind folded into enemy territory without knowing how many weapons are trained on me.

This can't be healthy.

I have no fucking idea what to do about it. Usually, staying away solves problems. It's not working this time. With no operations planned for the holidays, I'm not certain how I'll be able sit here for two weeks and not think about her.

I lean forward, elbows on my knees, and glare at the Ruptured Duck.

There's no way to know what Katya intended when she sent it, if she meant this as a something more than friendship.

Shit, we aren't even *friends*. We aren't anything that I know of.

She knows what this means to me.

I close the box and absently reach for the dog tags around my neck. I've got Mikael's with me still. I intended to give them to Riley or one of the others before they left.

I didn't. I'm not sure why. It's not like me to forget something that important.

Katya should have them.

Five minutes after receiving her gift, and I'm spiraling into an emotional firefight that I absolutely hate. I can't *not* know what's between us after this, and it's clear that, four months after I last saw her, I'm no closer to getting her out of my head than I was at camp.

There's a completely innocuous excuse for me to find out – the Christmas party the Khavs throw every year. Petr wouldn't turn me down, if I showed up on his doorstep. It's not the way we do things in spec-ops. Our team is our family. I can go, realize I'm not interested in her but have been obsessing over the unknown or a memory or regret or other emotions associated with her bother, and then leave.

"How do you do this to me, Katya?" I growl. "Halfway across the world, and I can't fucking think straight."

I will fix that. Somehow. I'm going to go crazy if I don't just end this. I definitely can't spend months, *years,* wondering what could be between us.

With a sigh, I send Petr a quick email, snatch the duck and trot through the compound to tell Colonel Howard that I need a few days off after all.

Forty hours, six flights, an eight-hour snow delay and a three-hour wait for my luggage later, I'm finally walking out of the Logan International Airport in Boston. By now, I'm tired enough to be thinking two completely opposite trains of thought: first, that this is the stupidest thing I've ever done and I need to go back to Iraq. And second, I'm not getting on another fucking plane again. Ever.

The chilly night air is flecked with white snow. I'd forgotten what snow and winter were like. After being away so long, it's almost pleasant. The night is quiet, aside from the crunch of tires on snow from the cars picking up passengers outside of baggage claim. I'm in my fatigues, which offer some protection from the gusts of wind. The pickup area is well lit with taxis and hotel shuttles waiting, their exhaust curling into the air behind them.

As soon as I touched down in Boston, I messaged the team. Petr wouldn't hear of me catching a cab and volunteered to make the hour long drive to get me. It's nearly two in the morning, and I'm feeling the travel.

Ten minutes pass before Petr's black, top of the line Range Rover slides up to the curb. He pops the hatch, and I lift my bags into the trunk before getting into the passenger's seat. Petr grins, his strong features awake and alert.

"Sawyer Mathis!" He sounds much more cheerful than I could ever muster, let alone after the two days of traveling. "How you doing?"

"Hungry," I respond.

"You're in luck. I brought food." He stretches to reach the backseat and retrieves a plate wrapped in tinfoil. "I grabbed shit on the way out. Not sure what's there."

I accept it, not caring what's under the foil, so long as it's not moving. Right now, I'd probably eat it even if it was. There's a cold cheeseburger, egg rolls, what might be chicken nuggets and cookies.

"Awesome," I say and dig in, taking a huge bite out of the cheeseburger.

"Good trip?"

I shrug.

"Yeah usually sucks." He's smiling, chipper enough that I'd be annoyed, if he was anyone else. Petr has a way of putting people around him at ease. I never could pinpoint what exactly it is about him that does it, but it works, even on someone as tightly wound as I am.

I wolf down everything and then take a bite of a cookie and freeze.

Petr laughs hard.

Setting the cookie down, I dig a bottle of water out of my bag. I swallow and drink then glare at him.

"How does your sister not know how to make cookies?" I grumble.

"I'll never understand it either."

Removing my cap, I set it on my lap and rest my head back. There's a knot in my stomach that has nothing to do with eating too fast and everything to do with the woman who can't cook. I'm not certain what to expect: either I'll see her and realize I was somehow romanticizing everything or I'll realize there's something between us that won't go away.

For once, I'm not planning either way. I'm going to wait to see, because there's one element of this that's absolutely beyond my control: her.

I'm going to enjoy the first recreational leave I've taken since joining the Corps six years ago. From the texts Riley sent me tonight, there's tons of food, alcohol and people around, so I'm pretty sure I can relax in the Khavalov mansion and let things unfold.

It'll be nice to take a break for once.

"I'm surprised you came," Petr says. "Thrilled but surprised."

"Colonel Howard was about to order me on leave," I reply vaguely. It's mostly the truth. I'm not going to tell him about the gift his sister sent, not until I can determine her intentions.

"Baba will be happy to see you. He always asks how you are."

"You have a great family." Closing my eyes, I take a deep breath and relax. The car is so quiet and warm that I know I'll be dozing by the time we get back. "How is he? Healthy?"

"Strong as an ox, as always."

"Good."

"Harper's supposed to be by on Sunday." The way he says it makes me think one of the guys told him about the casual relationship I have with her.

"Everyone will be back together again," I say.

There's a pause, then, "Is it serious?"

"No. We both needed the companionship."

"She on board with that?"

"Yeah."

He's quiet again. I'm not sure what he's looking for. He likes Harper; we all do. Maybe that's why. He's worried about there being hurt feelings or a nasty break that will interfere with our missions.

"It won't affect the team," I assure him. "It's sort of petered off the past month when she got transfer orders to Germany. Nice girl. Just not looking for anything serious. She'll be out of Iraq by mid-January."

"Understood."

Petr is quiet long enough for me to start drifting off. I can't quite get the drone of the aircraft out of my mind.

"You didn't ask about Katya," he says in an even tone.

My jaw clenches. Hearing her name reminds me of how crazy it was to leave Iraq on a whim like this.

"How is she?" I respond.

"Great. She's been managing the charity organization my dad set up. She's loving it."

"Seeing anyone?" *Fuck. Why did I ask?*

"Not seriously. There's a guy. Too boring for her."

My heart somersaults. I start to think I need to focus on drinking and relaxing and not her.

"He's not an issue, if you're interested," Petr adds.

"Your sister and I are not on best terms," I reply.

"Shame. You were good for her."

I say nothing, not wanting to read anything into his words. At all. Ever. I'm too tired for an emotional rollercoaster.

"You, uh, have any advice for dealing with her?"

I lift my head and open my eyes, looking at him to see if he's joking. I spent a few days with her, and he's lived with her for a lifetime.

He's serious.

"What's up?" I ask.

"I'm trying to figure out how to put up some boundaries before she drives me fucking insane."

"I understand." I want to laugh but don't.

He shakes his head.

"You want my advice? Sit down and tell her. Be direct, firm and consistent. Don't let her lay any mines," I respond. "If you give her the chance to set the stage, she'll walk all over you, and you'll let her. You're a doormat with women."

"She says the same, and yeah, she does that all the time."

"Wait until she's tired or something," I advise with a laugh. "She'll listen if you're upfront and honest. It's the approach I took with her."

"She listened to you. I want to figure it out before I tell her my news."

"Riley says they'll let you stay in?"

"Won't be going back to my group," he says. "I'll be working as a spokesman. Recruiting in inner cities and shit."

"Right up your alley. You're great with people. We all miss your stories."

"I was a little disappointed," he admits. "I understand you can't send a one-legged Green Beret into combat. I get to stay in the military and do something worthwhile. This is a happy medium, I think, until I tell Katya I'll be recruiting for the war effort."

"You may be surprised," I say quietly. "Katya loves you. Even if she doesn't agree with the war, she knows people like you fight it."

"True."

I settle back and close my eyes.

I don't notice that I doze off, until the car comes to a stop. Rousing myself, I take in their home. It's a legitimate castle, a mansion made of stone. I've seen it twice before, but I still find myself mystified why someone who lives here would be in the military when he had a clean, solid out.

We get out of the car. The house is quiet and dark, and he takes me in the back. Maybe I shouldn't be surprised to see a kitchen staff already at work in the large space. People who own a house like this don't cook their own food.

Probably why Katya's cookies are so awful.

We go up a service stairwell to the third floor. Wide hallways are well lit, the thick planks of wood flooring covered by a plush runner. Wrought iron chandeliers hang far overhead from wooden beams.

The interior is how I imagine a ski lodge. This kind of wealth is so beyond me ...

I shake my head. *It's a mistake to be here. There's no way Katya could be interested in someone like me.*

The fleeting thought doesn't stick.

Petr stops and points to the room across the hallway. "My room. Katya's is one down."

I glance the direction he indicates, my heart quickening. It's almost four in the morning. I'm not about to knock and wake the dragon.

Petr opens the door to a chamber much larger than any I've stayed in. The massive sleigh bed faces a cozy living room with its own burning hearth. Large windows overlook the back lawn. The furniture is heavy wood, the rug deep blue and the trophy case opposite the door filled with everything from red ribbons to military mementos.

My gaze settles on the hearth once more. I love a fire and have never lived anywhere with one. The triangular, wooden case holding a flag above the hearth makes me pause three steps into the comfortable room.

"Petr, are you sure?" I ask, surprised. "This is Mikael's room."

"It's yours for however long you want to stay." His back is to me. He's crossing the room to lower the drapes on either side of the windows.

There's a sudden lump in my throat. I'm not usually at a loss for words like this. The meaning behind letting me stay here runs soul deep.

"Baba and I talked about it," he says, glancing at me. "It only seemed right."

"It's an honor," I manage. "Really."

"I owe you everything. The least we can do is give you a place to stay whenever you come back to the States."

I'm so accustomed to being alone, to having nowhere but my rack in whatever country the Corps sends me to, to a childhood where I was moved around every year at least …

The idea of having a real home, one I can always return to, isn't one I can really digest after the long day.

But I like the idea. A lot.

At my silence, Petr smiles. "Bathroom." He points to one of the doors along a wall and then to another. "Closet. You're welcome to move anything around that you want."

I nod.

"Get some rest. I'm sure Riley and Carson will be up at some point tomorrow to drag you out."

He leaves.

I set my gear down and absorb everything he's said.

Home. It's not something I ever expected to find or in this case, have dropped into my lap. I can't help wishing I felt better about this trip. If Katya hates me, this isn't going to be home for long.

Too tired to dwell on it, I take a quick shower and drop into bed.

CHAPTER TWENTY: KATYA

TODAY IS THE SET UP FOR both my father's annual party and the holiday fundraiser I'm managing. Both kick off tomorrow, with my event – a Winter Wonderland auction and dinner benefiting children of wounded vets – lasting all day. It's the first I've organized, and my nerves are completely shot.

I can't think of a better way to spend the holidays than doing something that will make Mikael, Petr and my father so proud.

Even if I can't stop hurting inside.

Or maybe it's because most of Mikael's team will be present that I don't mind missing out on the annual event.

My therapist says I'm doing well. I know it helps having a positive outlet, channeling the pain I still experience about Mikael's death into helping those who need it. I've finally accepted that my brothers chose to serve their country, and I have to respect that decision. I don't think I'll ever be able to blindly support the military or the idea of war, but I can help those like my brothers who join up to make a difference. The people behind the war, I guess. People like Captain Mathis, who lead others into battle and then have to deal with the consequences alone.

I never responded to his letter and heard no more from or about him, aside from Petr's confirmation he wasn't returning for the party while the other guys are.

It bothers me. Thinking of him makes me hollow inside. I read his letter every morning for the week following its arrival and then put it away.

Your letter destroyed me.

That pain, the one stemming from knowing I hurt him, isn't relenting. There's nothing I can do about it now. I burnt that bridge; that much is clear.

Shaking my head, I look from the first light snow of the winter that coats the lawn and forest visible through the window of my bedroom to the open desk drawer where I placed the letter from Captain Mathis. I'm tempted to toss it into the fire burning in the hearth.

I won't. I already know I'll take it with me wherever I end up someday, a reminder of someone I wish I'd met under different circumstances and of how my fiery emotions burn up those around me sometimes.

It's also a reminder that my biggest regret is not sitting down to get to know him. I had to learn who he was through a letter.

Tucked in the envelope is a customs slip. I finally sent him the Ruptured Duck a few weeks ago. I bought it for someone I cared about, and I sent it, even if whatever disaster of a relationship we had is over. It only seemed right for the duck to go to someone who would appreciate it.

Letting go of it was hard and took me weeks of hyping myself up. It's not possible to get over the impact Sawyer Mathis has had on my life, no matter how much time passes. I want to. I'm trying. But it's like trying to forget Mikael. It'll never happen. Sending off the duck was like accepting that I'd never see either of them again. It hurt so much, I cried when I returned from the post office.

I sent it with a phony address and no note. I'm counting on him thinking it's from the Marine friend who inspired him to enlist. If he's staying there for Christmas, he might as well not be alone. The duck can keep him company.

The idea makes me smile, and I close the drawer and grab a sweater.

"Ready, sis?" Petr calls, knocking on my door.

I join him in the hall. He's dressed in a warm sweater that stretches across his broad chest and dark slacks.

"You need a scarf," I tell him automatically.

"Trained killer. No scarf."

"You look tired. Were you drinking all night?"

He rolls his eyes. "Come on."

We leave the house through the servants' stairwell to the car awaiting us out front. Our house is full of guests, the way it is every year this time. The second floor is packed with relatives, family friends and Petr's military friends, and the overflow is being housed in the guest cottages and mother-in-law wing of the mansion.

This evening is my last walk through of the event site for the charity event tomorrow.

"Hope this is worth leaving the guys and the booze," Petr says.

"You'll have plenty of time to get drunk," I snap. "How often do you get to see a charity event I put together?"

It's my first. He knows better than to answer.

He's smiling faintly, gaze on the snow brushing the window.

We travel the half hour to the exclusive country club Baba rented out at my insistence. The main areas are a flurry of activity with workers finishing up the exterior walkways, laying fake snow inside, and setting up the dining room. There's a bazaar in one area with vendors setting up, a silent auction section featuring items donated by local families and others, a children's room with a throne for Santa and live petting zoo on the porch extension, and a light display covering three acres out back, complete with lantern-lit walkway.

The activity, plentiful Christmas decorations and bright lights everywhere pull a smile from me, despite my apprehension about something being out of place or going wrong.

"You did all this?" Petr is standing in the middle of a miniature train track running around the interior of the building.

"Why do you sound surprised?" I raise an eyebrow at him and plant my hands on my hips.

"Not surprised, Kitty-Khav. Impressed." He smiles. "Totally over the top and incredible, as usual."

I look around, a little lost with how much is going on. I'm not as detail oriented as some and rely on Zach, my father's chief assistant, to tell me when something is off. I'm so nervous about tomorrow that I've been here no less than ten times today, walking around to see the progress.

"Is that a donkey?" Petr asks, staring at the four-legged animal being led into the children's room.

"I wanted a camel but Baba said no," I say with a sigh.

He gives me an odd look I ignore. I peek into the different rooms, satisfied with how everything has come together between my first inspection this morning and now.

"What do you think?" I ask him after we tour the club.

"I think Mikael would shit himself knowing there's a donkey in the club."

"Petr!" I slap him lightly on the back of the head.

He laughs. "I love it."

"Really?"

"Really."

"Okay, good, because you have to be here for the reception in the morning," I say, pleased.

"Seriously? I've got a bottle of hundred year old whiskey waiting for me."

"No drinking tonight!" I order him. "You can't show up drunk or hung over."

"I'll be fine."

"Wait, are you even *allowed* to drink?"

"Kitty-Khav!" He wraps me in a chokehold and hauls me against him. "I'll be here, and I'll be capable of shaking a few hands." He gives me a noogie. I bat his hand away. "Okay?"

It's not, but this is something else I've been working on: not being quite so overbearing. I still worry about him all the time.

"Fine," I snap. "Stop it!" I wriggle loose from him and smooth out my hair.

"Seriously. This is awesome." His smile is warm, his blue eyes on me. "You're amazing, Kitty."

"I know. About time you figured that out." I look around, nervous about everything. "Did you invite that girl you met to the party?"

"Nah."

It's not like Petr to be shy around a girl he's interested in. When he says nothing further, I glance at him.

"Because …" I prod.

He shrugs.

"You don't like her? She's another Brianna? She's mean?"

"Didn't feel right."

"What does that mean?" I study him.

He's not interested in talking about it. That much I can see from the change in his expression. It's never stopped me from dragging something out of him before, and it won't now.

"If you like her, you should at least bring her by," I urge. "I'll tell you if you can date her or not."

"She kind of freaked out about my leg," he admits for my ears only.

"She *what?*" My face flashes hot. "Did she say something? I know how to punch now. You met her at the coffee shop, right?" Fury tears through me, replacing the chill of the club with warmth. I know the spots he frequents. I'm pretty sure I can find out which bitch she is.

Petr's guarded expression melts with his laugh. "Down, Kitty-Khav. You aren't beating up any more of my girlfriends."

"Seriously, Petr. Did she say something?"

"It doesn't matter. I don't need someone like that around. Don't you agree?"

"Yes, but –"

"But nothing. I consider myself fortunate to learn that before I decide if I like her or not. She's not worth the anger, Kitty-Khav." Too laid back to tell me to back off like I might him, I can hear the firm note in his tone that warns me I'm not helping the situation.

I stew for a minute, reining in my anger. Petr doesn't seem too affected by it, but I know him well enough to know he is on some level. He's always been more sensitive than Mikael was.

"You're right." Being calm when I want to scream is like eating glass. I hate it. It's one lesson I haven't learned well from the therapist. "Not worth it." Except I'm too pissed to let it go like I should. "You can point her out next time we go to the coffee shop. I'll handle it."

He shakes his head with a grin. "It's for the best, Kitty."

"You are too good to deal with someone like that." I'm calming, probably influenced by the fact he really doesn't seem too upset. "People really suck."

"There are good eggs out there. You just have to find them."

And not drive them off. "That pisses me off. You're the best person I know."

"Speaking of dating, where's your puppy?"

"Oliver isn't a puppy," I say and roll my eyes. He kind of does follow me around everywhere. "I told him to go home."

"He's really not your type."

"He's nice." Oliver has been hinting a lot at becoming more serious as a couple, while I'm considering breaking it off. We've had sex a few times, but I'm not feeling it with him. "I don't think I have a type."

He definitely doesn't drive me wild the way Sawyer Mathis did. I have a feeling I'll compare every man I ever date to Sawyer. *The one who got away.* Or more accurately, the one I drove away.

"Dating sucks," Petr mutters.

"Agreed."

"You staying for a while?"

I nod. "I'm really nervous. I can't seem to stay away. Hoping to see everything set up tonight so I can sleep without worrying."

"It'll go well," he says with confidence I don't feel. "Out of curiosity, how did you convince the club board to let you have livestock on the veranda?"

"I didn't ask. I told them I was doing it." I smile.

"Good girl." He gives me a quick hug. "I'll save a shot of whiskey for you."

"Petr-" I start.

"Nope. I'm a grown man. If I want to drink, I will." He draws himself up to his full height of right around six-foot-one. "Deal with it, sis."

"Whatever." I love Petr, even when he's trying to act all tough like he is now. "Don't forget a tie tomorrow morning."

With another exasperated shake of his head, he leaves the club for the car waiting out front.

I watch him then turn back to the clubhouse. The event is taking shape, filled with sparkles and decorations and happiness that rubs off on me. I can't help smiling, knowing I made this possible. I'm proud of myself.

With an optimistic guess that I'll be out of there by nine o'clock, I dive in to help lay out silverware in the dining room.

It's past midnight when I get home. The pre-party crowd has spilled out onto the deck, and I make my way through the throng, intent on reaching the back stairwell and escaping up to my room. Deck furniture surrounds several fire pits, and an open bar is located in the center of the open space.

Too tired to find Petr and remind him about the morning, I don't bother stopping. I barely hear someone call my name until he's right behind me. Jarred out of my daze, I turn to see Harris there.

"Hey," he says.

"Hi." I haven't seen him since this summer. I assume his family was invited as usual to the holiday bash. A little leery after our last exchange, I find myself growing alert. He wouldn't do anything in front of all these people. Of course, I won't think twice about socking him if he does.

"Great party, as always," he says, lifting his glass. He seems a little unfocused. "You, uh, got a minute to talk?"

"Yeah."

"I mean away from all this." He waves at the crowd.

"Um, not really. We can talk here."

He glances around and inches close enough that I can smell the alcohol on his breath. "I thought maybe … you know. I could apologize in private."

I hesitate. He's drunk, and I'm not afraid to hit him. I'm pretty sure that puts us on even ground.

"Yeah. Come on." Turning away, I lead him inside. I'm not stupid enough to take him upstairs, so I go to the kitchen. It smells of food, and there are platters of baked goods and confections and buffet trays of hearty food everywhere.

Facing him, I wait.

His gaze is as much on me as the blinking Christmas lights around the buffet table.

My patience is thinner than normal after the long day at the club. "I haven't seen you since the camp this past summer," I say, hoping to prod him into a quick apology so I can go to bed.

Harris focuses on me. "I'm not much of one for camping."

"Me neither." He's talking clearly. I can tell he's tipsy, though.

"I know, they said not to talk to you again, but … Katya, I just want things to go back to how they were."

I'm not sure who he's talking about or even if he knows what he's saying. "I don't think that's possible, Harris."

"Why not?" He almost shouts the words, flinging his arms wide enough that he manages to dump the rest of his drink on the kitchen floor.

"Because I don't want to be your friend anymore," I reply in irritation.

"You don't?" He stares at me, surprised.

"Um, no."

For a moment, he looks so hurt, I want to laugh. His surprise turns into anger that glints in his eyes. Red creeps up his neck and into his face. "So you avoid me all year and don't want to be friends? My father donated to this stupid Winterland thing tomorrow and the camp!"

"Winter Wonderland," I correct him automatically. "I thanked him personally."

"He did it because I asked him to. Because I care about you, Katya." He appears distraught, sad and then angry again. "I've been in love with you since we were like ten. You never gave me the time of day."

Talk about moods. My therapist would have a field day with him. He's off his rocker tonight. It's unusual when someone else can make me feel like the most stable person in the room.

"Look, Harris," I say quietly. I want to be kind for the sake of our past friendship, but my tired temper is fraying quickly. "You're drunk. Sleep it off, and we'll talk in the morning. Okay?"

"You're brushing me off again."

"You're acting like a dick. Go sleep it off!"

"I just want to apologize."

"Then do it and go to bed!"

He frowns. "There are days I wish both your brothers died."

I gasp.

"You haven't been to the club or dropped by my house since Petr came back hurt," he goes on. "You haven't been my friend since then."

I take a deep breath. "My family is important to me, Harris. You know this."

"And I'm not? We've been friends since we were three. You ditched me for that cripple of a brother of yours, Katya."

"*Ditched* you? I lose one brother and the other comes back hurt, and you're worried about me ditching you!" *So much for calm.* "I never want anything to do with you again, Harris. Not now, not tomorrow morning, not ever!"

"Selfish bitch! I've done so much for you, and you just –"

I whirl. I'm getting nowhere, arguing with a drunk, and I'm losing what calm I've learned to maintain over the past few weeks.

Harris snatches my arm, and I grimace. He's squeezing too hard, reminding me of the night at camp when he slapped me after we had a similar argument about Petr.

"Let go, Harris!" I snap, trying to pry my arm free.

His grip is too tight.

"Let her go, Harris, and I won't gut you the way you deserve."

Harris goes rigid then turns.

If Petr's lethal, sharp tone unnerves me, his stony expression renders him almost unrecognizable. I've never seen that look on his face. It's scary and dangerous, an indication that my brother is every bit the trained killer he jokes about being. There's no way the older brother who teases me with warmth is the same man as the one in the doorway to the deck, who looks ready to kill someone.

Riley is standing behind him, grim.

Harris gazes at him uncertainly for a moment before recovering. "I see you brought backup."

"I don't need backup with you."

Riley moves into the room.

"Let my sister go, Harris. This is between us. I warned you what'd happen if you laid a hand on my sister again." Petr is peeling off his sweater to reveal the white t-shirt beneath it. He tosses the sweater.

Again? How did he know? My thoughts fly to Sawyer. I wonder if this is the reason Harris hasn't dropped by my house in months. Petr or Sawyer – or both – scared him off.

"The cripple thinks he can still fight." Harris appears amused.

"Petr is not –" I start.

"Katya." Petr's sharp tone silences me. Riley offers a small smile and shakes his head for me to keep quiet. "Let's finish this, Harris. You and the cripple."

Harris's grip loosens, and I yank free.

"Fine," Harris says curtly.

Petr walks out of the kitchen onto the veranda. After a hesitation, Harris follows. Riley remains in the kitchen with me.

"They're not seriously gonna fight are they?" I trail, alarmed.

"Your brother can handle it," Riley advises.

"I don't need him to handle anything for me!" I snap. *And he shouldn't be fighting on his bad leg!*

"Katya, respectfully, if you interfere, I'll pick you up and move you."

"Just try it!" That shit never worked for Captain Mathis. It'll definitely never work for Riley, who almost sounds apologetic.

I hurry out, making my way through the crowd gathering on the veranda. I reach the stairs before Riley catches me and wraps an arm around me, hauling me away from the stairs to the railing instead.

"Dammit, Riley!" I mutter and push at the thick arm.

"You're staying right here, Kitty-Khav."

"He's right." Carson says joining us. "This is Petr's battle."

"It's not anyone's battle! This is stupid and insane!" I retort.

Carson gazes down at me, amused. "He's taking care of his sister. It's the right thing to do."

I'll never understand how these men think. Violence doesn't resolve issues. It makes them fester, and if Petr gets hurt, I'll probably kill Harris and then him. Fighting to get free from Riley is like trying to move a tree out of my path, and I stop struggling with a frustrated sigh.

Petr and Harris are in the snow. Harris is saying something that doesn't reach those of us on the deck watching. I can't get over the change in Petr. It's strange. I can see Captain Mathis cracking necks. I can't see my sweet Petr doing the same, even though I know they went through similar training and ran missions together.

Harris lands the first punch, knocking Petr back a couple of steps. I flinch and try once more to get free. Riley isn't moving. Even if he did, I don't think Carson is going to let me past him.

Not that either of them would stop me from trying, if something bad happened to my brother.

Petr's nose is bleeding. I'm panicking inside, eyeing his fake leg and afraid he'll get hurt.

He dabs at the blood and then laughs.

What the hell? Who responds like that to getting punched? I watch, anxious and concerned for my brother. He shakes out his shoulders and lowers his stance some. I'm waiting for his leg to snap in two or something horrible.

I'm not expecting my gentle brother to slam one fist then another and another … over and over into Harris. He moves so fast and hits hard enough to knock Harris back with each strike. I've never seen my brothers fight. They wrestled once or twice but never like this.

Harris gets in a couple more blows, including one aimed at my brother's leg, before Petr picks him up and slams him into the ground.

Harris stays down. Petr goes with him, planting his knee on his chest while his fake leg is straight off to the side. He's pounding the shit out of Harris's face. Blood flies everywhere, terrifying me. If he kills Harris … if he hurts him enough to go to jail …

How can this be my sweet Petr?

"Petr!" I shout, horrified. "Stop!"

He pauses and looks up towards me, his face and upper body splattered with blood.

Harris isn't moving.

My heart is pounding hard. I'm not sure which is worse: the sight of all the blood or knowing my brother would probably kill Harris, if given the chance.

Petr checks Harris's pulse and then stands, walking towards the deck.

I pull lose from Riley and go to my brother, meeting him when he reaches the top of the stairs. Staring at him, I'm not at all sure what to say or feel. I *hate* violence, and he just beat the shit out of someone.

He offers me a quick smile and lifts his chin at Carson and Riley.

"Show's over!" Riley calls to those on the deck. He starts waving people away from the railing. "Anyone want to call an ambulance?"

"Petr!" I don't know what else to say. Gazing up at my bloodied brother, I'm horrified by what he's done and amazed he did it. His features soften until he's my Petr again. "What the hell -"

"Hush, Katya," he says gruffly but quietly. "Let me defend my little sister in peace." A note much firmer than any he's ever used with me is present. "Okay?"

I nod somewhat uncertainly.

"I told him never to come back," he adds. "No one is going to hurt my family, especially not a dickweed like that one."

Tears fill my eyes. Despite the blood that's grossing me out, I'm a little touched by his determination. I never really noticed how alone I feel in my own family, like I'm the one trying to take care of everyone else.

"Are you okay?" I venture, not yet sure if it's safe to talk yet.

"Awesome. Haven't gotten punched in a while. Almost forgot what it felt like," Petr says cheerfully.

"You're so weird."

"And you're so stubborn. If anyone ever bothers you again and you don't tell me, I'll be pissed at you, Katya."

"You're not my boss," I fire back.

"I'm your brother." He pushes me away to see my eyes. "We stick together. You beat up my girlfriends, and I beat up the guys bugging you."

I'm not used to my brother being assertive. He's a strong, good man. I'm surprised to find that I'm not angry for him standing up to me. There was a time when I'd be furious at him. It makes me think Captain Mathis was right yet again: Petr is so much stronger than I gave him credit for. Even missing a leg, he can beat the shit out of anyone. It shouldn't make me proud, but it does.

"We need ice cream," he finishes and takes my arm, walking towards the house.

"Is Harris okay?" I ask.

"He'll live." He doesn't sound at all concerned.

Whether or not I should, I trust my brother and let it go.

The partygoers are already distracted by beer and s'mores. Carson remains by Harris while Riley looks like he's entertaining people to keep their attention away from the horrible scene on the back lawn.

I take a seat at the breakfast bar and watch Petr pull ice cream out of the freezer.

"Things are gonna change around here a little, Katya."

After his display on the lawn, I'm listening. He sets down the ice cream then peels off his bloody t-shirt, displaying his muscular upper body. He pulls on his sweater before washing his hands then dipping us both bowls full of ice cream.

This is kind of ... strange. He kicks someone's ass, walks away and eats ice cream. Is this what he did in Iraq? Why doesn't almost killing Harris bother him one bit?

"I've always kind of brushed you off as the annoying little sister. I guess it never hit me until this year that you're not her anymore," he says, setting a bowl down before me. "I'm sorry if you felt left out around Mikael and me, or if we didn't ever really take you seriously."

Puzzled, I take a bite of ice cream and think about what I want to say. I don't think I can stomach eating much. I keep glancing at the bloodied t-shirt and hoping Harris is okay. Not for his sake, but so Petr isn't thrown in jail or something.

"I am very grateful for you in my life and for all you did this year," he continues.

"I felt left out when you guys left, but not in a bad way. I don't think. I mean, I didn't blame you for going."

"Everything changed this year."

I nod, gazing at my ice cream. I push it away.

"I guess what I'm trying to say is that I want you as my friend. Not my caretaker," he says. "I don't need you to be my mother, and there are days, Katya …" He gives a growl of frustration. "Let's just say it's like you see me as broken, as someone who needs help. I'm neither of those, Kitty-Khav."

He's speaking gently, as if knowing he's hurting me. I'm pretty sure he's right. What he's telling me isn't new; I've heard it from a couple different sources. It doesn't make it easier to swallow.

He's waiting for me to talk.

I clear my throat. "I don't think you're broken or lesser because of your leg. I couldn't bear it if I lost you, and everything I do is because I love you, Petr."

"I know, Kitty," he says. "We've both had to change this year. I'm proud of you and how well you've dealt with everything. It's because of this that I thought now was a good time to talk to you."

"I don't know how to be different," I say with some difficulty. "I don't want to let you go."

"I'm not asking you to. Just asking you to be my friend and my sister. Not worrying every second of the day about me. Not assuming that I can't take care of myself. Maybe trusting that I know what I'm doing with my life and my health and respecting my choices," he says softly. "Waiting until I fuck up to yell at me. *Talking* to me instead of lecturing me."

We've never really spoken to each other this way. Well, maybe he's tried. I don't really know. Tired and stressed from watching him beat up Harris, I'm about to cry, and my throat is tight. "Can I be your best friend?"

He laughs. "Yes. I have a lot to work on, too, when it comes to talking to you and others. Not being afraid of opening up or taking a chance on people."

"Like we need anyone else," I joke.

"We've got to date someday. Well, you've got your puppy."

"You really don't like him?" I venture to look up and see my brother gazing at me warmly. I wipe my eyes.

"He's so … boring."

I stifle a laugh.

"He does everything you say and never stops smiling. Doesn't that drive you nuts?" Petr asks.

"A little. I figured I'd break it off after the holidays."

"Yeah, you can't kick a puppy at Christmas. Pretty sure you go to hell for that one," he agrees.

I giggle, even knowing how awful it is to talk about Oliver and sweet little puppies like this.

"I always thought Captain Mathis would be good for you," he adds too casually.

I grimace. Even hearing his name out loud causes me pain. "Definitely not."

"Because …"

"Because … he deserves better," I whisper.

"Katya!"

"He does." I can't say more without opening the dam I've carefully emplaced. "So no. Maybe I need a break from men for a while."

"I'll support that," Petr says. "Will save me from having to beat up anyone else."

"So barbaric."

"He won't be back, and he knows what'll happen if he talks to you again. That's what matters."

I suppress a smile. I kind of like the idea of us being friends. I didn't realize how one-way our relationship was before this. I've always chased my brothers and father around, cleaning up after them, yelling at them for cursing or whatever the minor infraction, taking care of them.

My brothers were never really interested in me, let alone willing to consider me as a friend. If anything, they found me either a nuisance or amusing, depending on the issue. The fact Petr wants to be a friend is … amazing.

Wiping my cheeks, I nod. "I like the idea of us being friends," I decide.

"Good."

"I'm still going to beat up any woman who hurts your feelings and yell at you sometimes."

"I'll beat up any more Harrises you bring home. Don't be surprised if I start pushing back when you yell. I've learned a few tips from Captain Mathis on handling challenging people."

I roll my eyes. The last thing I need is my brother turning into Sawyer.

"Deal? Friends?" he asks, extending his hand.

I sigh and nod. Instead of taking his hand, I hug him.

"You look beat. Go to bed," he says quietly. "Big day tomorrow."

"Don't kill anyone before I get up."

"I won't, Kitty-Khav."

I release him and start away.

"Thanks for listening." He stands and takes the bowls. "Sleep well, sis."

I feel like crying. Without another word, I go to my room. The house is insulated well enough that I don't hear the party below. I peek out the windows at everyone, though, recalling a time when I'd be the first person drinking and the last on my feet.

Blinking, I stare and then rub my eyes. My heart takes off, and I find myself leaning against the cold glass to see better.

For a split second, I thought I saw Sawyer Mathis.

"I'm more tired than I thought."

Not that it matters if I did. But I stand for a full five minutes, scouring the faces of everyone, just in case.

He's not there. I'm not sure whom I saw, but there's no way it's him.

Isn't that a good thing? Do I want it to be him?

I'm too tired to know for sure.

CHAPTER TWENTY ONE: SAWYER

I'M STILL KICKING MYSELF OVER missing the scene with Petr and Harris. I'm not used to people disobeying me, and I'm definitely not happy about not getting to kick Harris' ass. What kind of Marine isn't there to defend his buddy in a brawl? Not that Petr needed the help, according to what Riley told me.

I could've used the outlet, though. It's probably the twenty hours of good sleep I got, but I'm wired today.

Petr disappeared this morning to Katya's event. The house is quiet, with people occupied in the media rooms, gym, bowling alley, stables, and wherever else the Khavalovs have set up to amuse people over the three day party. I've never seen anything like this place or imagined that a *house* would have a full-sized movie theatre, among other luxuries far beyond the normal reach of the average person.

There's no way Katya could ever leave this behind, and I'm doubting my visit.

Which I *hate.*

Riley stops Petr's Range Rover in front of the valet at the country club. Already, the scene appears festive, with decorations spilling out of the club and crowds of people lining up for the sleigh rides or Christmas maze.

We get out. The air smells like peppermint and cinnamon.

Uncertain what I'm doing here, or how Katya might react when I see her, I am determined to live up to my name of Iceman and stay calm. I'm enjoying my vacation so far. Tons of food, sleep and great company ... even if there's nothing between us, I'm capable of appreciating the break.

"I haven't been home for the holidays for three years," Riley says. His eyes are glowing as he takes in the scene. "I didn't realize how much I missed all this shit."

"None of my holidays were anything like this," Carson says. His arm is wrapped around a tall brunette model I vaguely recall from a magazine. They've been inseparable all day.

"I don't think the Khavs live the way we do," Riley comments wryly. "Hey, Sawyer, did Petr show you the ammo depot?"

"No," I respond, perking up. "Is it huge?"

"Have him take you." He laughs. I'm not sure why. I can easily believe that Petr and his father both are into weapons.

We head inside, which can only be described as cheerful chaos. People mill, decorations cover every surface, and the scents of food are thick in the air.

It's got Katya written all over it. Exuberant, bright, overwhelming. I'm better fitted to the austere, less-is-more approach of the military than the colorful fantasyland around me.

Not that I don't like it. It has the effect I'm sure she wanted. I relax despite the crowd and sensory overload. There's glitter and brightness everywhere I turn. It's uplifting, happy.

Riley goes one way while Carson and his girl go another. I follow the scent of baked goods to a catered room filled with pies, cookies and homemade bread. I ate a huge breakfast a few hours ago, when I woke up midmorning, and snag a couple of cookies, unable to resist the pull of real food.

There's a punch fountain on one table and a cocoa fountain on another. No booze, given the youthful crowd, and I settle for a bottle of water. Once I've gotten my bearings, I pull out my cell and text her a message I'm sure will get a reaction. Whether it's good or bad or even if she'll respond, I don't know.

Where are you? Pushing send, I tuck the phone away and make my way through the sweets again, picking out pieces here and there.

My phone vibrates, and I check it.

Petting zoo.

She responded. That's something. I return to the lobby, where there are candy canes acting as poles that have arrows pointing to all the different rooms. I follow the one towards the children's section. It's loud and even more over the top than the rest of the club.

"Captain Mathis!"

I turn at the child's voice to see little Jacob headed towards me, followed by Jenna and Morgan. Jacob is digging something out of his pocket. I'm hoping it's not a spider.

"You came!" Jenna exclaims. She's absolutely adorable dressed as an elf, cute enough that even I crouch to give her a hug.

All three of them hug me. They smell like food and peppermint, a scent I will always associate with Katya and camp.

"I have one more left," Jacob says, handing me a handcrafted arachnid. "It's a Christmas spider."

"I see that," I say. The white spider is covered in green and red glitter. "Did you make it here?"

"He brought it from home," Jenna answers for him. "Look, I have one, too." She proudly points to the spider pin on her hat.

"Me, too," Morgan adds and shows me the one she has on her jacket.

"You have to wear yours. We're a team," Jacob says firmly.

I laugh, not expecting to have left such an impression on them. I pin the spider to the collar of my long-sleeved polo.

"What did you bring us?" Jenna asks.

"Nothing, sweetheart. Not this time," I reply, smiling.

"Will you next time?"

"From Iraq?" I ask skeptically. "What do you want?"

"A camel," Morgan replies instantly.

"Desert spider," says Jacob.

"Maybe …" Jenna is thinking hard. "A pyramid. A little one."

"Those might be a little bit much," a woman says from behind them. "I heard a lot about you, Captain Mathis. I'm Morgan and Jacob's mother, Teresa."

I stand to shake her hand.

"They had quite the time at camp this summer."

"They're good kids," I reply, smiling.

"Jacob's talked about nothing but becoming a Marine like Captain Mathis when he grows up. You helped them through a rough patch. I appreciate it." She smiles at her kids.

"It's my pleasure," I respond.

"Are you coming back next summer?" Jenna asks, large eyes on me expectantly. "You can sneak us bacon."

"More bacon, more laps," I remind her.

She sighs.

"I'm okay with that," Jacob says. "As long as you're there."

"We'll see," I reply. "It'll depend on my schedule."

They don't seem too happy with that caveat. I can plan my career up to retirement but nothing outside. I'd like to say yes. I'm not about to give them false hope if Katya wants me gone for good.

"Are you going to see the animals?" Jenna asks.

"Yes."

"We'll go with you." She takes my hand.

It still feels weird holding the soft, tiny hand of a kid. The three walk with me towards the petting zoo, stopping to marvel at the rabbits wearing Santa hats. I spot Riley, Petr, Carson and his plus one, and the small shape of Katya on the balcony. Her back is to me, and she's wearing a maroon, crushed velvet dress that falls above her knees and a Santa hat.

Seeing her makes me want to hurry the kids. My gaze skims down her feminine shape. Warmth races within me.

It's like I just saw her. No part of me believes it's been a few months since we last interacted.

It's not the sign I was hoping for. Or maybe it is. It'd be nice to have a conversation with her that doesn't end in one of us upset. I don't know if that's possible when I always have such a strong reaction to her.

"Jacob, keep an eye on Jenna," I say to the boy. "I've got to say hello to Ms. Khavalov."

"Okay."

I'm not certain he heard. His attention is on Christmas rats pulling a miniature sled. Not too concerned, I make my way to the group on the balcony overlooking a Christmas maze. My adrenaline is spiking the way it does in battle and around Katya.

"Hey, Sawyer." Petr grins. "Good to see you."

I nod and join the circle.

"I see they found you." Riley indicates the spider.

"Yeah, they did."

Katya is watching me. I glance at her.

Fuck me. She's more beautiful every time I see her. I always tell myself I'm not going to let her gorgeous hazel eyes draw me in. And every time she does. Her delicate features are lightly flushed, her gaze unreadable. For the first time since meeting her, I have no fucking clue where I stand.

"So you *do* like cookies," she says. Her gaze is on the cookies on a napkin in my palm.

"We all live for cookies overseas," Riley says and takes one of mine.

Her gaze sharpens. "Petr says you don't. It's why I stopped sending them."

"I don't like cookies," Carson says.

She glares at him.

Carson steps back and grins. "I think I hear the cocoa calling me."

"Ah ... yeah. Maybe I don't either." Realizing his mistake, Riley replaces the half-eaten cookie on my napkin. "I think I need some cocoa, too."

Katya raises an eyebrow at Petr, who is trying not to smile.

"So, ah, good to see you here, Sawyer," he says while backpedaling. "I'm going to make a strategic retreat before my sister body slams me."

All four of them escape, leaving me with Katya. She gazes up at me, and I can tell she's as lost as I am right now.

"No one else will tell you this, but your cookies are terrible, Katya," I tell her.

"Your text etiquette is worse! What is this, Sawyer?" She pulls her cell out and shows my message to me. "You don't call, don't text, don't write ..." She's trying hard to keep the mood light and then flushes. "Well you did write, but ..." She clears her throat.

"Want to start over?" I ask with a half-smile.

"Yes."

We gaze at one another in heavy silence. Any hope I had of not being attracted to her, of not thinking she was the most incredible woman I've ever met, vanishes when I'm standing before her again. From the plump lips to her flushed cheeks, I can't stop scouring her features, trying to memorize them so next time, I'm not caught off guard by her looks.

"Do you want to have coffee or something?" I ask, unaccustomed to feeling so awkward around anyone.

"Yes," she replies. "I, um, can't now. I've got to keep an eye on this." She motions to the club.

"Petr told me you set it up."

"Do Marines like Christmas?" she asks archly.

"Yeah. And this is amazing."

"I'm glad you like it." She smiles, pleased. "Maybe after this is over?"

"Sure."

"Can I give you a time range or will that make your head explode?"

I laugh.

"I can text you." There's an odd look on her features that I can't read. "Are you staying at the house?"

"I am."

"Good." Her voice is soft. She's staring at me. "I mean ... better than destroying the environment driving somewhere in your truck." Her blush is getting deeper. "Or something. You always do this to me, Sawyer." Anger flares in her gaze. "You're so calm! Just when I start to think ..." With a sound of frustration, she moves away, thoroughly flustered.

Smiling, I watch her. She doesn't look back, doesn't acknowledge me again.

For some reason, it makes me laugh. I have no idea what she started to say, but when Katya Khavalov is too emotional to talk, it means there's something there.

Something that gives me hope that my trip back wasn't for a few nights of drinking and French toast. Something that tells me I better know what I want in my life, if I sit down for coffee with her, because things will only escalate from there.

For once, I don't mind adjusting the career path I've carefully laid out, not if she wants to be a part of my world. There's a shit load of questions to answer before it's a possibility.

But I'm willing to consider the option that I might need to make a change to where I'm going in life. Our first meeting gives me a good idea of how this is going to play out. What I'm not sure about: if Katya's figured it out yet or not.

CHAPTER TWENTY TWO: KATYA

THE NERVOUSNESS I EXPERIENCED about running the event is nothing compared to the emotions flying through me at the prospect of having coffee with Sawyer. I still can't quite believe he's here. Or that he actually spoke to me.

He even smiled. Not the terse one he used to give me at camp, but a real one, like he gives others.

After my letter to him, I didn't think it was possible for us to meet again without there being too much bad blood between us. He was so calm and contained, though, I have no idea what he's thinking. So he asked me for coffee. Maybe he's being polite, for Petr's sake, wanting to rebuild a bridge that can at least hold our weight so we don't upset my brother.

I can't read too much into this. If nothing else, coffee might give me the ability to say a few things I've been rolling around in my head. *Closure.*

Then it hits me; he's looking for closure, too. It dampens my spirits but does nothing to stop the fever inside me or the fact I have trouble focusing long enough to think straight.

His smile and the way he regarded me with familiar intensity ...

It's too much to think about.

The rest of the day flies by. On the ride home, I'm trying to figure out if I want to text him now or wait until I get back. I don't want to seem either eager or the opposite, unwilling. Because I'm dying for some time with him and dreading it at the same time.

Disgusted with the emotions I thought had somewhat under control, I tuck the phone in my purse without texting.

The party is raging out back when I get there at eight. The evening schedule was a formal dinner and after-party style night. Open bar, electronica blasting, a dance floor on the back lawn …

My old scene. I wind my way through the crowd onto the deck, where couples are snuggled up together around fire pits. They appear cozy and happy. I'm trying to figure out if I'd ever be that relaxed around Sawyer when I trip over my own feet.

I catch my balance, tug off the high heels and continue through the kitchen and up the back stairs. Padding down the hallway where my room is, I frown when I see my door open. I walk in and toss my jacket and shoes on the bed. The closet light is on.

"Petr!" I complain before I get there.

"Just showing Sawyer the ammo depot," he calls cheerfully.

He calls my shoe closet the ammo depot, because of how well I throw shoes when I'm pissed. I'm not sure if he's seriously proud of the fact he organized it alphabetically by designer a few weeks ago or if he's messing with me. Having him home is great, except for the fact that he is always straightening up everything of mine. I like my messes the way they are.

"I don't think Sawyer is interested in my shoes," I retort and enter, crossing my arms.

"It's fascinating," Petr replies.

I have a couple hundred pairs of shoes, if not more. They're over by the Jimmy Choo rack.

"This pair cost half what my Land Rover did," Petr says picking up a rare pair.

"Definitely couldn't buy these on a captain's salary," Sawyer mutters.

"I buy my own shoes!" I snap. "I have a trust fund."

"This is what you use it on?" Sawyer glances at me. His intent gaze lingers. The combination of his chiseled features, direct look and the cling of his dark sweater to his lean frame cause the base of my belly to grow warm.

It's something like his reaction to my shoes that indicates we might be too far a part for any bridge to connect us. I'm not sure how to answer. Or even if I can right now. I'm staring at his body.

"The good thing is that you don't have to buy her shoes on your salary. Her trust fund will last a few lifetimes," Petr says. "You've got one thing going for you at least."

We both look at him. My brother sounds crazy right now. He's definitely not helping the growing tension.

"Just in case anyone was wondering." Petr shifts uncomfortably.

I roll my eyes and leave them in my shoe closet. God knows why anyone but me is interested in my collection. Snatching clothes to change into, I escape to my bathroom and swap out the dress for jeans, grateful to be back in comfy clothing after the long day.

My phone chimes, and I glance down. My stomach flutters to see Sawyer's name pop up.

Coffee/cocoa on the deck, 5 min?

Part of me wants to mess with him and say I need at least seven minutes.

Another part wants to run down now and melt in his arms.

"What is wrong with me?" I'm twenty-five and feel like I'm fifteen.

I don't answer but end up rushing anyway, the way I did at camp when he told me to hurry and I told him I had no intention of doing so.

In a sweater, jeans and ballet-style shoes, I head downstairs. My hands are clammy, my blood humming with hope, dread and disbelief.

Sawyer is seated at one of the fire pits, two mugs of steaming cocoa in his hands. I draw a deep breath of the chilly winter air and the scents clinging to me from the event before approaching with what I hope is calmness.

I sit down beside him, too aware of the distance between our legs, the firm shape of his swimmer's thighs.

He offers me a mug, and I take it wordlessly.

I've had a list of things I wanted to tell him, if I ever had the chance. I can't think of one of them right now.

In fact, I can't think of anything to say. I give him a sidelong glance. He's always so calm and put together. Is he anywhere near as nervous as I am?

Nope. Not Iceman.

Frustrated, I take a sip of cocoa and glance at his. He hasn't drunk any, and he's gripping it tight enough for his knuckles to be white. I realize he's a little uneasy, though I'm not sure how to take it.

"So … how's life?" I ask finally, needing something to fill the silence.

He meets my gaze, brow furrowed, like I've asked him what his shoe size is instead of the more general question.

I laugh, a little giddily.

"We were never good at small talk," he replies. Setting the cocoa by his feet, he reaches into his pocket. "I brought you something."

I can't imagine what he might have. He holds out his closed fist, and I set down my cocoa and hold out my hands.

He drops dog tags into my palm. I lean forward, towards the fire, to see the name stamped on them better.

Mikael N. Khavalov

My breath catches. I read his name again.

"I thought you should have them," Sawyer says softly. "Riley found them out on a mission recently."

I didn't think it was possible for Sawyer to pull these emotions from me once more. I no longer feel anger but sorrow and an intense yearning to see my brother again. These are *his*. Something he touched, something he kept with him at all times.

Something Sawyer knew would mean the world to me and brought them to me from all the way around the world.

"Thank you." I manage not to start crying. I can't believe how sweet the gift is or how thoughtful Sawyer was to hang onto them.

Leaning back, I wrap my hands around them. I wish they were big enough to hug. It takes me a moment to recover.

"Let me guess – you came back to bring them to me." I try to lighten the mood.

"Something like that."

I sneak a look at him and find him gazing at me. Sawyer is so damn hard to read. I want to strangle him right now, because my emotions are completely at his mercy while he's playing it cool.

"You don't approve of all my shoes, do you?" I don't know where the words come from. I think I need to pick a fight. I do better when I'm mad at him.

"If they make you happy, I don't care," he says then leans back in the chair. He rests his head against the edge, gaze on the fire.

"You should've told Petr you were coming back," I say. "How long are you staying?"

"Two or three days."

"That's it?" I'm embarrassed by the disappointment in my voice.

He glances at me.

"It's a long trip back for two or three days," I add quickly.

"Yeah." He's amused.

I'm struggling, and he's got to be laughing internally. This coffee date isn't working. I'm too stressed out.

"Stop trying to be crunchy and relax," he orders quietly.

"I *can't* relax!"

"Let things unfold, Katya."

I don't know what the hell that means, but fire is moving through me, along with anticipation. My face grows warm, and I decide there's really no good response. I rest back in the chair.

For a second or two, until I'm still long enough for my thoughts to take off again.

"No. I can't do it," I say, straightening. I face him and brace myself for what I have to say. "I owe you an apology."

He's listening. I can't look at him. This is hard enough.

"I can't even list the things I need to apologize for. There's too many," I add with a frustrated sigh. "But mainly I think it's for … hurting you. I think, of everything, that's what bothers me most. Because you didn't deserve it, and I was angry. Well, I'm always angry. Totally different topic, but I was wrongfully angry this time. And I made a promise that if I ever saw you again, I'd tell you that I'm sorry."

"You have nothing to apologize for, Katya." He takes my hand and squeezes. "I understand the grieving process."

"That's a terrible answer."

"What would you rather I say?" he asks, chuckling.

I consider, afraid anything I say is going to dive back into the deep end. I'm not sure I'm ready for that. Normally, I relish it, but tonight … with him … and me not knowing if he feels anywhere near what I do …

I'm tired of being hurt. I don't want to risk my heart and soul tonight and end up devastated.

"Make it up, like we did introductions at camp," he suggests.

I don't know why it makes it seem easier, but it does. "So, fictional Katya apologized, and Sawyer forgave her. Even after the horrible letter she wrote, the way she pissed him off every time they met, the fact she didn't try to contact him for five months, and will probably argue with him until the end of the world. She did a ton of stuff that just totally irked him, like collecting shoes worth more than his truck."

He's smiling.

"But he also knew she'd come around and realize what they had or could have, so he wasn't about to give up on her. One day, he traveled thousands of miles to visit her, to see if maybe, just maybe she ..." *feels the same way he does.* I stop, the story becoming too personal.

He sits up, still holding my hand. "Finish it."

"... wanted to have coffee."

He eyes me.

"Oh, you wanted a different ending?" I ask sweetly. "Maybe they can have tea."

"All right. I'll play." He pauses to think before speaking. "While fictional Sawyer was playing games with Katya, she was thinking about the gift she sent him, whether or not he received it. She'd sent it after months of silence, because she wanted him to know he wasn't alone, to remind him that there are people who care about him, even if he was determined to spend the holidays in Iraq. Because secretly, Katya kinda likes him, enough to hope she saw him again and that the next time they met, maybe, just maybe they could escape somewhere where it was just them and..." He pauses dramatically.

I'm on pins and needles. "What?"

"... have coffee, of course."

"You're such an asshole!"

"You started it," he points out. "If you want to fill in those blanks between fictional Katya and fictional Sawyer at any point ..."

I ignore him, almost enjoying our cat and mouse game. Before the awkward silence can descend, I speak up. "You got the duck."

"I did. Thank you." He's smiling again, his dimples showing.

"If I hadn't sent it, would you have come home ... er, I mean here?" I ask.

"I don't know. Probably not. When I saw it, I knew you didn't hate me too much. I figured I'd come back and just see if you wanted ..."

I glare at him. "If you say coffee, I'm leaving!"

"Nah. We both know you won't."

"How did you know I sent it anyway?" I ask, irritated.

"Because the only other person who knows about it is dead."

"Oh, god." I stare at him. "I'm so sorry."

"It's been years," he says easily.

We evaluate each other once more.

"I'm sorry, Sawyer." This time, I'm holding his gaze when I say it. My voice trembles. "I'm sorry that I blamed –"

"Stop," he replies.

I do, not at all certain how he can be so forgiving or how much longer I can sit here, gazing at him, without going insane at not being able to break the fragile plane between us. Or even if I should.

"Just ... out of curiosity ... if fictional Katya asked fictional Sawyer to stay with her tonight, what would fictional Sawyer say?" I ask.

"He'd say yes. Without hesitation."

The answer makes my heart somersault. "So you're saying fictional Sawyer has none of the honor issues real Sawyer does. Too bad real Sawyer doesn't -"

He kisses me lightly, enough to shut me up.

"I'm saying, let's skip the coffee and go upstairs," he whispers. "Unless you want to keep playing this game."

No part of me wants to. I press my lips to his in response, emotions I've never experienced working their way through my system. Sawyer deepens the kiss leisurely, and I lean into him, my body burning too badly for him for me to try and play it cool.

He pulls away. "Come on." Drawing me up, he leads me through the house to the third floor and my room. I follow in a daze, hardly daring to believe this is really happening and so aroused, if it doesn't, I might die.

We make it to my room, and he tugs me into his arms, his lips claiming mine once more. Mine part, and his tongue slides in to taste me while I deepen the kiss to get a taste of him. Cocoa and mint, light and dark, sweet and heady. His taste is intoxicating, complicated, like he is. Despite the need I know he feels, he takes his time, exploring my mouth while his hands run down my body, over my clothes.

His mouth, the thick arousal pressed to my lower belly and the firmness of his touch convey how hot his hunger for me is. My body is fevered, the ache at my core almost too strong to tolerate.

But still he is patient, the opposite of me even here, relishing each second while I push him for more.

The sense I had about him soon after meeting, that he's not the kind of guy you walk away from, is pounding into the back of my mind, warning me this isn't a fling.

This is something much more already, something so deep and primal, it almost scares me. We barely walked away from one another the last time we kissed. This time, we won't. If his kiss stayed with me for months, made me look at every potential date I met differently, what will sleeping with him do?

I'll never want anyone else.

My hands slide up his sweater and over the warm skin of his chiseled his abs and chest. He's solid, hard, strong.

He breaks off the kiss to tug off his shirt then presses his mouth to mine again. I let my hands roam his upper body, amazed and enthralled by the shapely muscles and his strength. His scent is stronger without his shirt, a mix of coconut and man, as complicated and consuming as his flavor.

I love it. I love that he's got so many layers, so many puzzles for my senses. The hollow between my thighs is wet with need, my mind already fantasizing about how it'll feel when he's inside me.

Sawyer's hands go up my shirt, one drifting over the scars on my back, and I hesitate for the first time.

The scars remind me of how much we've been through, of how battered we both are as people. He's honorable, good and deserves everything good in the world. Being this close to someone this amazing reminds me of how flawed and imperfect I really am.

"What's wrong?" he whispers, resting his forehead against mine.

"I, uh … one sec." Prying myself loose from him, I go to stand in front of the hearth. The fire is the only light in my room.

Sawyer trails without crowding me, calm as always when my hands are trembling from emotion and need. I wish so much that I could have more self-control like he does, especially right now. My soul feels exposed, and I'm terrified we'll end up where we've been the past few months: devastated.

I pull off my shirt and unsnap my bra, dropping both. "I want to show you my scars."

"I've seen them, Katya," he replies gently.

I face him, not surprised when his eyes go to my breasts. He's so sexy right now, standing in his jeans with his perfect upper body exposed. His brown eyes are bright with desire, his features softened with affection.

"No, Sawyer," I say with some impatience. "I want you to see all of me. Every last imperfection. Because I'm afraid if we do this, and you don't ..." I can't finish. I don't know how to say what I feel. This is so much more than one night with him, and if he is going to be scared off by something about me, I'd rather know that now than later.

My heart can't take him breaking it again. I'm about to lower every inch of my guard to someone I admire and respect more than I can express, and I'm scared.

His gaze lifts to mine, and understanding flickers through his features. "Show me," he whispers.

I fumble with my jeans and unbutton them, pushing them and my underwear to the floor. I turn my back to him and pull my hair over one shoulder, so he can see the extent of the damage.

"I've got a lot of scars," I say into the quietness.

His hand touches my shoulder lightly and goes down my back, tracing the edges of the scar tissue.

"You're beautiful to me, Katya," he murmurs, his other hand resting on one of my hips. I can feel the heat of his bare chest, inches from my back. "I don't care how many scars you have or understand why you think who you are is going to scare me off." His voice carries a tender note.

I listen, hardly daring to breathe. His hands skim my shoulders and down my sides, wrapping around me to my belly, where he clasps them and leans into me. His skin is hot at my back, the strong arms I've admired for months holding me securely.

"I won't hurt you in any way, Katya," he adds. "I'm here because I want to be with you. Nothing will change that. If this is too fast, I'm happy to wait until you're ready."

"No," I murmur. I rest my hands over top his.

"I know what kind of person you are, and I like who you are. Enough to fly halfway around the world to see if there's even the smallest chance you feel the same."

"I do, Sawyer," I whisper. Even hearing his words, it almost seems too incredible to be possible. That Sawyer Mathis, the man I've given hell since we met, is actually interested in me ...

He turns me to face him. "You're beautiful. Passionate, sweet, giving. You make me feel like it's okay to let someone in finally." He searches my gaze as he speaks. "When I got your letter, I thought there was no chance of ever seeing you again, and that crushed me."

"I'm so sorry, Sawyer." I touch his face and then wrap my arms around his neck, leaning into him. My heart is pounding hard, my body screaming for him to touch every part of me.

"We both had to heal, I think, before we were ready for this," he says. "I swear, Katya, I want to be with you. Nothing you can do or say, no shoe you throw at me, will ever change my mind."

I smile at the mention of the shoe. He's serious and sincere, which is almost as mind blowing as the idea he's holding me right now. I pull his head down to me and kiss him.

A different kind of warmth is blooming inside me, stoked to life by the idea he feels what I do about us.

Desire soon overtakes conscious thought, and I sigh when his hands reach my breasts, pausing to tease my nipples, before they continue down my body. He releases me briefly to remove his pants and picks me up, carrying me to my bed. I listen to his heartbeat, my blood racing.

Setting me down, he lies beside me on his side, his hand exploring my body while his mouth finds mine. His controlled, slow approach is killing me, driving me mad with need, and I shift onto my side, wrapping a thigh over his and trying to pull him on top of me.

Sawyer breaks off with a soft laugh. He pushes me onto my back once more and stays in place.

"I want to experience every part of you," he whispers and kisses me. His hand glides down my lower belly to the sensitive hollow of my body.

"Sawyer!" I complain.

My knees part automatically to give him better access to the part of me that's almost painful with need. His fingers slide into me, and I groan.

"So wet. And here I wasn't sure if you really liked me," he teases.

"I do!" I snap breathlessly. "I want to be yours. I've never wanted that with anyone else. It scares me, but I want you to have all of me, down to my scars."

His fingers still, and his eyes travel from my body to my face.

"That's how I feel. Right or wrong," I add.

I'm expecting a verbal response. Instead, he kisses me and presses me back, his body lowering onto mine. The heat of his skin against mine and the hunger in his kiss scatter my thoughts, send me into sensory overload, while his arousal tickles the opening of my core in a way that makes me claw at his back and try to wriggle into position.

Sawyer enters me slowly, inch by inch, and my body grows taut. At no time in my adult life have I ever felt the need to come from penetration, but with him, it's entirely different.

It's more than physical. I opened my heart and soul to one man, the best man I've ever known, one who makes me want to be the best person I can be, who challenges me mentally and stirs me physically.

It's knowing he's seen my scars, survived my pain and born my misguided anger – and still chosen to be with me.

It's admitting to myself that it's not only okay to lower my guard to someone else, it's worth risking everything I am to be loved in a way only someone like Sawyer can love me.

Whatever this is between us, it's too strong to walk away from, and I never want to make that mistake again.

I arch beneath him, overwhelmed physically and emotionally, unable to control the intense pleasure building in response to his rhythmic thrusting and the friction of our bodies, to the intimacy of being one with him, with Sawyer Mathis. My legs are wrapped around his hips, my arms hugging him as close as possible.

"Come for me, Katya," he whispers into my ear.

My world shatters, and I murmur his name as pleasure breaks over me, sweeping me even deeper into my senses, filling me with waves of ecstasy and his scent, skin, heat.

He slows.

My eyes flutter open, and I gaze up at him. I'm trembling from my climax and reach up to trace a finger across his lips.

I could get used to this, to lying beneath him and feeling him inside me.

"I want you to be mine in every way, baby," he adds.

His tenderness makes me want to melt. I breathe in our combined scent. "Do you want to be mine?"

"You pretty much already own me."

"Really?" I start to smile.

"Yeah."

"I like that."

"I figured you would."

"I want you to make love to me until we can't walk," I whisper.

"A good Marine always follows orders."

I'm grinning, when his lips claim mine. Within seconds, it's like I didn't already come. I'm burning for him with too much desire to control.

No longer caring about self-control, I drop the last of the guards around my heart and tackle him with every ounce of passion I contain.

I've never felt so euphoric and happy as I do the next morning. Taking a quick shower, I pull on my bathrobe and glance at my glowing, grinning reflection. It's the first time since Mikael's death where I've felt … happy. Truly happy.

Incredible isn't enough of a word to describe last night. Sawyer was more than I expected of any man.

I want you to be mine in every way, baby.

The words, and how he looked at me when he said them, hit me hard enough that I start to tremble in the middle of the bathroom. I balance myself against the wall. My inner thighs are sore, but I'm already growing wet for him once more. The fire that's been smoldering between us since we met enveloped both of us last night. There were no survivors in our passion, no barriers or walls that could withstand everything we did last night.

"Breathe, Katya." I recover and comb my hair before braiding it.

Tossing it over my shoulder, I exit the bathroom. To my surprise, he's not in bed but nearing the door.

Fully dressed, with boots, as if he's leaving. The small voice that's been warning me about him being gone in two days is a little louder. I ignored it last night, too swept away in the physical sensations to want to think about not spending another night with him.

Sawyer reaches the door, and I debate whether or not I should say anything or just throw a shoe. I'm not sure why I feel the urge to flip the switch on my anger. Maybe because I'm a little embarrassed about plunging head first into a relationship without knowing if we can have one.

The door opens.

"Captain *where-are-you* is leaving without telling me where he's going?" I challenge.

"I texted you."

Picking up my phone, I check and see he has. "*Going for coffee,*" I read.

"You need shoes in the kitchen?"

"Oh, no. We're not starting like this." He closes the door and faces me.

My breath catches at the sight of his handsome features. My face is warm, my body humming with desire already.

"You need to decide now if you're going to trust me. Because if you don't, this won't work," he says firmly.

What won't work? I rarely think more than a day ahead. I know he's the opposite. What I can't figure out: if he's only thinking two days ahead or much farther.

Or even if I care, if I can get his clothes off him right now. I don't like there being anything between us, more so after last night, when I got to experience Sawyer without his Iceman face or guard.

He's even more beautiful unguarded than he is now.

"I'm going to tell your brother about us then get us both coffee," he says when I'm quiet.

"*Petr?*" I say, startled. "You're going to tell Petr you slept with me?"

"No." Sawyer gives a faint smile. "Mikael. He brought us together. I thought I would thank him."

My god. I think I love this man.

CHAPTER TWENTY THREE: SAWYER

KATYA'S ENTIRE EXPRESSION CHANGES, from the point where I'm about to have a shoe thrown at me to the vulnerable, emotional, sweet girl she is only for me. Her cheeks are rosy, her lips swollen from kisses. The bathrobe is cinched loosely enough for me to glimpse one smooth, round breast.

"If that's okay," I add. I'm not one hundred percent certain she's comfortable with me bringing Mikael up. Her emotional reaction is always intense yet mixed, and I suspect she's not sure yet either if she's comfortable talking about him.

"I'd like to go with you," she says, eyes wide and filled with emotion.

"We'll go together." I resist the urge to take her in my arms, knowing how it'll end if I do.

She nods, gaze misting over.

"I figured we'd have coffee and talk this morning," I tell her.

"If this is the part where you tell me I'm a one-night stand, then skip the coffee and leave."

Already she's stirring my blood with her fire. We were awake for hours last night, but I can't get enough of her. I know she wants this as much as I do. I also know she likes to poke the fire to get a reaction out of me.

I have the sense this morning that she's raw and uncertain what to do about it. Last night was beyond anything I expected: intense, sweet, tender, passionate. Any restraint I thought I'd show was burnt to a crisp the moment she said the words I can't get out of my head.

I want to be yours.

She was vulnerable and open, her heart in her eyes. I'll never forget that or the surge of protectiveness, of possessiveness, I experienced.

But I'm still going to enforce a few boundaries I think she needs.

"I'm serious," I warn her again. Taking off my jacket, I toss it then work my shoes off. I approach her. "We're not starting off like this. You need to decide now if you trust me."

She cranes her neck back to look up at me, not backing down.

I love it. She's so sexy when she's pissy or about to throw a fit. Now that I know how to fix it properly – by making love to her until she's too happy to speak – I'm eager to try it again.

Holding her gaze, I tug the tie of her bathrobe free. "I don't do one-night stands."

"You leave in two days. Is this a two-day stand?" she retorts.

Hearing the tiny note of distress in her voice, I kiss her and push the robe off her shoulders. I ache for her in a way that's almost uncontrollable. Her scent is all over me, and her light flavor is such a turn on, I don't think I'll ever be able to kiss her again without dragging her to bed.

Her soft, firm body melts at my touch in a way that makes me want to learn new ways of making love, so I can claim her every way possible. I glide my hands down her perfect curves and pull her against me.

Katya plants her palms on my chest and pushes me away, breaking the kiss. Her face is flushed, her eyes sparking with fire. Her body is pliant, her breathing off.

"Two days," she repeats.

"It's what I wanted to talk to you about over coffee," I reply, nuzzling her. "Do you want me to stay longer?" I capture her lips once more. It's not possible to have her naked body in my arms and not make love to her, not after everything we've been through and how deeply we plunged into each other's hearts last night.

Her hands travel under my shirt and push it up. I lean back enough to take it off.

"Yes," she says. "I do."

The sensation of her breasts pressed to my chest adds to the fire racing through my blood.

"I can stay a couple of weeks," I say as I strip out of my pants. Her cool hands roam down my hips to my straining erection.

"And then … what?" she asks.

"Trust me, Katya," I grunt.

If last night was hot, this morning is like being a Crayon melted in the sun. Katya's passion pushes past any restraint I can muster. I pick her up, taking her to the bed once more.

Settling on top of her, I enter her quickly this time, with urgency, my mouth devouring hers hungrily as her thighs clench my hips and fingernails rake down my back. She's so hot and tight and slick, her kisses and passion consuming. I let her carry me away with her desire and hunger.

Two weeks … a *lifetime* isn't long enough for me to be satisfied with her. I'm not possessive of women, but I could be with her from the sheer amount of need and emotion burning me up from the inside out.

I want to be yours.

Fuck! I've wanted her to be mine for months, to cart her off and prove to her how good we could be together.

I get lost in her body, in her sighs. The breathless way she cries my name before she comes, the softness of her skin. My god, I'm intoxicated by the sweet, addictive taste of her core. On her back, her belly, her side, doggy-style, cowgirl … on the bed and off … I can't get enough of her and feel my self-control sizzle in her fire as I try. I need to explore every part of her body, to memorize each curve and hollow, so that, when I do return to Iraq, I have something to tide me over until the next time I see her.

She's wild, uninhibited, as up for a challenge in bed as well as real life. From the way she touches me and holds my gaze when she swallows me when I come, to her throaty moans of pleasure and how she pushes me, as if not wanting to give me the chance to recover my restraint.

It takes another three hours before we're sated enough to stop, and I lower myself on top of her after another powerful climax. Sweating and utterly relaxed, I kiss her jawline. Her breathing is ragged, her fingers trailing down my back and arms light enough to tickle. Her inner thighs are trembling against my hips. I plan on fucking her until neither of us can walk at some point over the next two weeks, maybe when I'm better able to control my desire.

Like that will happen. The attraction is too intense for either of us, always has been.

Wrapping my fingers around her braid, I close my eyes, unable to remember a time when I was so relaxed and content.

She traces my hairline with a finger and idly scratches the back of my neck. I know if I look, her features will be radiant, sexy beyond belief. Still inside her body, I can't recall sex every being so intimate or noticing how warm a woman's skin was, how much I love hearing her whisper my name with such need, I never want to leave her bed. I've never wanted to give up my self-restraint or thought I'd find someone who made me want to ditch it.

"I never thought we'd be here like this," she whispers. I feel some of the same awe she expresses. "Sawyer." She cups my cheeks and lifts my head. "What happens in two weeks?"

I can see her fear. Smoothing hair from her face, I offer a small smile.

"I go back until April," I reply honestly. "After which I'll rotate back."

"What does that mean for ... us?"

"You're still mine, baby, even if I'm away."

She smiles at this.

"I'm career military," I remind her more gently. "I'll have many more deployments and will likely move around every few years. It's not an easy life, Katya, and I can't afford a place big enough for all your shoes." I really can't get over her shoes. Petr says she collects then donates them to charity. I guess that qualifies as a hobby for someone this wealthy, but how many pairs of shoes can one person own?

She chews her lower lip, pensive.

My heart is hammering at her hesitation. But I'd rather have this talk now, before things get serious.

Things are already serious, for me at least. I knew when I showed up for coffee last night that I'm already looking twenty years into the future. I'm not sure she's thinking of what it really means to be with me. I'm not confident she's willing to give up a mansion for officer housing.

When the fuck did I go from sleeping with her one night to marrying her? I don't exactly know how coffee turned into something more. I can see us being together like that, though. It's way too natural for it not to be a real possibility.

"We'll just enjoy the two weeks together," I say when she doesn't speak.

I drop my forehead to the pillow and breathe in her scent. "Do you want to go out and visit Mikael?"

"Yes."

I swallow emotions I don't want to feel, mainly the pain of rejection that's starting to form. I'm going to spend my two weeks with her. If she doesn't want anything else, then I'll go.

"I'll take a quick shower." I withdraw from her warm depths, feeling a little cold inside, and kiss her quickly on the forehead.

There's a stone in my lower belly, one that makes me wonder if I made a mistake coming back.

No. She's worth it. Whatever time I have with her, I'll value. The ache at my core is one of regret and sorrow. She's the kind of girl you never get over, no matter how much time passes. I know that now.

I take a hot shower. It's long for me, about fifteen minutes. I don't know that I'll ever be able to stay in for thirty like she does. It feels good, though, and I relax and let the scalding water wash over me.

When I get out, I pull on jeans and leave the bathroom. At first, I don't see her anywhere. The door is closed and locked from the inside, so I stop and listen for an indication of which of her closets she's in.

Rustling comes from her shoe closet. I walk to the doorway and lean against the frame, arms folding across my chest as I watch her curiously. She's dressed in jeans and a sweatshirt and appears to be rearranging her shoes.

Is this what she does when she's upset? I have no idea. There are two pairs on the island at one end of the closet.

"Is Petr going to be upset that you're disrupting his system?" I ask.

She shoots me a dirty look. "They're *my* shoes!"

I love her fire. It moves me in ways that are too primal to name, compels me to take her in my arms and temper those flames with some hot sex. "What're you doing?"

"I'm deciding which ones to take with me."

"Where?"

"What do you mean, where?" She faces me, puzzled. "Where do you go after Iraq?"

"Quantico." I start to smile. "That's not for four months."

"It'll take me that long to pick them out."

"So ... you were quiet because you were thinking of what shoes to bring?" I ask doubtfully.

"No. I had to remember where I put these." A flash of defiance crosses her face. She places a set of white shoes on the counter and plants her hands on her hips.

I wait for her explanation, leery of the kind of dare someone like Katya can throw down.

"I was thinking that these are the shoes I'm wearing to the wedding." The challenge on her face tells me she's waiting for me to squirm.

"I know nothing about shoes, but they look nice," I reply calmly. "You have a date picked out?"

"June third."

"Guest list?"

"Twenty people, give or take."

"Dress?"

"I'll hire someone."

"Honeymoon destination?"

"Seychelles."

"Does your groom get to vote on that?" I ask.

"Nope. And I want three kids." She's glaring at me, getting irritated, upping the ante, expecting me to flinch.

You won't win this one. "Two and a dog." I'm struggling to stay stoic. The heaviness in the pit of my stomach is gone, replaced by lightness and hope I've never experienced.

Pursing her lips, she falls quiet, frustrated with me.

I hold her gaze. "You know Marines don't live in castles like this."

"I don't care."

"And that I'll be in the middle of a war you don't agree with?"

"I beat you there!" she exclaims triumphantly.

"How so?"

"You go off to war and break people. I use my charity to fix their lives when they get back." There's a light in her eyes that tells me she's found her calling.

"So we're good," I assess, unable to help my smile. I'm fairly certain it's the only middle ground we'll ever reach on the issue of war.

Her hands drop to her sides. She approaches me, a familiar glimmer in her eyes as she takes in my bare chest. When she's close enough, she reaches out and runs her hands down my shoulders.

I drape my arms around her, clasping my wrists at the small of her back. She seems pensive once more as her palms trace the muscles of my upper body.

"I figured we could have coffee. Talk things through," I say, tilting her chin up to see her gorgeous eyes. "Get to know each other better. Though I told you more about my background than anyone else knows."

She smiles. "I think I know what I need to. The rest we'll learn together."

"So do you want to be mine or not?" I challenge.

Taking my face in her hands, Katya kisses me with her usual passion. I hold her while we kiss slowly, leisurely, taking the time to savor her taste and the velvety depths of her mouth.

"You know I do, Sawyer." She drops back onto her heels, gaze on me. "But I do have one question."

"Shoot," I reply. "Ask me anything."

"Are you serious about June?" A flush accompanies the hesitant question.

"How far we take this is up to you." I rest my forehead against hers, speaking gently. "If you can live with a Marine, then tell me when and where to be on June third. If not, I'll come home to you, until you tell me not to."

The words are difficult for me to say. I'm not accustomed to letting go of control over my life, especially not with something this serious.

"Okay," she whispers.

I'm not entirely certain what that means. I don't ask. It's a lot to think about on day one, and I'd rather know she was certain.

"You do understand it's not easy, right?" I ask again.

"Yes. And I know you'll be in danger." A tremor works its way through her body. "I'm really glad you came back, Sawyer."

"Me, too." I kiss her forehead and release her. "Want to walk out back?"

She nods, the thoughtful expression remaining.

Whatever she's thinking, whatever she eventually decides, I know I'm committed. It's out of my hands. Surprisingly, I'm not uncomfortable or uneasy about it. I suspected last night how this would go, from the moment she showed me her scars, and I'm confident it will unfold the way I want it to.

I dress quickly, and we walk hand in hand towards the snow-topped hedges of the family cemetery. It looks far different than I recall, the roses and flowers gone for the winter. It's still peaceful, and the stone walkways winding through the garden are clear of snow.

"Can I have a minute with him?" Katya asks.

"Of course." I let go of her hand and hang back as she approaches Mikael's tombstone and kneels.

This place gives me mixed feelings. It's hard for me to recall that nine months ago, I was standing in this same spot, watching one of my men being buried after the worst experience of my life. It's difficult to digest how far Katya and I have come, how much pain we both went through and how that shadow of Mikael's death will always linger.

But it's not all pain here. I feel a deep sense of gratitude towards her brother. While I'd change his death if I could, I'm also aware that he brought Katya and me together. I don't know that either of us would've gotten the help we needed or would've ever been able to take a chance on letting someone else in, had we not met here at Mikael's funeral.

Nine months ago, I owed him my life, and today, I owe him my heart. I never knew the appeal of having people who cared for me, a true family. Petr and Katya changed that this year. I can't stop thinking about what life will be like with her.

Eventful. That I know, but in the quiet moments when we're alone, it's more peaceful than I've ever known. I love that she's so passionate and speaks her mind and even that her way of beating me and showing up the war effort will end up helping out service members who need it.

I love how good she is and how much sweetness she hides from the world. These are my secrets, and it's a privilege to be one of the only people in the world who knows this about her.

She stands and waves at me.

I approach and slide an arm around her waist.

Katya leans into me, nestling her head beneath my chin with a deep sigh.

"This is where we met," she whispers.

"I know." I circle my other arm around her, enjoying the weight of her body against mine. It's an honor to be the one she seeks support from, one I will cherish for as long as she'll have me. "He would be so proud of you, Katya."

She's silent. Her breathing is uneven, a sign she's crying.

I hold her, and we stand quietly.

My Katya recovers quickly and moves away from me. Whispering a farewell to her brother, she entwines her fingers with mine and wipes her tears away.

We leave the cemetery and are halfway to the house when she takes a deep breath and eyes me.

"You're not even going to really propose, are you? Just assume I'll give you a place and time to show up?"

"Pretty much. I figure when you're ready, you'll let me know."

"You really are serious." Her eyes widen, and she faces me.

"Yeah."

We gaze at one another. I'm trying to gauge her reaction. There are too many emotions to know what's going through her mind.

"You won't change your mind?" she whispers.

"No."

Another minute passes with her studying me. "I'll have to tell Petr what to wear. He's got no fashion sense," she murmurs.

"Or you could let him choose his own clothes like most full-grown men do," I reply, amused.

"If you want me to tell you where to be, we're doing this my way," she retorts. Her eyes are glistening with tears despite the fiery response.

Out of principal and for her brother's sake, I should probably object. But she's about to cry, and I've never been able to stand it when she does.

"Okay, Katya," I whisper and cup her soft cheeks with my hands. "We can do it your way. You've got plenty of time to think things over, too. I'll wait as long as it takes."

"I don't need to. Sawyer ..." She stops, her voice trembling. "I would be really ... honored to marry you. I know I want to be yours forever. I already own you, so we might as well make it official."

I laugh. I can hear and see her emotion. Despite her attempt at a joke, her declaration pierces through me, the same way her passion does, and my throat tightens. She's trembling, and I hug her to me tightly.

"You have a family now," she adds so quietly, I barely hear her.

"I know." It's an overwhelming thought. Holding her, being with her, feels so right. So perfect, natural and peaceful.

We hold one another in the serene setting, the tender moment as intimate as making love to her. When she's calmed, she eases away and wipes her face free of tears. Her features are lit up for a different reason this time, one that pulls a smile from me.

She's happy. I've never seen her like this, and I love it. Taking my hand, she tugs me towards the house. If the spark in her eyes is any indication, she's plotting.

"I think my father is going to want a word with you," she says, amused. "And then Petr. And while you're being interrogated, I'm going to wake up Riley and Carson and let them know I will hunt them down if they let anything happen to you overseas."

I chuckle.

"Then we're going to my room, because you promised to make love to me until we can't walk." She glances at me with a grin. "Think you can hang with me?" The challenge is in her gaze again, along with hunger.

"Absolutely. Why don't we start there?" I reply casually. I stop walking and pull her into my arms. "Sound like a better plan?"

She nods, and I lower my head to hers, capturing her lips for a deep kiss. She melts into me. I steady her.

After a lifetime of dedicated solitude, I'm humbled by the knowledge that I somehow managed to find the woman in my arms.

I could definitely get used to coming home to her.

I look forward to the chance and to our future.

"Hey, get a room!" Petr shouts from the deck.

Katya breaks off the kiss with a laugh.

A glance towards the house reveals Petr standing at the edge of the deck with a wide smile.

"You ever get the feeling he was playing matchmaker?" I ask her.

"Yeah. Pretty sure he was." She grins up at me. "Are you ready for this?"

"Born ready."

"Let's go meet the family, hero."

"It's my pleasure, ma'am."

She laughs once more and pulls me towards the deck.

I go, warmth and happiness filling me at the thought of my newfound family.

A SONS OF WAR NOVEL

SEMPER MINE
SOLDIER MINE
SEAL MINE

ABOUT THE AUTHOR

Lizzy Ford is the author of over twenty books written for young adult and adult paranormal romance readers, to include the internationally bestselling "Rhyn Trilogy," "Witchling Series" and the "War of Gods" series. Considered a freak of nature by her peers for the ability to write and release a commercial quality novel in under a month, Lizzy has focused on keeping her readers happy by producing brilliant, gritty romances that remind people why true love is a trial worth enduring.

Lizzy's books can be found on every major ereader library, to include: Amazon, Barnes and Noble, iBooks, Kobo, Sony and Smashwords. She lives in southern Arizona with her husband, three dogs and a cat.

Connect with Lizzy:

WEBSITE:
www.GuerrillaWordfare.com

FACEBOOK:
www.Facebook.com/LizzyFordBooks

or find her on TWITTER!
@LizzyFord2010